Mysteries
by
Martha Kemm Landes

<u>Pity Mystery Romp Series</u>
Pity the Movie Lover
Pity the Garage Sale Addict
Pity the Stranded Tourist
Pity the Reluctant Fan

<u>Out of the Box Mystery Series</u>
Upcycled to Death
Crime Flies

Framed Fur Murder

Crime Flies

by

Martha Kemm Landes

Elemar Publishing

This is a work of fiction.
Identities and situations are greatly embellished.

www.marthalandes.com

Pitymystery@gmail.com

Print ISBN: 978-1-956912-20-3
e-Book ISBN: 978-1-956912-21-0

Cover design by Tahomina Mitu

First Edition

Disclaimer

The dangerous ballooning situations depicted in this novel are fictional and written purely for entertainment purposes. Hot air balloon rides are very safe and offer guests unforgettable experiences.

DEDICATION

I dedicate this mystery to the Albuquerque International
Balloon Fiesta. It is my very favorite event.
Watching hundreds of hot air balloons floating in the air
at once is indescribable. One must see it to believe it.

Here's a shout-out to my sister, Kathy. Although we live far
apart, she's only a phone call away when I have a question
about a storyline. She's a good listener, and being a former
librarian, she knows good plots of books.

I want to thank my husband, Dan, for being my excellent
editor. He has gone through all seven of my mysteries to catch
mistakes and give suggestions on word choice. It is very handy
having a detail-oriented, former English professor in the
house. Dan rocks!

Special thanks to my neighbors/balloon pilots, Gary and
Cindy Cooper. They answered my questions about piloting a
hot air balloon, which helped my characters fly!

Crime Flies

Martha Kemm Landes

Chapter 1

"Thank you for shopping at Upcycled. Please come again."

A woman wearing tight exercise pants shifted the bowling pins she just bought in her arms and waved at me. "I just love your shop. Who knew you could paint bowling pins to look like different dog breeds? You are so gifted. And those hot air balloons made from books are amazing! And how did you make those wind chimes?"

I wasn't able to answer her because she pushed back a lock of her long gray hair, and quickly said, "I'm going to tell my whole pickleball gang about your shop. They will love it."

I grinned. "Cool." Her T-shirt made more sense now. Pictured on the front was a paddle, a holey ball, and the words, "It's always a good day to play."

She started out the door, then turned back. "Have you ever played?"

"Pickleball? No. I don't know much about it, and I don't really have time to play. I'm here all the time."

Her eyes narrowed. When the woman set the pins on the floor, I feared she would pull a paddle from her backpack and demonstrate to me how to play.

Instead, she looked around the store and frowned. "You probably don't get much exercise here, but you've gotta keep that tiny little figure in shape so you can feel this great at 68." She flexed her right arm and winked. "I'll call you and see if you can join us. You'll love it."

I said, "Well, I will have to wait until after Balloon Fiesta because I'll be swamped."

She nodded. "Of course! They don't call it the largest ballooning event on Earth for nothing. I'll stop by or call you when it's all over to get you out on a court with us. My name is Sandy, by the way."

"Wow. You don't give up, do you?" I chuckled.

She shook her head, clutched her bowling pins, and skipped outside, seeming far younger than 68. Her smile and enthusiasm were so contagious that I almost wanted to sign up right then and there.

Just as the door shut, a Canada goose honked in my right ear. Five o'clock already? I glanced at my bird clock. It might be an odd thing to do, but I had memorized all twelve bird sounds along with their corresponding times. The goose was my favorite – closing time. The 1990s clock was not my most attractive upcycle since all I did was glue feathers around the rim. It was so ugly I figured nobody would buy it, but I kept it in my shop for my own entertainment. Surprisingly, it gets a lot of attention from customers, and some people have even asked how much I wanted for it.

I walked to the door, ready to lock it, but it pushed back towards me. I released my hold, assuming I had a late customer, but a man's squeaky voice shot through the crack, "Hey, little Missy. Just where do you think you're going?"

As much as I wanted to shut the door on him, I rolled my eyes, blew out a breath, and opened it. "Hi, Larry. I was planning to go home. It's been a busy weekend. Do you have a problem with that?"

The scrawny manager of our Out of the Box shopping center made from shipping containers squeezed through the opening. He stood before me wearing his typical uniform of tight jeans, cowboy boots, and a shirt unbuttoned to his waist. He looked like a Western disco dancer. Surprisingly, I had learned to tolerate the oddball during the past year, but I still dreaded each of his visits to my store.

He licked his lips and whined, "Well, my sweet Maria, I jist came on by to remind you of our gathering tomorrow. You know, it's only a few weeks before Balloon Fiesta, and we need to be ready for the big rush."

Larry's accent was so thick and corny that he sounded more like a cartoon character than a manager of an up-and-coming shopping center. I watched him sashay over to my stool, perch on it, then spin around as if he owned the place.

He continued, "It'll be the busiest time of year – what with so many tourists coming to Albuquerque from around the world to see the balloons."

I sighed. "Yes. I know. Remember, I've already rented a space at the Fiesta."

"Oh yeah, that's right. You're takin' some of your stuff there to sell." He glanced around the shop. "Who's gonna mind your shop here while you're working there?"

I packed up my purse as I answered. "Jill is going to run it."

His eyes lit up, and he abruptly stopped spinning. "You mean to tell me that voluptuous ginger will be right here for ten days?" He held his hand to his heart.

"Yes, Larry. Along with her one-year-old baby and probably her six-foot-four husband, so you had better behave."

"Cross my heart and hope to die. I'll be on my bestest behavior around her." He gave a flirty wink.

I huffed, "Was there any other reason you came by besides to harass me?"

"Nope. I'm just makin' the rounds to remind people of the meetin'."

"Well, I'll be there. Ten o'clock Monday morning at the brewery."

He cocked his head. "I guess you did remember, didn't cha? I'll see you there." He pointed a finger gun at me and clicked as he pulled an imaginary trigger. "Ya gotta make lots of balloon stuff for here at that Fiesta booth, you know."

I nodded. "I know. I'm on it."

"Good, 'cause that's what sells the most this time of year."

I frowned as he made his way out the door. He was right. Last year, I was new and unprepared for the onslaught of tourists wanting souvenirs that had screamed New Mexico or balloons. I needed to make even more hot air balloon-themed products pronto.

As I locked the door, I took a tentative sniff. That was weird. My shop didn't smell like Larry today. I took a deeper breath and was baffled. As a rule, whenever Larry appeared, I could count on a waft of B.O., cigarette smoke, and aftershave odors lingering long after he departed. This time, there was nothing.

Did I have COVID again? I quickly ran to my scented candle and held it to my nose. Nope – it smelled like lavender as usual. Maybe Larry had finally taken the hint and started taking showers.

A peep came from the corner. Zia was looking at me and scratching her feet on her bed. Poor thing must be hungry.

I lifted the tiny girl and said, "I know, Punkin, time to go home and get dinner." I stuck the little curly-haired pup inside my bag, turned off the lights, locked the door, and climbed into my little pickup truck.

As I parked at my small adobe house, I sensed something wasn't right. Despite the bright Sunday afternoon, the lights were on inside. I whispered to my tiny black teacup poodle, "Zia, you saw me turn off the lights when we left this morning, right?"

Her beady, black eyes stared out from underneath my chin, but she didn't answer me.

I climbed out of my old Nissan Frontier, dog in tow, and carefully walked to my door. The knob turned without my key, and I grabbed my phone to call 9-1-1. Then I heard the squeal of my favorite new redhead.

I threw the door open, and there, sitting in the middle of my rug, was little Sophia. When she saw me, she clapped her chubby hands and squealed, "Mia!"

Her cuteness melted me. Was there anything more precious than a baby just learning to talk? Especially this one. I ran over, set Zia down, scooped up my Goddaughter, and kissed her soft, yummy neck.

She giggled, then reached down to the dog and said, "Mia!"

My mouth twisted. I thought Mia was her name for me. Had I been mistaken? Was she calling my dog, Mia?

I put the 14-month-old on the floor and watched as she crawled over to the tiny pup and gently patted her. Luckily, Zia loved the child, so I didn't have to worry about them being together.

Where the heck was her mother? I called out, "Jill, are you here or did you just drop off an innocent child to fend for herself?"

She called from the kitchen. "I'm here. Just heating a tamale for her."

I stood leaning against the thick wall, separating the living room from the kitchen, and watched my best friend. She pushed her red curls behind her ear as she cut up the masa-filled meal.

"Isn't that a little spicy for a baby?"

"This is nothing. She's been eating green chile since she was ten months old. It's her favorite."

"I thought you were kidding when you told me she ate your enchiladas."

Jill blew on the food and carried the little bowl into my living room. "Nope. I don't joke about things like that. How was work?"

I followed her and sat next to the mother and daughter on the floor. "Not bad for a Sunday. I actually sold that vintage train case covered in old Simplicity patterns.

"Wow! Good for you!"

I watched as Sophia took a bite of the tamale. She chewed it happily with the few teeth she had. "Hey, Jill. Does Sophia call me Mia? Or does she call Zia Mia?"

"Well, as far as I can tell, you and the dog have a joint name. She always sees you together, and I think she just combined Maria and Zia into one name."

I chuckled. "That's funny. It's like we have a celebrity couple nickname. So, why are you here? Don't you usually see Kelly's family on Sunday nights at the pueblo?"

"Yes, but they are all packing up their pottery to sell at the upcoming feast days. Seems like a lot of pueblos have their celebrations in September."

"I'm surprised you aren't helping."

Jill turned to me and raised her eyebrows. "Maria, have you met me? Would you put expensive hand-painted pottery in my hands?"

I squeezed my eyes shut and laughed. "Right. I'm sure they know you well enough not to have you anywhere near breakables."

She wiped Sophia's mouth and said, "We should go to a Feast Day soon. The food is great, and the dancing is amazing. Acoma is kinda far, but if you have time, we could go to the San Ildefonso Feast Day. It's coming up."

I pondered this. Every Native American Pueblo had at least one day each year, where tribal members celebrated by dancing and feasting. Food was plentiful in every household, and members of other pueblos had booths to sell their jewelry, pottery, and other artwork. The public was allowed to watch, as long as they didn't take photos. And if they were lucky, they might be invited inside a home for an amazing meal.

"Sure, but I can't do anything fun for the next few weeks. I have to make enough products for both my shop and the booth. I'll probably wait and go to the feast day in Zia Pueblo in January. I can even help your in-laws fix the food."

Since Jill's husband, Kelly, was born and raised in Zia Pueblo, Jill had been adopted into his family's tribe when they married. With her own Irish heritage, her fair skin and red hair stood out in the pueblo. I studied little Sophia, who looked like a junior version of her mother. The only obvious physical traits she inherited from the Standing Bear family were her dark brown eyes and wide cheekbones. The baby was absolutely stunning.

Jill leaned down to her daughter and said gently, "Sophie, do you want a drink?" Her tiny mini-me bobbed her messy strawberry-blonde head up and down.

I said, "I'll get it. Water?"

Jill said, "Yes, please."

I hopped up to fill the same tippy cup that I used when I was a toddler.

Jill said, "The real reason I'm here is to ask you if you can upcycle something for me."

Without giving it a thought, I said, "Sure. What is it?"

She grimaced and said, "Um, Granda Finn's piano?"

I turned off the water, sure that I had heard her wrong. "What? The player piano? Why? It's magnificent! I love that piano. Wasn't it made in 1900 or something?"

"Yes. 1907." She sighed. "Well, you know he's moving into a fancy independent living place, and he can't take the piano."

I straightened up. "I still don't understand why he's moving. He's not ill."

"Right. He's still spunky as ever – just lonely, and this place is amazing. They have dances, bingo, happy hour, and movies. He said maybe he could meet a nice lady too." She chuckled.

"Awe, that's sweet. But don't you want the piano? It's awesome."

"My dad had a piano repairman give an estimate to fix it, but he said it's so out of tune and brittle that the wires would break as soon as he tried to tune them."

"What did he suggest you do?"

She frowned. "Take it to the dump."

I sucked in a breath, horrified at the thought of giving up the player piano. Jill and I spent many days as kids in her grandparents' living room. We put piano rolls in and watched the piano play by itself. "That's an awful thought. How did it get so out of tune?"

She shrugged. "The guy said the temperature in the house fluctuated too much from being on that outside wall. But it could have been when their heater broke for a week. Or the time last year when there was a leak in their kitchen and the house was all humid. Who knows? I didn't believe it would sound that bad and put on the roll for "You're a Grand Old Flag," so I could march around to it with Sophia, like we did as kids, but it sounded more like some crazy avant-garde piece. It hurt my ears." She frowned.

I shook my head in disbelief.

"I know. We are all heartbroken. So, is there any way you can salvage some of the parts? Like some of the keys or special things we can keep for sentimental reasons. And of course, you can have all the rest of the piano pieces to make stuff to sell in your shop!"

I closed my eyes and pictured the massive instrument. There were Pinterest posts of cool things made from piano parts, but I didn't know the first thing about dismantling a player piano. I twitched my lips and looked at Jill's hopeful green eyes. I did love a challenge and couldn't say no. I sighed. "I'll check it out. I can't promise anything, but I will at least look at it."

"I know you can do it!"

"I'll start on it as soon as Balloon Fiesta is over."

At that, Jill's face scrunched up, and she started twirling her hair around her finger. "Um…yeah, well, there is one catch."

"What?"

Granda is putting the house on the market next weekend, so the piano has to be gone by then.

"Jill! It will take forever to take apart a whole piano…let alone a player piano! If I recall, there are 88 keys on a piano, and 88 of everything. And since it's a player piano, it has bellows and other special equipment. I can't do that in one week. You know I work, right?"

"I know. I know. I know. I've been thinking about it. How about if I work at your shop while you do this? I need to get used to selling things during the Fiesta anyway, right? And you don't have to pay me. I can bring a playpen for Sophia – and if you want, I'll even keep Zia there, so she doesn't get underfoot."

That would solve the work problem, but I had to upcycle so many more items for my booth at the Fiesta. I wasn't sure I could manage all that. Then I looked at her hopeful face and closed my eyes, and sighed. "Let me look at it before I promise anything."

Jill stood up and said, "Yes! Let's go over tonight!"

"Tonight? No. I'm beat and I have a pile of laundry waiting for me. How about tomorrow?"

She perked up. "Oh, that's right. Out of the Box is closed on Mondays, so your Upcycled shop is, too. Tomorrow is perfect. I'll meet you there. Just say the time."

I smiled at her excitement, but wasn't sure I could do anything but look at the piano. "I'll go right after my meeting – probably about eleven o'clock." I wiped dripping water from Sophia's chin and told the toddler, "Your mom is gonna put me in an early grave." Then I brightened and whispered, "But I'm kind of excited to check it out."

Jill beamed. "I knew it was right up your alley. Hey, where is your meeting?"

"Rusty Railroad."

"Ooh, is Joey back yet?"

"No. He'll be gone another month." I wrinkled my nose.

"Shoot. I really wish you two would get together. Why did he have to run off to Africa right when you were hitting it off?"

"Well, he's a good guy, you know. He volunteers to work in underserved countries. We should all be that nice."

She put her hands on her hips. "Well, I did a good deed today."

"Oh yeah?" I waited to see what my nutty friend would say.

"I offered to give my best friend an entire antique piano for free."

I rolled my eyes. "Sure. That's just the same as Joey saving lives with Doctors Without Borders." I pointed my finger at her. "And don't hold your breath. I haven't committed to the job yet."

As Jill packed up Sophia and the baby supplies, I said, "Oh, and if you or your family have any burned-out lightbulbs or old books you don't want, save them for me. I need them for some other projects."

"Lightbulbs? OK, but remember to make sure if you find any old books, make sure they aren't special editions before you cut into them."

"Ha! Believe me. I learned my lesson last year."

Chapter 2

Early the next morning, I gathered the materials needed to upcycle light bulbs into hot air balloons. Even though I could work on the project at home, I was more productive at my shop.

The short drive to Upcycled was beautiful. It was a perfect Fall morning in Albuquerque. Balloons already dotted the sky, their pilots preparing for the upcoming big week. To illustrate my thought, a pickup truck passed me with a huge balloon basket in its bed. 'Tis the season!

Once Zia and I unloaded the supplies inside my shop, I made a soft work surface by laying a worn towel on my glass countertop. I set out paints, beads, glue, and the few light bulbs I could find. Unfortunately, even though they could last 18 years, I had to use some of my LED bulbs, since I didn't have any used incandescent bulbs. I realized this defeated the purpose of upcycling old things, but I was anxious to try out my idea.

I looked at my clock and twisted my mouth. There was no time to start now. The meeting would begin soon.

When I entered the pub, Zia wiggled in my vest, distracting me, and I almost walked right into a table, which was in a different spot than usual. A familiar voice said, "Look out, Maria!"

I righted myself and turned to see Joey reaching out to catch me. My breath caught at the sight of him. What the? I studied his hair, which had grown way past his ears. His chin was covered with a scruffy beard, and he looked extremely fit in his white T-shirt and jeans. Hubba, hubba. How did this man get even more handsome?

I gulped, then stammered, "Joey. I thought you weren't coming back for at least two more weeks."

A smile spread across his face as he said, "Sometimes, you just gotta come back home to see what you're missing. Actually, the funding ran out, and they sent us all home early. Hopefully, I can go back to the same area next year if they get more aid."

He sauntered closer and held my shoulders out at a distance while studying my face. "You are a sight for sore eyes—even prettier than in my dreams."

"You dreamed about me?"

"Every night – when I wasn't swatting at mosquitoes."

I joked, "Who did you dream of while you were swatting at mosquitoes?"

He chuckled, then our attention switched to Zia, who was frantically straining to reach her favorite man. Just before she managed to squirm out of my vest, Joey grabbed the teacup poodle and held her up to his face. Her tiny tongue attacked him with kisses.

In baby talk, he said, "I even dreamed about this little mosquito." He snuggled her and crooned, "I missed you too, Zia Patia."

I watched the two reunite, shifted my stance, and said, "Looks like Africa treated you well." I reached out and grabbed his arm. "And where did you get those guns?"

"Well, I wasn't just hanging out, brewing beer, and drinking it, as I do here. I had to load heavy boxes of supplies and haul them through uncharted territories in the heat. Plus, I lifted people in and out of cots daily. Truth is, I'm in the best shape of my life.

I said, "I like."

"Well, then. How about a kiss for this weary world traveler?"

I glanced over his shoulder to see if the group was watching. They were busy talking, so I leaned in for a long-awaited kiss. When we pulled apart, I cleared my throat. "So, I guess you have been working out those lips, too. That was some kiss."

"What happened in Africa stayed in Africa." He winked and pulled me close again, locking eyes with mine with a serious expression. "But, Maria, I need to confess something. I did kiss one girl while I was over there, and I'll never forget her. That's why I want to go back next year."

"Really?" My heart sank. Without meaning to, I backed away a bit, and my eyes narrowed.

He smiled. "Not to worry. Aliya is three years old, and I only kissed her once – on her chubby cheek. She has Tuberculosis and came in weekly for treatments. She was so adorable."

I relaxed and smiled. "That's so sweet. I hope you took photos of her."

"I did, and I'll show them to you later. We are late for the meeting. Better get in there. Louise is giving us the wide eyes."

By this time, the eclectic group of merchants was staring at us. We adopted the name 'The Boxcar Adults' during the first month of business last year. It was a fitting name since we all worked in the shipping container shopping center, Out of the Box.

Sure enough, our loveable loudmouth and self-appointed leader, Louise, stood up with her hands on her hips, giving us a funny expression. She belted out in her Texan accent, "Glad you two finally made it over here. I thought you may have to get a hotel room before the meeting even started."

My face heated instantly, and I knew with my fair complexion, it had turned red.

Joey stepped in and said, "Now, Louise, you're just jealous because I haven't given you your kiss yet." He rushed over, kissed her on the cheek, then lifted the older woman and swung her around.

Gee, he really had gotten stronger. Everyone laughed.

When he set her back on the floor, she straightened her bedazzled t-shirt and said, "Now that's what I call a homecoming."

The rest of the group seated included Joey's sultry brother, Jett, their beautiful sister, Julie, and the bakery guys, Pat and Mike. Across from them sat Carl and his brothers, Danny and Arnie, who together ran the Antique store. The newest member of our crew was Sally Ann, who just moved here and opened a permanent jewelry shop called Link Me Up. Only one person from the shopping center was missing – Larry. But that was fine with me.

Joey and I pulled up chairs to the end of the long table, and we discussed different ideas for handling possible crowds during Balloon Fiesta. I said, "Don't forget, my friend, Jill, will be running my shop while I'm having a booth in the artisan tent at the Fiesta."

Pat said, "I'm so excited for you."

Louise lifted her chin. "Hey, Maria. How much did they charge you for that booth? Is it outrageous?"

"Kinda. The fee was $1,800 for the nine days. But it is fully equipped with pipes, drapes, and electricity, and it's heated. That's a lot less than being right on Main Street. A booth there is over $5,000, and you have to provide your own tent and deal with the weather."

Sally Ann raised her hand. "Main Street? I thought you were going to be at the festival at that big Balloon Fiesta Park."

We all looked at her, forgetting the girl had recently moved here from Kansas. This would be her first October in New Mexico.

Pat answered, "It is at the park. There is a long, paved road stretching alongside the grassy area where the balloons take off. The road is just called Main Street. It has a gazillion food vendors and shops."

I nodded. "I just hope I can sell enough to pay the fee, so that I don't go too much in the hole."

Louise barked, "Raise your prices, Maria. You sell stuff too cheap as it is. There will be up to 90,000 visitors a day, and all of your stuff is cool and one-of-a-kind, so chances are good you'll do well."

My stomach tightened at the thought of that many people.

Carl, my friend with autism who helps to run the Antique Store, said, "Y y you have to get there early."

I nodded. "You're right, Carl. I have to be there before 4 a.m. every single day. I can leave for a while between sessions, but it's gonna be tricky getting there so early."

Joey said, "You'll be fine - just go to bed super early for 9 nights." When he put his hand on my knee, a jolt ran up my leg and possibly down my spine.

Mike said, "Well, let us know if those deep-fried, green chile cheese curds are there. If they are, I've gotta get the recipe."

Pat put his arm around his boyfriend and agreed. "Good idea. And gosh, make sure to eat a bag of tiny donuts. I love those things. I wish we could buy one of those machines and serve them here."

Joey said, "Don't you dare. I'd gain even more weight."

I looked at my fit boyfriend and wondered where any fat was hiding.

Julie rubbed her stomach. "I'll be eating one of those amazing burritos if I go."

The ever-handsome Jett, whose black hair and mysterious ways matched his name, said, "Speaking of burritos, we're opening our rooftop bar at six thirty every morning for 'Burritos and Balloons.'"

Louise squawked, "Well, that must have been Julie's idea. You boys could never think of anything that fun."

He smirked. "I know. Little sis has lots of great suggestions."

I studied Julie. She had features unlike either of her brothers. Her hair was honey colored rather than black or blonde.

Joey added, "We're putting a big white X on the open area out back of our shipping containers so pilots will know it's a safe place to land. That was her idea, too. She even got approval from Larry."

I turned to Julie. "I don't know how your brothers got along without you."

"Well, the brewpub is their baby. I just do their books and come up with a few ideas." She looked at Joey and Jett, respectively. "You still haven't let me buy board games so people can stay and play games while they drink."

Jett said, "We're still mulling that one over."

I smiled at my cute brewmaster boyfriend and asked, "Joey, is the Rusty Railroad going to have a special balloon-themed beer?"

"Well, I sure wasn't around to make one this year, but Jett has been working on his very first brew."

"That's great! What is it?"

We all faced Jett, who said, "It's almost ready. I named it and made the design for the labels."

Louise jutted her jaw out. "Well, don't leave us hangin'. What's the name of your new balloon beer?"

Jett puffed out his chest. "It's called Chase Crew Brew."

The group smiled at the clever name, while Louise automatically turned to Sally Ann to explain. "Each balloon has a chase crew of people who help inflate it, then follow it as it flies. They are in contact with the pilot the whole time to discuss a safe place to land. Then, when it lands, they roll up the envelope, the fabric part of the balloon, and pack it up along with the basket into a trailer. It's a team effort."

Carl asked, "D d do they get p p paid to be on the crew?"

Louise answered, "I'm pretty sure they are volunteers, so they don't get paid, but usually they typically get a free ride in the balloon they crew for."

The new girl nodded. "So…maybe I should order hot air balloon charms for my shop."

Pat said, "Yes! You should. Everyone in town gets crazy busy during the Fiesta. We're having balloon-shaped donuts and specialty cakes in our bakery to commemorate the event."

Carl's brother, Danny, who rarely spoke, said, "We're putting balloon-themed antiques on a table."

Carl spoke up. "And will have a f f fiesta sale that week."

I thought that was a great idea, but I wondered how much of it was their sweet Aunt Milly's idea.

When the meeting ended, Joey stood on the porch with me. He grinned. "I'm so glad to be back. I missed you. Wanna go to breakfast?"

Oh, how I wanted to sit and stare into his blue eyes while eating a delicious green chile and bacon Zia Pancake at Wecks. I said, "Yes, I want to, but I can't." I frowned. "I have to figure out how to take a player piano apart."

He pushed his head back in surprise. "What? That sounds like a huge undertaking."

"I know. It's Jill's grandpa's piano. I may try to get out of doing it, but I promised her I'd at least look at it. Maybe I can catch up with you later."

"You'd better." He leaned over and kissed me again.

Why did he have to do that? Now I really regretted my date with Granda's piano.

Zia and I met Jill and Sophia at her grandfather's house. As we entered, I smelled the familiar scents that permeated the old house. There were hints of pipe tobacco, fireplace smoke, and Grandpa Finn's soap. I said, "I can't believe I can still smell your Grandpa's Irish Spring soap. I loved how he said it reminded him of home."

She laughed. "I know. It's American-made, but you know him - he claims anything Irish, or even hints at Irish as his own. Just check out all the shamrocks in his kitchen. One of the reasons he chose Sandia Vista Retirement Center was that he could still drink his Irish Whiskey there."

We walked into the living room where the oversized piano stood. The exterior wood was in pristine condition, which seemed unbelievable after having survived more than a century. I sat on the stool and placed my hands on the keys, just the way my mother had taught me so many years ago. I played a C chord. At least half of the notes were so out of tune that I winced. I started playing the scale but stopped when Sophia cried.

Jill said, "See? It's so out of tune she can't even stand it."

I lifted the lid and looked down at the golden metal plate, the part that makes a piano so heavy. I reached my hand in and flicked a felt hammer against a string. It made a lovely sound.

The instrument was massive. The solid mahogany case would be difficult to disassemble. I kneeled and pulled off the lower front panel. There were bolts, brackets, and odd metal pieces holding it together. Maybe it could be dismantled with a large screwdriver and some elbow grease, but still…

"Jill, I don't know. This is quite the undertaking. I'd have to spend a lot of time here, and I'll need help removing the heavier pieces."

"I know, but remember, we don't need the big pieces of wood. Just take apart what you can. I just want some of the small things for sentimental purposes."

I knew I'd still have to move the big parts to get to the innards, but I was intrigued. I took a deep breath and said, "Are you sure you don't mind working at my shop even more days than we had planned?"

"I'm looking forward to it. I already know the prices and how you upcycled them to explain to your customers. It will be good practice for when I work there in a few weeks. I'll sell the heck out of your store. Besides, the Rusty Railroad Brewpub is next door, so I might get to see Jett." She waggled her eyebrows.

I smiled. "And Joey."

Her eyes flew open wide. "He's back?"

"Yes. I forgot to tell you. That's another reason I don't want to be stuck here when I could hang out with him."

"Well, I'll bet he'll be glad to help you with this. He already works with wood, and he's strong."

I blushed. "He's even stronger now." I went on to tell her about our brief reunion, then said, "Okay then. I guess we have a deal. When do we start?"

"Tomorrow? Will that give you time to get what you need to work on it?"

"I guess so."

Chapter 3

Joey met me at Granda Finn's house and rubbed his hand along the piano's beautiful wood. He said, "This is gorgeous. It's a shame to take it apart."

"I'm just going to have to close my eyes and do it like ripping a Band-Aid off, so it won't hurt so much."

"Well, you might want to keep your eyes open, or you could get impaled with one of those wires sticking out."

It took both of us the whole morning to detach the lid, fallboard, and front wooden panels from the piano. Once we did, Joey's eyes widened when he saw the detailed mechanism inside.

He said, "Wow, this is much more complex than I anticipated. Look at all the parts for the pneumatic system."

I didn't know what that was, but I could sure tell taking it apart would be a lot of work.

We got started, and in a few hours, we had removed long rows of keys, hammers, and bellows. We took out the cool wooden box that held the piano roll, but the giant metal plate holding the wires and tuning pegs would be impossible.

I shook my head. "No way we can take that out."

"I agree. That monster stays put."

I frowned. "I feel bad that so much of it will go to the dump. Makes my heart hurt."

Joey hugged me and said, "Maria, think of it like going to a shelter to adopt a dog. You can't adopt them all. At least you are saving all of this." He pointed to the mess surrounding us. "And maybe someone will see this carcass at the dump and find something to do with it."

"Carcass! That sounds awful. But I guess I should be happy we picked this much meat off the bones."

That evening, while Joey worked, I was too tired to do much, so I watched TV while gluing pennies onto a bowling ball.

The next day, Joey met me again, this time with a circular saw. He cut two gorgeous mahogany boards into smaller pieces so I could use them for my projects. He helped me load other long pieces of beautiful wood into my truck and said, "I'm sorry I can't stay to help you remove a million screws. Jett is hounding me to finish canning the new beer."

I leaned against the piano. "I can't tell you how much I appreciate your help. How can I repay you?"

His bright blue eyes twinkled. "Well, I'll settle for some of your famous chicken enchiladas - but not until after the Balloon Fiesta, of course."

"Deal. But I'll at least bring tacos over to your place tonight."

"Perfect."

He leaned down to give me one of those sweet kisses I'd missed for months. After he left, I sat on the linoleum floor surrounded by piano parts. What had I gotten myself into, and where to start? I rolled my head around my shoulders and played Billy Joel's "Piano Man" album on my phone to get me in the mood.

Finally, I picked up a screwdriver and started taking apart the keyboard. I was surprised to find the keys were long 18-inch pieces of wood, rather than the six inches you can see on a piano. One end of each key was imprinted with a number from 1 to 88. The opposite end was thinly coated with either ebony or ivory. How cool to see how the keys had been put together?

Ideas swirled through my head as I slowly made my way across the keyboard. When I finished, I had a box full of long, stacked keys perfectly aligned like sections of a keyboard. I also had a backache from leaning over.

Needing a break, I stood, groaning on the way up. Wait. I was only 31. That was the sound of an old woman. I twisted at my waist, reached the floor, reached for the sky, and shook out my aching hands. Maybe I should let that Sandy lady talk me into pickleball lessons. I could use something to get me in better shape.

The house had been emptied of everything Granda wanted. Jill's whole family had also taken what they wanted. Jill had told me, "Take whatever you want. The rest will be picked up by a charity shop in a few days."

I walked around the old, familiar home and looked at what was left. The furniture was cool, but I didn't need any. I found some picture frames and stacked them in a corner next to my box of piano keys. In the dining room hutch, I studied the tarnished silver tea set. Most people had no room for elaborate serving sets anymore and didn't want to mess with polishing the silver. But I figured I could upcycle them into amazing wind chimes. I carried the bulky set over to join my stash.

In the kitchen, I found some spoons, just perfect for making jewelry. Then I found just what I had been looking for in the utility room – a box of old light bulbs. This was my kind of treasure hunt.

I peered into a bare storage closet and noticed a box hidden in a dark corner. After dragging the dusty thing out into the light, I sat on the floor to check out its contents. It was mostly full of papers, probably stuff Finn had collected over the years. I found an old bumper sticker with a hot air balloon and the words, "Craic in the Sky." What did that mean?

Beneath that was a newspaper article from the Irish Times. It was dated March 3, 1977. I carefully unfolded the yellowed paper and saw a photograph of a young man leaning against a hot air balloon basket. The headline read, *Local Balloon Pilot Prepares for 10th Anniversary Celebration of the Dublin Ballooning Club.* I squinted to read the caption underneath the photo. I raised my eyebrow when I read Finn O'Brien. The man in the picture was Jill's Grandfather, Granda.

I'd never heard that Granda was a balloon pilot and immediately took my phone from my pocket to ask Jill about this. When she answered, a baby cried in the background.

"Yeah?" Jill's voice sounded strained.

Oh no. I knew this was a bad idea. Even though everything had gone well for her yesterday, she had her hands full watching the store, the dog, and Sophia all at once.

"Is everything OK?"

"Well…yeah…it's fine?"

"You don't sound very fine. What's going on, Jill?"

After grunting and a few swear words, she answered in a huff, "Well…all was good until a woman with two little boys wanted to buy one of your birdbaths made of terra cotta pots. I was carrying the base when the bigger kid crept over and picked up Zia. I told him to please put the dog down, but he didn't listen. The mother did nothing except carry one of the little birds you put on top of the bird baths. I was fuming that she let her kid pick up Zia. But when the other boy, about three, headed towards Sophia in her bouncy chair. That's when I lost it."

"I set the pots down and grabbed the kid's arm just before he reached my baby. The lady proceeded to bite my head off. She yelled, 'How dare you touch my child. He's just curious.'"

I said, "Well, I'm curious how you think your kids should run wild in a store. She wrangled her boys and said, 'I'll never be back here, again.' which was fine with me. She finally stormed out with both wild kids in tow. Unfortunately, she took the bird with her without paying."

Jill continued, "I raced after her to retrieve it, but the bitch threw it on the ground, shattering it into pieces before she drove off. I couldn't get her license tag number, but it was a red CRV."

Listening to poor Jill, my face sank. "I'm so sorry," I said again.

"Then, after I swept up the glass in front of the shop, I came inside only to find that Sophia had a dirty diaper and that Zia was anxious to go outside. Just as I handled those things, I discovered one of those bratty boys had smeared chocolate fingerprints, or at least I hope that's what it was, all over the glass case. So, I was cleaning that when you called." She puffed out an aggravated sigh.

"I'm so sorry you had to deal with all that, Jill. That kind of thing doesn't happen very often, but people can be awful. And don't worry about the bird. I can make another one."

She took a deep breath and said, "All's okay now. It just proves why I'll never have children."

I chuckled. "Uh, Jill, I hate to remind you, but you already have a child."

"Yeah, but Sophia is different. She will never act like that, and if she does, I'll take care of it - mark my word. So, did you just call to see how badly I'm handling things at your store?"

"No. I'm calling to ask why you never told me Granda was a hot air balloon pilot?"

There was a pause. "What? I have no idea what you are talking about."

I was still sitting with the old box on my lap, and I described the newspaper to her. I picked up a sort of certificate and brightened. "I even found his pilot's license! You've gotta ask him about it."

"That's crazy. I'll check it out. So, how's the piano amputation going?"

I sighed. "What is 88 times 6?"

"I don't know. A lot?"

"Well, that's how many screws I need to take out to be able to bring the project pieces home with me. It will keep me busy today and most of tomorrow. Joey and I removed all the big parts from the body. He and Jett offered to take the carcass to the dump tomorrow if you want to come say your last goodbye."

She laughed. "No. I'm good. Have you thought about what you can make from the parts?"

"I have a few ideas. Hey, are you sure none of your family wants your grandmother's silver tea set?"

"Heck no. Who wants to polish all tha…" Jill interrupted herself, "Oh, someone just came in. Talk later." She hung up.

I put Granda O'Brien's box over with my treasures and returned to dissecting the piano.

I worked diligently, detaching hammers, tubes, and bellows. Without my bird clock to announce the time, my annoying iPhone alarm startled me at 4:30.

I surveyed the area and smiled, proud of my accomplishments. The box of long keys looked cool. The 88 felt hammers proved difficult to remove, since each was attached to a strange-looking configuration of wooden pieces with hinges, rods, and springs. It was worth it, though. The cute pieces graduated in size from 1 inch to 2 ½ inches. I was so sure I could make keychains from these that I picked up my phone and ordered findings online.

My back hurt even more this time as I got up from the hard floor. I looked down and marveled at the ingenuity of people back in 1910. How did anyone a century ago put all these moving parts together to make a piano play by itself with no electricity?

I drove to my store. Inside, I found Jill feeding Sophia a bottle.

"Thanks again, Jill. I think I only need a few more hours tomorrow, and then I can relieve you here. I put Granda's secret box in your car. Did you find out anything about his ballooning?"

"Sort of. I tried calling him, but he was in a Zumba class, so I called Dad. Apparently, he was a pilot, Dad said I'd have to talk to Granda to get the whole story. Wanna go check out his new digs and talk to him sometime?"

"Sure! I'm dying to know."

Zia and I picked up tacos at Blake's, our favorite New Mexican fast-food place. She always loved to get bites of tortilla. We met Joey at his apartment. As we ate, he told me tales of Africa. Some made me laugh, and others were devastatingly sad. The lack of healthcare in the region was evident from the photos he showed me. And too many people died from malnutrition.

He told me more about little Aliya. She was obsessed with Joey's blonde hair and told him she wanted to marry him when she grew up. Once I saw the picture of the dark-skinned cutie with dimples, that did it. I wanted to meet the precious little girl, too.

If it seemed odd that Joey, a brewmaster, volunteered in a medical unit, there was a reason. A few years back, he was close to finishing his fourth year of medical school when he decided the profession wasn't for him. Instead, he has found joy in volunteering whenever he can.

It was nice to spend a relaxing evening with him after living four months on different continents.

The next day, I made a final walk-through at the house and hauled everything to my truck before heading back to my shop.

When I walked through the door, Jill said, "Look, Aunt Maria is here to see you."

Sophia yelled, "Mia!"

I picked her up and kissed her chubby cheek, cooing, "I sure did come to see my favorite girl. Yes, I did." Zia ran up to me, jealous that I didn't get her, so I scooped her up with my other arm.

Jill started packing up stuff as she spoke, "A lady bought a bunch of your teacup candles today…swag for guests at her daughter's bridal shower."

"Oh, that's cool."

"So, you want to go to Granda's when you get off work today?"

I handed Sophia to her mom and said, "Any chance we can wait until tomorrow afternoon? I really want to make something from his piano so I can take it to him."

Her eyes widened. "You think you can do that by tomorrow?"

"Maybe. If I get cracking. I'm excited to see if my ideas turn out. If so, maybe I can sell some of the stuff at the Fiesta, even though none of it will have a balloon theme." I frowned, remembering that was supposed to be my focus with only 10 days until showtime.

She pointed a finger at me. "Just as long as I get first choice."

"Well, that's understood. You and your family can have as much of what I make as you want. It's your piano!"

Jill smiled, walked to the door with her haul, and turned back. "A package arrived for you. It's behind the counter."

A couple of twenty-something girls held the door open so Jill could exit, and they entered my shop. They were especially interested in the jewelry I had made from silverware.

"This is so sweet." I glanced up to see a gal holding a butterfly necklace made from parts of spoons. "I have to have this."

I couldn't help but be a little proud. All the pieces in my shop were unique and took some time to make. With each new idea, I learned a new skill, so I loved it when others appreciated it. During my ten years of upcycling, I had made some big fails, but most were pretty good.

As the girls looked around, I opened the new package. Ooh, the keychain parts were already here! I set my padded worktop on the glass counter and pulled out my needle-nosed pliers along with the prized piano hammers. I had to sand down some parts, then screw the tiny screws into the hard wood, which was difficult. I held up the cute keychain to admire. The second girl asked, "What is that?"

"Oh, I recently took apart an entire old player piano. This is one of the felt hammers that hits the wire to make a sound when a key is pressed."

"My mom plays piano. I'd love to give her one. How much is it?"

I was startled by her immediate interest in the keychains and hadn't yet thought of how to price them. I had plenty of hammers, 88 in fact, and putting this together was quick, but I needed to consider the painstaking effort and time it took to extract them from the rest of the piano.

I said, "Um. This is my first one, so I'm not sure of the price yet, but since you are first here, how about five dollars?"

"Oh, wow! I was thinking more like $15, but I'll take it."

I gulped and decided I should make them at least $10. After all, I would never take apart another piano, so there was a finite number of each treasured piece.

As the girls checked out with their purchases, the keychain girl said, "I can't help but stare at you. You are so gorgeous with that black hair, fair skin, and electric blue eyes."

My face flushed, and I joked, "That's what you get when you have a Mexican mother and Norwegian father."

After the girls left, I made more keychains, ranging in size from large to small. One of the fatter hammers was lying upside down on the counter. I did a double-take when I realized it looked just like a hot air balloon! This got my heart pumping faster. These upside-down felt hammers would be adorable balloon Christmas ornaments, even if nobody knew they came from a piano. I rushed to my storage area and found my fancy ornament hooks. I carefully poked the wire through the felt part of the "balloon" piano hammer. Voila - I had a hot air balloon ornament. This was just what I needed – more balloon things for my shop and booth.

As I made more of the small balloons, I was sure these would sell quickly when people saw them on my little artificial Christmas tree in my booth. They could hang alongside other upcycled ornaments such as reindeer made from puzzle pieces and, of course, my new light bulb balloons. This was going to be really fun.

When I closed the next day, I packed up my dog and special goodies to take to the retirement center to see Granda Finn.

As I drove up, I was wowed by the Southwest exterior of the building. It looked posh with manicured xeriscape rocks and showy desert plants. I wondered if they had The Grass Man do their landscaping, since Jill's family did much more than just synthetic grass.

The interior was equally lovely. I walked to the front desk and asked the woman, whose name tag read Cecelia, if I could bring my tiny dog to visit a friend. I said, "I promise to keep her in the sling on my chest."

Cecelia leaned forward, "Oh, my goodness. Are you sure that's a dog? It's so tiny." She reached up and patted Zia. "Sandia Vista is very dog-friendly, so you just bring that baby right in."

"Mr. O'Brien's room number is 212. He has already made quite a splash around here. The gals are already flocking around him."

I chuckled as I made my way down the beautiful hallways decorated with southwest-inspired artwork. Jill's adorable laugh echoed down the corridor, so I didn't even need the room number.

I gave a little knock as I entered the stylish suite. It wasn't huge, but what it lacked in size it excelled in quality. Beautiful vigas, or carved wooden beams, framed the entryway of the living room. A kiva fireplace stood in the corner. Everything was very homey. A caramel-colored leather sofa faced a wall of windows with an unobstructed view of the beautiful Sandia Mountains, hence the name of Sandia Vista Estates.

"There you are!" Jill shouted as she sauntered out of the kitchen carrying a glass of wine. Little Sophia was hanging from her chest in a baby sling; just like Zia was on me.

Sophia squealed, "Mia!" and I kissed her on her cheek.

Behind them, Granda appeared, also carrying a glass of wine. Wow. He looked even younger than when I'd seen him over a year ago at Sophia's official baby-naming celebration in the Pueblo. He still had a full head of reddish hair, which I suspected he now dyed. His fuzzy gray beard tickled my cheek as he leaned in and kissed me. "Hello, my darlin' Maria. I haven't seen you in yonks. You are still just the prettiest half-pint, aren't ya?"

I chuckled. At only 5'1", I really was pretty short, especially compared to everyone in his tall family.

He held up his glass and said, "Would you prefer wine or a mineral?"

I was used to his funny Irish term for soft drinks and decided I would prefer a glass of wine. Jill went to the kitchen and came back with a glass for me.

I looked around. "Your place is amazing. And from what I hear, you are getting along just fine – especially with the ladies." I winked.

"Well, it didn't take long to learned that the lads outnumber the lasses here.

"Granda, I have something for you." I settled on the couch and patted the seat next to me. After he sat down, I handed him a gift bag.

"I don't need a housewarming gift. I've never lived in such luxury before." He turned to Jill. "Sorry, Jilly, but I'm spending your inheritance by living here."

She smiled. "Who can blame you? This place is awesome — especially the movie theater, pools, wine nights, and hot tubs. I'm planning on doing the same thing someday." She turned to Sophia. "No inheritance for you either." She turned back to her grandpa. "Now open Maria's present!"

He pulled out my heavy gift, wrapped in tissue paper. When he unwrapped it, they both gasped.

Jill squealed, "Maria! That's wonderful. How did you do that?"

I thought I saw a tear in Finn's eye as he said, "This is just grand - a true treasure. I know just where to hang it." He stood and walked to the door. He held the 12"x12" key rack made of wood with piano keys beside the door jamb and said, "Now I have a beautiful, nostalgic place to keep my keys. Thank you so much. I was very sad to lose my old piano. But this must have taken a lot of time to make."

"It wasn't that bad. And the wood they are mounted on came from the piano, too." I turned to Jill. "Don't worry, I'll make one for you and one for your parents."

She jumped up and down, making Sophia bounce and laugh.

I asked, "Do you think your brothers would want them too?"

She rolled her eyes. "Uh. No. They never played piano and aren't very sentimental. But I love it! Use the rest of the keys for your projects."

"Sweet. Oh, there is something else in the bag for both of you."

Granda sat again and pulled out a few keychains and ornaments. He held them up. "This is made from a felt hammer?"

Jill said, "And this one looks like a hot air balloon."

"I know! I was shocked when I realized that. I'm glad you recognized it too."

Jill said, "Thanks so much, Maria. These are so cool. And this is a perfect segue to our questions for you, Granda." She pulled the article from her purse. "What's this about you being a hot air balloon pilot?"

Chapter 4

A few days later, I sat at my dining table, painting light bulbs and thinking about what Finn O'Brien told us. He said, "I was a pretty good pilot, even won some awards, and was elected president of the Dublin Ballooning Club."

When we asked why he had quit, he turned quiet, which was unusual for the gregarious guy. He stared out the window and spoke in a solemn voice. "It was a beautiful morning. My mates and I had our two balloons ready to lift off. The first balloon took off, then I piloted the second up. The muckers in that balloon caused a ruckus, doing low-level flying. For some reason, the pilot challenged his mate to reach out and touch the steeple of a church."

That's when tears came to his eyes. "The wind picked up, and they were caught in a wind shear that flew them right towards a power line. I yelled to warn them, but they were messing about, and they didn't hear me. When the balloon hit the lines, the basket burst into flames. Both people on board died instantly."

He wiped his eyes. "There was nothing I could do. That was the worst day of my life."

I knew pilots avoided power lines at all costs because propane and electricity didn't mix, but that type of accident was very rare. I wondered why it would keep him from ever flying again, and quietly asked him, "Were you close to the people inside?"

He looked into her eyes and said, "Yes. That's the day I lost my brother, Conor."

"No!" Jill put her hand on his and said, "I never knew that was how Great Uncle Conor died. I'm so sorry, Granda." She leaned her head on his shoulder.

He sniffed and continued, "For a while, I couldn't fly. I was too upset. Then, as time went by, my friends tried to get me to go up again, but Mam made me promise to never fly again for fear she might lose her last child. She also pointed out that I had a family, and it was up to me to lead them into the future.

Even though Conor would have thrown a fit if he knew I was giving up ballooning. But I did it. I sold my balloon and its gear."

A tear rolled down my cheek as I thought about his tale. The two brothers loved ballooning more than life itself. He managed to say, "At least Conor died doing what he loved."

I wiped my eyes and propped my last balloon bulb up in an egg carton so it could dry like all the others.

A few days before the start of the Albuquerque Balloon Fiesta, tourists had already descended on the Land of Enchantment. I was so busy with customers that I hardly had time to work on any products. Some locals brought their guests to Out of the Box, while out-of-towners found our shopping center on their own. All seemed to love my Upcycled shop and the new themed items.

When I pointed out my balloon merchandise to a woman who came into the shop alone, she said, "Balloons? Give me a break. I hate this time of year. Everything's crowded, you can't get into a restaurant, and traffic is a nightmare. People stop traffic to point to the sky and gawk. I'm leaving town tomorrow and won't come back until they are gone."

That was a perfect example of how some Burqueños felt, but I've always been the opposite. The nine days of the Fiesta are my favorite days of the year. No matter where you were in the city, you could see balloons every morning. Depending on the direction of the wind, they could land anywhere - in the middle of streets, parks, big yards, or back at Balloon Fiesta Park. It was the most exciting time of the year.

I chuckled at the lady. "Why don't you tell me how you really feel?"

"Sorry. I get anxious when I start seeing all the out-of-state license plates."

When an excited couple visiting from Germany entered, I was glad the other woman didn't voice her opinion. She was actually sweet and pointed out my balloon items to them. Winking at me, she bought a few glasses cases I'd made from men's ties.

On the morning before the big event, Joey helped me move my displays and products to my booth at Balloon Fiesta Park. Luckily, we were allowed to drive on "Main Street" and park fairly close to the artisan's tent to unload. The next day, the whole area would be blocked off, restricted to pedestrians only.

As Joey stood on a stepstool, hanging my new vinyl "Upcycled" sign, I said, "Thank you so much for helping me."

"It's a good thing I'm here. I doubt you could reach this."

"Absolutely." I looked at his strong arms flex as he worked. I wasn't about to tell him I could have done it. I've stood on the top rung of ladders many times. It was way more fun watching him.

When he climbed down to make sure the sign was straight, he said, "I'm glad you added, 'by Maria Olson,' and where your shop is, so people will know you are local."

"Yeah, I also printed a ton of new business cards, so maybe we'll get more business at Out of the Box, too." I held one out to him.

"You printed these on paper bags?"

"I try to repurpose everything."

He climbed back up to attach rods to the piping so I could hang lamps and windchimes.

While the tall, handsome man managed the higher stuff, I set up tables, shelves, and a Christmas tree, then started unpacking my items to sell. I had already priced everything and had followed Louise's suggestion by charging a bit more than usual to help recoup the high booth fee.

"I sure hope I sell something here."

"Oh, you will. Especially these amazing key racks made out of piano keys. They are awesome. If you have one left, I might want to get one for Julie. She played piano for years, and her birthday is coming up."

I took one from the box and showed it to him. "Here. It's your payment for helping today, and for cutting the wood they are on, and all the work you did with the piano." I realized I hadn't done anything for him except buy tacos. "I really owe you. Pick out some more stuff."

"You'll never make money if you give everything away."

"A few things won't matter." I held up the key rack and said, "And you shouldn't wait if you want this. Once they are gone, they're gone. We aren't taking apart any more pianos."

He laughed. "I'm glad to hear that. It was a real bugger, finagling the carcass out of Granda's house. That thing weighed at least 600 pounds, and that's minus what we took out." He looked at me with a serious expression. "Listen, with all the tourists in town and our extended night hours at the pub, and your early mornings, I probably won't get to see you much. I'll try to stop by some morning before our lunch crowd hits, but otherwise we may have to keep in touch via texts."

He stepped down and gave me a rather deep, passionate kiss that made me want to forget about the booth and go home with him. I cleared my throat, pushed him away, and said, "Now, it's not nice for you to distract me from my work."

He leaned his hand on my table and stared at me. "So tell me, my little Norwexican, just how do I distract you?"

I almost melted when his blue eyes twinkled at me. I turned my head away and said, "It's time for you to go home. I can manage the rest myself, now." I faced him again and lifted an eyebrow. "But, keep in mind, Buster, once this is over, I will be ready for your distractions any time you can."

"Oh, I'm your man. I'm confident I can distract the heck out of you."

After he left and the blush finally left my face, I hung up my new book balloons. Then I put my ornaments, including the felt piano-hammer hot air balloons on the fake tree. They looked great.

I had expanded my jewelry section a month ago when I found a stack of old New Mexico maps. I created bracelets, earrings, and cufflinks by encasing the bits of maps in resin."

"What have we here?"

Upon hearing the sultry voice, I nearly dropped the necklace I was hanging on a hook. I turned to find a woman wearing a flowy, blue top over black leggings. She had beautiful, milk-chocolate colored skin and looked to be in her mid-50s. Her hair was covered with a beautiful, flowered scarf. She stood, twirling a hanging balloon.

I sputtered, "Oh, hi. I'm Maria. I own an upcycle shop where I repurpose old things into treasures." I recited my usual spiel, then realized she might have just wanted to know about the balloon she was holding. I said, "Oh, did you mean that?"

"Hon, my name is Angelica, and I'm happy to meet you, but I do want to know how you made this. Did it used to be a book?"

Her slow, smooth voice made me smile. I walked closer to her. "Yes. First, I removed the front and back covers from an old book and lightly spray-painted the edges. I clamped the book on a table and drew the shape. Then I cut it out with a jigsaw. After that, I fanned the book out and glued the front and back pages together making a 3D balloon. Oh, and the little balloon basket is made from pieces of the book's cover. See, this was an old paperback copy of Alice in Wonderland." I pointed to the name on the "basket."

"It's just beautiful. Was it difficult to make?"

"Well, I ruined a lot of books in the process, but at least I found them in a dumpster behind a used bookstore. Do you have a booth here?" I assumed she did since visitors weren't allowed in until tomorrow.

"Yes, Ma'am. I'm in the booth right next to yours."

I stepped out so I could see what she would be selling. The booth was twice the size of mine and had carpeted partitions displayed with framed balloon pictures.

"Oh, those photographs are beautiful. Did you take them?"

"No. My husband did. I'm just the saleswoman."

I still couldn't get over her slow, sweet voice. It was like she was singing a sexy blues song every time she opened her mouth.

"So, he must ride in a balloon to capture these." I walked up and pointed to a few prints, which had obviously been taken from above.

"Yes. He's actually a pilot too. He is always "Up and Away" as he says." She chuckled. "Marvin has an assistant, Chris, who takes the reins, so to speak, when he sees the perfect shot."

I marveled at all the photographs. There were several great shots of the special-shaped balloons, including an elephant, an astronaut, a bear, a clock, a fox, penguins, and many more. I spotted the fan-favorite bee balloons I loved. I stared at it as I responded, "That's so cool that he flies. Seeing all these photos makes me sad that I'll be stuck inside and can't even see them fly."

"Oh, honey. When the balloons are up, it gets pretty dead in here. Everyone wants to be outside. I'll be glad to watch your booth anytime you need to take a break or want to see the balloons."

That was a big relief for me. "Thanks so much, Angelica. And I'll do the same for you. Sounds like you've done this before."

"I'll say. I've been here since the Artisan tent began 20 years ago."

My jaw dropped. "Wow. You do know the ropes. So, what is the name of Marvin's balloon so I can look for it?" Hot air balloons not only had names, but each crew handed out trading cards with the balloon's stats. I must have collected hundreds of cards over the years.

She answered. "He doesn't have his own balloon anymore. He flies for a commercial ride agency. I'm sure you've seen them. The company is called 'Up and Away.'"

"Sure. I've seen them. They have a bunch of matching purple balloons with Up and Away on the side. Don't they have those huge baskets that hold about a dozen riders?"

She nodded slowly. "That's right. Sweetie, I'd better get back to work. Tomorrow morning will be here way too soon. Oh, and make sure to park in the West lot – it's closer."

"Thank you. See you tomorrow!"

I sighed, grateful to have a new friend whom I could rely on.

Once I finally got everything set up, I took a few photos of my display, thinking it looked pretty good!

I drove back to Upcycled. When I entered the store, Jill was speaking to a woman from France. I walked past her as she described how I had made the clocks from book covers.

There was no sign of Sophia or Zia, so I peeked behind my curtain into the storage area and found them both lying on blankets in the playpen, sound asleep. That was a photo-worthy moment, and I snapped a pic with my phone.

I spoke to a few customers, and when the shops emptied, I asked Jill, "Do you think you can handle nine more days of this? I mean, I can only stop by briefly between sessions for the next few days. It's just so much to ask with a baby and all."

She rolled her eyes at me, then walked over and picked up Sophia, who was now babbling and standing in the playpen. "Maria, most mothers work. It'll be fine. Besides, Mom is on call to come here and take over or pick up Sophia anytime I need her to. Plus I miss being with adult-type people. The little squirt is fun, but she's not a very good conversationalist."

Jill tickled Sophia under the chin, making her giggle. Then she pulled Cheerios from a baggie and gave a few to her. She continued, "And meeting people from all over is so cool. I worry more about you getting up so early, working eight hours, then going back later the same day. And you don't even have anyone to watch your booth to go potty. At least I have one right here." She pointed to the back room where I had installed a tiny bathroom.

I held up a finger. "Actually, I met the lady in the booth next door. She'll be alone too, so we'll tag team and watch each other's stuff. She's sweet and reminds me of a cool, older soul singer."

"Soul singer? Was she selling soul food?"

"No, silly. She's selling the most beautiful photographs of hot air balloons. Her husband is the photographer, and he'll be taking photos again this year."

"I thought the actual artists had to run the booths."

"I did too, but she's done it for 19 years, so her husband must stop by often enough to qualify as a seller."

Zia scratched at the playpen, so I picked her up and said, "What should I do with you this week? I doubt they will let me bring a dog."

Jill held up her hand. "Kelly and I discussed it. You'll be way too busy to care for a dog. We're planning on keeping her the whole time. It will be a good test to see how Roscoe does with another dog." She patted Zia on the head.

"That's so sweet of you guys." I turned to Zia, "Baby, are you ready for an adventure?"

I helped Jill pack up to leave for the day and was sad to say goodbye to my tiny black pup. "You have to be very good for Aunt Jill and Uncle Kelly." She stared at me with those beady black eyes, as though she understood everything I said. It could be. After all, last year she helped me solve a murder.

After Jill drove away with both little ones, I sat on my tractor seat stool to work on my hunting trophies. No animals were harmed. I used old bicycle parts I'd gathered from the junk yard to create bicycle taxidermy. For this one, I wrapped curved bicycle handlebars with colorful tape to make them look like the horns of a gazelle. Then I attached a painted bike seat for its "head." I'd discovered the idea on Etsy and decided I had to try it. Some of my bike animals resembled deer, and others looked like rams. It was one of my craziest upcycle projects.

I was wiring the seat to the plaque when I heard a child's giggle and a loud, familiar drawl. "Hey, Lisa, slow down. Remember, I'm ten times your age."

The door opened, and a boy with freckles, big ears, and a buzz cut stepped inside. Following him was a tiny brown-haired girl in a purple tutu.

The boy stared at me as if he were in a trance. The little girl looked at me with big brown eyes, then ran over and hugged my legs. Was it my imagination, or did she smell like bubble gum? It could be worse, I guessed.

"Well, I see my little buggers have warmed up to you just fine," Louise said as she entered and bent over with hands on her knees to catch her breath. Her incredible pouf of hair stood out like she had applied a whole can of Aqua Net. Today's outfit looked almost like something Elvis might have worn, but upon further inspection, it was just a bright turquoise pantsuit, much too small for her large body.

The boy walked up to me and said, "Hello, I'm Bartholemew, commonly known as Bart. I presume you are the proprietor of Upcycled? Ms. Maria Olson, isn't it? It's very nice to meet you."

He held out his small hand and waited for me to shake it. I gaped at the boy. He looked like he was maybe seven years old, but I'd never met anyone so formal at any age. I shook his hand and stammered, "Hello, Bart. It's nice to meet you, too." Maybe he wasn't a child after all. Maybe he was a very refined little person.

Louise said, "Don't take my grandson too seriously. He's 8 going on 80. The one who is glued to your legs is Lisa. She's six, going on four." She paused and twisted her mouth. "Yes. My daughter has an affinity for *The Simpsons*. Funny thing is, they turned out opposite of their namesakes, if you know what I mean. She's fluff and trouble, and he's the brainiac."

I had heard all about her unique grandkids for a long time, but since they lived in Texas, I had never met Bart and Lisa before. I said, "Well, they are adorable."

Little Lisa still had her tiny arms clamped onto my legs as she said, "Gam Gam is taking us to see the balloons!"

I looked up at Louise. "That's great. When are you going? You need to stop and see me in my booth."

"That's the plan, my little Norwexican." Louise was the one who coined my nickname by combining my Norwegian and Mexican heritage. I didn't mind since it was cute, and because she said it with such love.

She continued, "We plan to come on Friday morning bright and early. My daughter will mind the bookstore so we can stay all morning."

"Oh, that will be fun."

Louise put her hands on her hips and said, "Lisa, Miss Maria might like to have her legs back. Can you maybe let go now?"

The little girl with bouncy curls finally released her grip, and I was free to straighten up.

"You kids can buy something at her other shop on Friday. We need to get back to your mom. Say goodbye to Maria now."

Lisa grabbed my legs again and looked up at me. "You are pretty. Bye Bye." Her eyelashes were so long they looked fake.

Bart walked right up to me, looked up at me, and said, "I do hope we have an opportunity to get to know one another better, Miss Maria. I look forward to seeing you at your satellite establishment a week from today."

Satellite establishments? I was taken aback. I cleared my throat. "Thanks? Good to meet you both."

I watched through my window as the curious trio made their way across the parking lot – one skipping, one walking stiffly like a robot, and the third huffing and puffing to keep up.

I finished making my bike animal and hung it in the empty spot where a book clock had been. Then I gathered everything I still needed for the booth and stuffed it into a big tote bag. The shop looked almost bare, since I had taken a lot out for the booth. I doubted I would have much time to work on projects this week, but I made sure I had supplies in both locations, just in case I could work on something.

It was weird going to bed at 8 o'clock since I was usually up late working on projects. My bed was also lonely without my tiny sleeping partner. I had never owned a dog before, but my year with Zia had made me realize what I'd been missing. I sure loved that tiny fluffball.

Chapter 5

My alarm buzzed way too early for my liking, and a cup of coffee was my first order of business. I dressed in layers for the day, then made a breakfast burrito to go. I figured my gurgling stomach wasn't from hunger, but from nerves.

I showed my Artisan badge to the attendant and parked in the lot Angelica had suggested. It was fairly close by. I couldn't believe how many spectators were already lined up to park at 3:45 a.m. The gates didn't even open until 4:30. I wished I'd brought a coat since it was breezy and only 48 degrees. I was ever grateful I would be in a heated tent.

As I carried my overstuffed bag into the tent, I neared a tall guy wearing a jacket covered in collectible balloon pins. His goofy hat was shaped like a hot air balloon. For a minute, I thought it was our lovable TV weatherman, Steve Stucker, who used to dress like that this time every year. But it wasn't him. This guy was younger. When he turned, I saw he had light brown hair in a man bun. He welcomed each vendor with a funny saying, "Start the day with a smile, and your sales will soar like the balloons."

He repeated the line to me, then added, "Looks like you are new here. Good luck today, Milady!" He bowed formally, making me chuckle. When he looked up, I noticed his bright green eyes, a dimple in his chin, and an infectious smile. What a charming man.

When I made it to my booth, I smiled. It was just as I had left it.

I peeked my head around the corner pole and said, "Hi, Angelica. I sure hope I'm ready."

"You'll be fine. Oh, here's Marvin – you can meet him."

I wasn't sure who I expected to see, but a slight, pale man with a white beard was not it. He appeared from behind a carpeted display wall covered with hanging photos. His Balloon Fiesta jacket was embroidered with this year's theme, 'The Sky's the Limit.'

"Marv, this is Maria, our neighbor I told you about."

He held out his hand and said, "Nice to meet you, Maria. I checked out your booth. You are very creative."

I shook his hand and said, "I'm jealous you get to spend so much time in the air. Your photos are amazing, especially the one of several balloons dipping into the Rio Grande."

With a shrug, he said, "Yeah, I sell a lot of that splash and dash photo. I was lucky to be just above them when they splashed into the river."

When Keanu Reeves entered their booth, I froze in disbelief. I blinked a few times. Oh, never mind. It wasn't Keanu after all. He was just a tall, dark-haired guy who looked just like the young version of the actor. I finally took my eyes off his face and saw that he also wore a Fiesta jacket.

Angelica said, "Maria, this is Chris, Marvin's right-hand man. He's been with us for a few months now, and I don't know what we would do without him."

I gulped and said, "Hi, Chris. I have the booth next door."

He nodded but didn't say anything at all. I was sure Keanu would have been a little more talkative. Stop it, Maria. It wasn't him.

Chris turned to Marvin. "We need to get going, Boss."

Marvin nodded. "Guess so. Gotta get the truck in place if we're gonna be in the Dawn Patrol."

Chris turned away, but Marvin waved to us before leaving.

When they were out of earshot, I whispered to Angelica, "He looks so much like Keanu Reeves, that I was startled."

"Who?"

I lifted my hands and said, "Chris."

"Hm, girl. I've seen him every day and I never noticed, but I see him every day."

I found that hard to believe, but I shook it off. "So, they get to be on Dawn Patrol?" I was impressed. Patrol is made up of only a dozen balloons that take off in the dark and fly until it's light enough to find a landing spot. They test wind speeds and directions at the different altitudes to report back to the rest of the pilots.

Angelica answered, "Yeah, they had to apply and were accepted again, but only for today."

"That's so cool."

Angelica frowned. "I'm a little worried that we won't get a green flag because of the wind this morning. I'd hate to think the first Mass Ascension would be canceled due to the wind."

"That would be sad. I guess the Dawn Patrol will find out first."

We both looked up when we heard people approaching. Angelica looked up and sang a little tune, "Here they come."

I rushed into my booth and turned on my iPad so I could accept cards and keep track of sales.

Once the gate opened, spectators still had an hour before any action on the field. They were all excited to see the balloons, but spent the time before, getting food and shopping. I was excited to have customers in my shop. I was ringing up a couple who bought some glasses cases made from men's neckties when another woman asked, "Are those vintage wooden ironing boards?"

I looked at my fun display shelves and said, "Yes. I detached the legs and added brackets."

"So cute! Are they for sale? I'd love to have them for my sewing room."

I hadn't anticipated someone wanting my display shelves, especially first thing. If I sold them, I would have no place to put the items displayed on them. "Uh. Yes, they are for sale, but do you happen to live in the area?" I held my breath, hoping she did.

The woman said, "I live in Rio Rancho."

I let out my breath. I told her the price, then said, "If you want them, I need to ask a favor. They are my display shelves, and I really need to keep them here, at least for today, until I can replace them with something else."

"That's fine, honey. I'm in no hurry and I sure don't want to lug those things around while trying to take photos of the balloons. She looked up at my banner. "I'll just pick them up next week after the Fiesta."

I handed her my upcycled business card and pointed out the address of Upcycled. Once she paid for the two ironing boards, I put a sold sticker on each one.

After that, business was good for a while. It slowed to a near stop when the drone light show began at 5:45. At 6:00 it was time for the Dawn Patrol to go up and check out the conditions.

While my shop was empty, I walked past a few other vendors to the tent's opening so I could watch Dawn Patrol lift off. Like fireflies, the patrol balloons disappeared, then glowed each time their burners were lit. How beautiful.

When the sun started to rise, visitors kept their eyes on the flag flying in the center of Main Street. They hoped the yellow flag would soon be replaced by a green one, meaning the balloons were cleared to fly.

Not long after I returned to my booth, Angelica stepped into my area with her phone to her ear. She hung up and said sadly, "Looks like it's gonna be a red flag day."

My face sank. "Oh, no. All those people will be so disappointed."

She nodded. "Winds blow when winds gotta blow. Mother Nature doesn't kowtow to anyone – even during special events."

With the first mass ascension canceled, guests returned to our tent in a collective solemn mood. A family from Kentucky came in, and the little kids looked as though they might cry.

One boy with his bottom lip stuck out, pouted, and asked me, "Why can't they fly today?" His Southern accent was so cute.

I leaned down to him. "The silly wind is too strong, so it's not safe for the pilots and riders in their balloons. We don't want anyone to get hurt, do we?"

He shrugged and admitted regretfully, "No."

I had already checked the weather for tomorrow and told the boys, "I hope you can come back in the morning. It should be a calmer day."

The mom said, "She's right. Remember, we received rainchecks so that we can see the balloons tomorrow. And we can swim at the hotel when we get back?"

The boys brightened at that and then started looking at my merchandise. I pointed out the tiny robots I had made from hardware. It had been fun creating the little guys from rusted nuts, bolts, springs, and gears.

"Mom, can I have one?"

"You can each choose one," she said. Then she turned to me. "You have so many cute things. I'll bet you'll sell out in a few days."

Yikes, I hoped so, but kind of hoped not.

The morning was very busy with customers. I made more money in seven hours than I usually did in three days at the shop.

After the last group left the park just after noon, I walked to my car and marveled at how much it had warmed up. That's the way our New Mexico sun worked. I rarely wore a coat, even in the dead of winter, as long as the sun was out.

Which did I want more - food or a nap? Alas, as much as I yearned for sleep, a quick Green Chile Cheese Whataburger won. Energized after the protein boost, I zipped home to pack up additional balloon-themed items to take to my booth.

After that, I stopped by the shop, surprised to find it was crazy busy, too. I jumped in to help Jill by welcoming customers and answering their questions.

Jill, who carried Sophia in her sling, sidled up next to me and said, "What are you doing here? You're gonna wear yourself out. Go home and rest."

"I just came by to see you and the kids, and to get more stuff, but it looks like you are selling here too."

"Yep. I am. It's been pretty busy this morning. How's it going at your new fancy booth?"

"So great. But that may be because they canceled the Mass Ascension due to the wind."

"That's too bad. Is it on for tonight's glow?"

"I think we have to wait until this evening to find out."

"Okay. Here. Take Sophia for a minute. I really need to poop."

I wrinkled my nose at Jill and looked around to make sure nobody had heard my goofy friend. Thankfully, they were all busy shopping.

Sophia raised her hands with a smile. I took her in my arms and whispered, "Please don't become a silly girl like your mother."

Sophia put her head on my shoulder and said, "My Mia!"

Awe. Those were words I could get used to. I snuggled her and stood behind the counter, checking out the sales on my laptop. She may be a little obnoxious, but I had to hand it to her. Jill had sold a lot in the few hours she was open.

Jill returned and whistled. "I must have had too much coffee this morning. Thanks." She held out her hands to take her daughter.

I said, "Not yet. This girl is mine for now."

I carried my godchild back to the storage area, where Zia slept soundly on her bed. Jill had bought the little bed for her shortly after we found the abandoned pup in a junkyard last year. The bed was yellow and emblazoned with the red Zia sun, just like the design of the New Mexico state flag. I had named the pup after the Zia sun symbol and Zia Pueblo, where Jill's in-laws lived.

When Sophia babbled something, Zia awoke and popped out of her bed and scratched at my leg. I lifted her up and carried the two around the store as I talked to customers. The striking baby and tiny dog got more attention than my products, but I didn't mind. I was happy to show them off.

After a bit, I decided I should get what I came for. As I handed Sophia back to her mom, I said, "Good job, Jill. I see you sold the globe candy bowl and the stamp-covered lampshade. You're sure earning your paycheck."

"Yeah, but the balloon stuff is going the fastest."

When a couple walked up to buy some balloon ornaments, I winked at Jill and turned away to gather a few items to take to the booth. My supply there was dwindling too, so I'd have to crank out more merchandise Monday through Wednesday, since the Fiesta had no evening sessions then and I'd be done at noon.

My toy xylophone-turned-chimes rang, and I looked up to see good ole Larry enter. Before he reached us, I whispered to Jill, "Has he been bothering you?"

Her eyes widened. "Nope. This is the first time I've seen him."

He squealed when he saw us both. "Well, Missies, how's it going at your two Upcycled shops?" His creepy voice made me cringe, but despite looking like some pervert, Larry was just annoying.

I said, "Hi, Larry. It's going well. I just stopped by between sessions to pick up some stuff."

He licked his lips and looked at the bundle of hot air balloons in my hand. "I told you that you would need lots of balloon stuff, 'cause you'll sell out right away at that there Fiesta.

"Yeah, well, I'm working on it. By the way, Jill's doing a great job here. You don't need to check on her."

"It's okay. I don't mind." He looked toward her and said, "If ya need anything, like watchin' that little baby there, you let me know. My nephews always loved my horsey rides." He patted his knee. "I'll bet she would too."

Jill's face was aghast. No way would she hand her child to him. But she said, "Thanks for the offer, Larry, but we're fine."

He sighed. "Okie dokie, then. Now Maria, if you need me to come over and keep you company, I can probably get away."

My nose wrinkled at the thought. "I appreciate it, but I'll be fine."

I went back to the park and checked in, then rushed to my booth, waving at Angelica as I passed.

She came around the corner and pointed at me. "I'm sure glad you made it before three. This year's manager is a real stickler."

I let out a sigh and asked, "How did you do this morning? Sell a lot?"

"Only about $2,000."

My eyes nearly popped. It normally took me two weeks to make that kind of money - if I was lucky. Their photo prices were extremely high, and I was disappointed to think of how little effort went into framing photos, once they were printed. I had to remind myself that Marvin's photographs were art and my stuff was just repurposed odds and ends.

Once I got over the shock of her high sales, I said, "Wow. And to think I was excited that I made $400 today. Not to mention that half of my stuff is gone."

She narrowed her eyes and said, "Let me see what you have." The impressive woman floated into my booth with the swagger of a movie star. She picked up a paperweight that I had made by encasing a dandelion puff in resin. She cocked her head and said, "Girl, you have this marked at $10. How much were the materials?"

"Maybe $5 for the resin?"

And how much time did it take you to make it?

"A few hours, but it's tricky to get the dandelion centered just right. I messed up several of them and had to start over. Then it takes 24 hours for the resin to set."

"Well, we are changing that to $30 right now."

I started to balk at the price, but she said, "And how about this thing covered with pennies? What is that?"

"It's a bowling ball that I glued pennies to. People use them as gazing balls in their gardens."

"And what was your cost?"

"Oh gosh, a friend gave me the ball, and it took 440 pennies to cover. Then I had to use glue. So, maybe five dollars altogether?"

"And how long did it take you? And what is your price?"

"Probably four hours. I have it marked $15."

She shut her eyes and said, "You know you are probably making less than $4 per hour for labor. Then you have to pay for materials, this booth, and rental at your shop, right?"

I nodded sheepishly. "I know. Everything I make is labor-intensive. Friends always tell me I should charge more, but I feel bad selling things when I get some of the parts for free. I just want my stuff to be affordable."

She shook her head. "Maria, you are selling yourself short. Your time and creativity are worth much more. You are an artist. Don't you forget that." She pointed up. "Okay, for instance, how long did it take you to make these piano key racks?"

I laughed aloud. "You don't even want to know how long it took to take the piano apart."

She looked at the tag and said, "You must be kidding. We're going to raise all of your prices before the tent re-opens. Where are your price tags?"

For an hour, she worked on repricing my merchandise while I attached the new tags.

When a deep voice sang out, "Honey, you're in the wrong booth," I turned to find Marvin standing behind me.

With her hands on her ample hips, Angelica said, "I'm just helping Maria raise her prices. She's so creative, but there is no way she can live on what she gets from her work. Her prices are far too low."

Marvin raised his hands and said, "The doors are opening in fifteen minutes. Might want to get back to our spot."

From the way Angelica pushed her shoulders back, I could tell that was the wrong thing for him to say.

She lifted her chin and spoke in a calm voice, "May I remind you, Marvin Moore, that they are your photographs. I suggest you take some time to meet your customers and sell your lovely photographs on your own, for a change."

Marvin started to object, but she continued, "Tonight's Twinkle Light Glow isn't until 6:30. You have plenty of time to peddle your work before going to your balloon."

Used to his wife's reasoning, he saw he couldn't get out of it, so he saluted her with a smirk and barked, "Aye, Aye, Captain."

I found their relationship a little confusing. No matter who was in charge, he didn't seem to mind being told what to do.

Before he turned away, Angelica said, "I'm not sure if you've seen your competitor's booth, but this year he's making photo mugs, blankets, and keychains. He seems to be doing very well."

Marvin's expression darkened a bit, then he brightened. "Yeah, well, he's riding in my balloon tomorrow. I'll push him aside if he tries to get a better shot than I can." He winked, then turned and left my booth. That exchange didn't make much sense to me.

She scoffed under her breath. "Sure, you will, Honey."

I chuckled as I picked up one of my book clocks and was shocked to see her new price. "Uh. You think this would sell for forty dollars?"

"Sure! And that book cover purse is worth at least $50. Nobody can make something so unique on their own. Trust me."

I wasn't so sure about that, but there was no harm in trying the higher prices for at least one day. I put the clock back and asked, "So who is Marvin's competitor?"

"His name is Stoney. He has the other photography booth right up front." She pointed to the tent's entrance. "The guys have had a friendly rivalry for ten years. Stoney is a daredevil and will do anything to get a great photograph. One year, he rode in a helicopter and took some extraordinary shots of balloons. But the funny thing was, another guy took an amazing photo of Stoney lying on his stomach and hanging out of the helicopter. That photo won an award, too. I could go on and on about his crazy stunts."

Angelica grinned, handed me a newly priced necklace, and said, "Stoney isn't a pilot, so he hitches rides with Marvin." She chuckled. "The two are as different as night and day. Stoney is a showman – always goofing around, whereas Marvin is a stickler for rules and safety."

I said, "I'm surprised Marvin would let Stoney ride with him to take photos if he is his rival."

She stood and straightened her scarf. "They are actually best friends. They play poker together every Monday night. Stoney's like the son we never had."

I shook my head and said, "Those two men sure have a complicated relationship."

Suddenly, there was an onslaught of people heading towards the booths. Angelica said, "Well, they're back. I'd better go remind Marv how to use the sales app again."

My place was busy, so the afternoon passed quickly. No events were going on from four o'clock to six, except the chainsaw carving exhibition, so a lot of people were shopping.

The first thing I sold was a purse made from an old copy of the book, *Heidi*. Who knew I could double the price and still sell it? The cute girl who bought it did say that her name was Heidi, and it was her favorite book growing up. She probably would have paid even more for it.

My sales did increase, and my booth was popular! Maybe Angelica was right, and I had undervalued my work. The poor girl across the way, selling freeze-dried candy, had a lot of people tasting samples, but she wasn't selling very much. Guess there were too many other food options on Main Street.

During the Twinkle Glow, people stayed outside to see the incredible display of balloons. Since they couldn't fly at night, the baskets were tethered to the ground. People walked among the rows of balloons and watched the giant envelopes light up. It was an amazing spectacle.

When the music blared for the evening drone light show, that signaled that we were almost finished. The only thing left were fireworks.

At 9:00, the last pop of fireworks boomed. I waited for Angelica to leave and then drove home. I had to be back in only six hours, so I went to bed straight away.

Chapter 6

Sunday morning, I wore a Balloon Fiesta T-shirt I had bought last year, hoping it would bring good luck so the balloons would fly. As I walked from the car, the wind was much calmer. Maybe the Mass Ascension would go off without a hitch. If it did, there would finally be hundreds of balloons in the air all at once.

When I entered the tent, I ran into the fun balloon guy again. He stood in front of a photography booth and spoke in a loud voice. This time, he was dressed in ordinary clothes, but it was easy to recognize him due to his animated style.

I said, "Thanks for the tip yesterday. I followed your directions and smiled at my customers. I ended up selling a lot."

He pointed at me. "I could tell you have what it takes."

I looked past him to the framed photos on display and was instantly struck by the beauty of one in particular. In it, a hot air balloon was centered right in front of the sun, blocking the light. It caused a gorgeous glow around the balloon. I pointed to it and said, "That's a stunning photograph."

He glanced at it and smiled. "I call that one 'The Ballooner Eclipse'."

Tickled by his sense of humor, I said, "I love it. Well, have a nice day."

He followed me as I walked to my booth, which I thought was weird. It turned out he wasn't following me at all. He kept walking past me and boomed, "Angel, my dear! I've missed you so much. Haven't seen you since yesterday!"

I watched the tall guy pick Angelica up and swing her around just like Joey had done with Louise.

He set her down gently, and she swatted him. "Stoney, you are such a flirt. Good thing Marvin didn't see that."

He winked, "Now, now, Angel, just because you're wearing his ring, doesn't mean we weren't meant for each other." He kissed her on the cheek.

Ahh. He must be the rival photographer she spoke of yesterday. I stared, wide-eyed, at the two fascinating people.

Angelica saw me, then grabbed his hand familiarly, and pulled him toward me. "Maria, this is the obnoxious guy I told you about. Stoney, meet my new friend, Maria."

He leaned down and kissed the back of my hand. "We've met – sort of. Hello Maria. Any friend of this beauty is a friend of mine."

I warmed to Stoney instantly. He was outgoing and friendly. I gauged him to be about forty, a good 25 years Marvin's junior. Funny that they were such good friends.

When Angelica got a phone call and stepped away, Stoney said, "Maria, are you flying this week?"

"No. I have my booth here," I pointed to my area. "So I'd better sell, sell, sell."

"Yeah. I just can't stay stuck indoors all day, so I hired someone to watch my booth."

I laughed. "I spend every day inside. My goal here is to sell enough to cover my booth fee."

He looked inside my shop and picked up a few things. "You will. This is cool stuff." He said, "I want to give you a special pin. He took the enamel pin from the lapel of his blue golf shirt. "This is my special good luck pin. Now you are guaranteed to sell a lot."

I smiled. When he handed it to me, I studied the small design, shaped like a horseshoe balloon. I guessed there was no limit to what kind of shapes they could make.

I stuck the pin on my T-shirt. "Thank you so much. Are you sure you don't need it for luck?"

"I'm fine. I'm invincible! Just ask Marvin."

At the mention of his name, Marvin strode up with Keanu, I mean Chris, by his side. Both men were wearing their company's purple "Up and Away Jackets."

Marvin slapped Stoney on the back. "Ready to ride, buddy?".

"Yep. Thanks for letting me fly, but why the hell are you letting Smith come too?"

Angelica joined the group and listened.

"I only had eight paid riders, and he's been begging me to fly. None of the other pilots wants him on board their balloons. I will try to keep him away from you, because of your…history."

Stoney grumbled, "Maybe I'll just wait 'til tomorrow."

Angelica opened her mouth wide and punched Stoney playfully on the arm. "Are you scared of Smith? I don't believe it."

He cocked his head and looked into her eyes with a grin. "Oh, Angel, you know I'm not afraid of anything. I just can't stand to be around the guy."

Angelica nodded. "Smith is just full of hot air. Ignore him."

Chris was standing to the side, shifting from foot to foot. He pushed his black hair out of his face and rolled his eyes at the two other men. Finally, he said, "I'm gonna go check the propane pressure levels. I'll be back for you guys later."

I really wanted to snap a photo of the guy to see if Jill thought he looked like Keanu Reeves, but he was gone before I could lift my phone.

Not wanting to get involved in the drama happening in my next-door neighbor's booth, I scooted back to mine. I wondered who the heck Smith was. He must be quite a troublemaker.

As I restocked my shelves, I thought about the nice, daring Stoney. I looked down at the pin he gave me and smiled.

As I put more keychains in a basket, people started arriving in droves. I realized the number of customers here this morning could double, considering all the people with yesterday's rain checks and the folks who had tickets for today.

I sold one of the piano key racks for $65 and wondered if I should give that money to Granda Finn since it had been his piano. I would surely offer to pay him.

While I was explaining to a woman how I had made a dandelion paperweight, Angelica came around the corner and whispered in my ear, "Marvin called. There are a few small clouds today, but they got the go-ahead at the pilot's meeting."

I smiled and gave a thumbs-up.

A few minutes later, while I was wrapping the paperweight, people outside started cheering.

The woman gave a loud whoop and said, "Does that mean they are going up?" I nodded. I handed her card back, and she hurried outside along with most of the other customers. Everyone wanted to watch the balloons inflate and take off.

When my booth was emptied, I ran to Angelica and said, "Mind if I go check things out?"

"Go for it, Darlin'. I know most of your products now, so I think I can answer questions people might have."

"Thank you. Oh, do you know which row Marvin's balloon is on today? I may go see them launch."

"It is K-3 and they take off around 7:30."

"Okay, I'll look for them. Thanks." I rushed out and joined the ninety thousand people walking among the balloons on the field. I dodged a few trucks and trailers that were still parking to unload ballooning equipment.

Each row of balloons had a different launch time, which kept them from crowding in the sky at the start. It also gave people a chance to watch more of them launch. It took about two hours to get them all launched.

As I walked onto the huge grassy field, my shoes got wet from the cold dew. How wonderful to feel real grass under my feet in this desert town, which was covered mostly with sand or landscaped gravel.

The Albuquerque International Balloon Fiesta is one of the only balloon festivals where spectators walk out onto the field right in the middle of the action, making it an amazing event.

I paused to watch some Zebras direct a row of balloons to lift off. They are the launch directors whose job is to confirm the airspace above the balloon is clear and safe for take-off. They note that the area around the balloon is free of spectators and other balloons. Zebras are easy to spot in their black and white striped shirts - hence their name.

No matter how many times I'd witnessed a mass ascension here, it was still magical. Entranced, I ignored the people around me and focused on the roar of the balloon burners igniting the propane fuel. The heat from the nearest balloon flame warmed me, and I couldn't help but smile. That, plus all the colors and shapes of the gorgeous balloons, was mesmerizing.

When a woman pulling a wagonful of toddlers bumped into me, I woke up and remembered I was supposed to be heading to Row K and started that way again.

Marvin's team hadn't laid out the nylon fabric yet, so when I arrived, I asked if I could help. He was busy but smiled and said, "Sure. Just remember to wear gloves so we don't get oil on the envelope." He pointed to his trailer. I walked over and put on a pair of cotton gloves.

I had crewed a few times and remembered that there were a lot of moving parts. I started by helping the crew unroll the huge bundle of purple fabric onto the grass. While Marvin, Chris, and Stoney lifted the enormous basket out of the trailer, another guy with a receding hairline aimed a fan into the envelope's opening. I listened as he barked orders rudely at the crew. Who the heck was he?

People held ropes as the envelope began to inflate with the air from the fan. I surmised the bossy man who acted like he was in charge was the one called Smith. I looked at him more carefully. He was wearing a lime green jacket and a dangly balloon earring. Ok, that was an odd look.

One gal from the crew was tasked with keeping spectators from stepping on the envelope. I walked to the other side and did the same. Everyone around me had their phones pointed up to the sky or were taking selfies with the colorful fabric as a backdrop. Of course, many people used fancy cameras with long lenses. What surprised me was how many people held up iPads to take photos. That just seemed cumbersome.

The man in green shoved a stack of cards into my hands and growled, "Hand these out."

Well, okay then. As I handed out balloon cards to onlookers, I studied what Marvin, Chris, and Stoney were doing. The basket was on its side as they attached the burner to hoses and checked for leaks before activating the pilot light.

My stack of cards drew children to me like candy. Even though this balloon was one of 20 matching purple balloons from the "Up and Away" company, people were still happy to get cards. During a brief lull, I studied one of them. The front had a photo of the balloon with the 'Up and Away' phone number. The back of the card provided the balloon's stats. Since this was a company, the cards were basically an advertisement for the 'Up and Away' paid balloon rides.

I wondered who the riders would be this morning and looked over to the truck, where a group of excited people stood in a clump taking photos of each other in front of the billowing sideways balloon.

Marvin yelled, "Hey, Smith, I could use some help here with the inflation."

Sure enough, the guy who gave me the cards was Smith. He rolled his eyes as he joined them. When he made it over to the fun-lovin' Stoney, there was obvious tension. Stoney frowned and stepped away. I wondered what their beef was. Smith grabbed the basket roughly and started yanking it up before the others were ready.

Once the purple balloon was standing upright and passengers were on board, Marvin would await permission from the Zebras to safely launch. Marvin and Chris hopped into the basket. When Marvin ignited the burner, flames flew upward with a whoosh. The crowd of soon-to-be passengers cheered and took more photos, and the balloon began to fill with hot air.

While Stoney and Smith held the balloon down, they glared at each other across the big wicker basket. Wow, such drama among men. Who knew?

Marvin told the group, "All aboard!"

Even though there were footholds in the basket to help people climb over the four-foot side, Stoney set a stepstool next to the basket to make it even easier. I rushed over and took photos of the basket's interior. I'd never seen one so big up close. It looked very roomy, but it might not be once a dozen people were inside.

Stoney helped the giddy guests aboard. First, there was a cute young couple, then two older couples climbed in. Then two 50-something ladies, who dressed alike, followed. By the way they acted, they may have already had numerous mimosas.

All the paying passengers were now in the basket, jostling for the best positions. Marvin hit the burner often to keep the air inside the balloon hot, but not so much that it lifted off. When the balloon started to rise without Smith and Stoney inside, I watched the crew pull it back down.

On the flights I had taken, the baskets only held 4, so being up close to one so big was fascinating. How could it even lift off, with so much weight? I started taking photos of the passengers waving, in case Marvin wanted to e-mail the pictures to the riders. While snapping, I finally got a good one of Chris/Keanu to show Jill.

When Smith noticed me taking photos, he practically shouted, "I told you to hand out cards. What are you doing over here?"

I was startled by his outburst and put my phone down.

Stoney turned to Smith and said, "What the hell, Smith? She's not your employee. She's a friend who offered to help."

Smith wrinkled his nose and said, "Fine." He started to step on the stool to climb in, but Stoney took it away just as his foot got close.

That was shocking, but I was even more surprised when Stoney turned to me. "Ladies first…Maria?" He put the stool down again and ushered me to step up.

I was confused. "Oh, I'm not going on the flight."

Stoney winked. "You can if you want. I don't mind giving you my spot."

Wow. That was so kind of him. I looked over the top of the basket that came up to my chest and understood why they needed a step stool. As much as I wanted to hop in, I shook my head. "No. I can't. I need to be in my booth."

He frowned, but said, "Are you sure?"

I nodded.

When Stoney motioned for Smith to climb in, the man fumed. He took a tentative step toward the stool, probably worried it would be pulled out from under him again.

Once Smith was inside, Stoney tossed the stool aside and hopped up onto the side of the basket. He swung one leg over, straddled the side, and yelled, "Giddyap!" as he gave Marvin a thumbs-up.

Everyone except Smith laughed at the jokester. Marvin said, "Up and Away!" Then he hit the burner enough for the monstrous flying machine to lift from the ground with Stoney still straddling. Spectators on the ground cheered, as they do for every take-off. I took a video from my vantage point below.

When the basket was feet off the ground, Stoney finally pulled his leg inside. What a goofball.

It amazed me how quickly the balloon rose into the sky. Another pilot in a multicolored balloon flying next to Marvin's yelled, "Let's kiss."

Oh, how fun! The two pilots expertly navigated toward each other so that the balloon envelopes briefly touched in the sky. This tactic was especially fun to watch when two special-shaped balloons, like the two adorable bumblebees, touched at the mouth

Once Marvin's group had flown too far for another good photo, I made my way back across the field toward the tent. I stopped along the way to watch an elephant go up. It was funny because right next to it was a mouse the same size.

As I left the field, I made a quick trip to a porta-potty since the line was short. When I stopped by Angelica's booth, I told her, "Well, they're up!"

"Good."

"Did anyone come by here?"

"Only a few. No sales for either of us. Now that you're back, I'll head to the bathroom."

"Oh, sure." Why hadn't I offered to watch her booth earlier?

I sat on my tractor-seat stool and scrolled through the photos on my phone. Ooh, I got some good shots of the passengers. And there was that funny one of Stoney straddling the basket. What a silly guy. I texted that pic to Jill, then a good one of Chris to see if she thought he looked like Keanu. But it was pretty early, so she was probably still asleep.

The girl across the aisle waved at me. I made my way over to her. "How's business?"

Her shoulders slumped. "I don't think I'm a natural salesperson."

I said, "Ok, try it on me."

The girl cleared her throat and said, "Would you like to try freeze-dried Skittles?"

I pretended to be a customer. "What are they?"

"They are Skittles candies that are freeze-dried."

I said, "Sure. I will try a sample." I looked at her and said, "Maybe give a little more description. Maybe tell how they are made. Do you make them yourself?"

She nodded but looked like someone who had just been asked to give a speech in front of a thousand people.

"Practice on me. Just relax."

I heard a strange moan and looked up to find Angelica standing in front of me with a flushed face and trembling lips. A silent tear ran down her cheek as her hand clamped onto her phone. "What's wrong, Angelica? Are you ill?"

She shook her head rapidly and gasped, "He fell."

I moved toward her. "What? Who?"

Her hand reached out to steady herself on my booth's frame pipe, but she missed and started to fall through the curtain. I grabbed her and led her over to sit on my stool.

"Take a breath and tell me what happened. Who fell?"

"S Ston…Stoney."

"Stoney fell down? Is he ok?"

She leaned her head back and wailed, "He's…" When she blinked, tears ran down her face. "He's dead."

I gulped and tried to make sense of what she was saying. I couldn't fathom how it happened, but I waited until she was ready to speak again.

The distraught woman rested her elbows on her knees and covered her face with her hands. After she took a deep breath, she said, "He fell from the balloon."

My face lost its color. I stuttered, "How in the world…"

My question was cut off by the blaring of sirens as emergency vehicles headed to the field.

She lifted her head to listen, then sniffed and said, "I don't know, but Marvin says Stoney was clowning around and leaning outside of the basket trying to get a photo. All they can figure is that he lost his balance."

My pulse picked up as I pictured him falling from the balloon. What a horrible way to die. I leaned over and gave her a long hug. "Angelica, I'm so sorry. That's just awful." I had so many questions, and once I stepped back, I asked, "Is the balloon still in the air? Or did they land?"

She took a shaky breath and managed to speak. "They landed in Rio Rancho, and another crew is bringing them back here." She closed her eyes. I thought she was finished, but she continued so softly I could barely hear her, "Marvin's chase crew was following them and saw him fall and called 911. They were able to reach his crumpled bo…" She broke down in sobs, unable to say the word.

It was difficult watching my new friend in such angst. They must have been very close.

Once she had composed herself a bit, it was as if she heard my thoughts. She said, "Stoney was extraordinary."

I'd only met the man a few times, but even I could see that he was a special guy. How tragic.

When Angelica's phone rang, she grabbed it from her pocket as if she hoped for good news. "Yes?"

I watched as her face crumpled again. "Okay, Honey." Her voice sounded strong, but I could tell it was forced. She said, "I'll meet you back at the launch site."

Just as she hung up, an announcement came over the speakers throughout the Fiesta. "We are very sorry, but due to an accident, the Fiesta will close early today. Please proceed carefully to one of the exits. Watch the website for updates on whether tonight's balloon glow will go on as scheduled."

That was a first for me. I'd never heard of the Fiesta being canceled for anything besides weather. How very, very sad.

Angelica said, "I guess they're on their way back here. I need to go see Marvin."

She turned to me. "Can you watch my booth until I get back?"

"Of course." My heart ached for the devastated woman. When she stood, I hugged her again and was surprised at how frail she felt in my arms. The woman who seemed so large and in charge was now just a shell of herself. Her shoulders slumped as she left.

At that, my tears began to fall.

I sat on my stool and tried to think of how someone could fall over the 4-foot side of a basket. There have been accidents in the past, but they usually involved balloons hitting something, landing too hard, or the wind carrying them into dangerous areas.

My phone dinged, and I saw a text from Jill. "Is Keanu Reeves in Albuquerque?"

Normally, I would have made a wisecrack, but I just wrote, 'No. It just looks like him.' I remembered the other photo I had sent and called her rather than texting the awful news.

When she answered, I told her all about the accident with the guy with the man bun in the other picture. "I don't know much yet, but I'll let you know when I find out."

"Oh, Maria, that's just terrible. Was he still straddling the basket when they went way up?"

"No, he put his leg in, but he is…" I corrected myself, "He was kind of a daredevil, so he might have done something like that again."

"Unbelievable. So how are the Fiesta people handling things?"

"Well, they sent everyone home and might even cancel tonight's Balloon Glow. I'm stuck inside, so I'm not sure what's going on now."

"I'm so sorry you're having to deal with that. Are you ok?"

"Yes. I'm just worried about my next-door neighbors. Angelica is very upset, and Marvin probably feels even worse since he was the pilot. I'm not sure what to do. Guess I'll wait until they come back. Angelica left her purse here, so I'm sure she'll come get it."

"Okay, well don't even think about coming by the shop. You take care of yourself and get some rest."

"Thanks, Jill. I'm glad you have a full day off tomorrow."

"Yes. That will be nice. Kelly, Sophia, and I are coming to the Fiesta and will stop by your booth to see you – if the Fiesta is on."

I frowned at the idea that it might be canceled another day, but said, "That would be great."

It was only nine a.m., and other artisans were already packing up to leave. The candy girl stopped by with a worried face. "So, did someone really die falling out of a balloon?"

I nodded. "Yes. It looks that way."

"That's just awful."

"It was the man who welcomed us at the door. Do you remember him? Tall and outgoing?"

"Oh, yikes. He was so nice. He gave me a pin shaped like a lollipop balloon."

At that, I instinctively touched the horseshoe pin Stoney had given me. I've never been superstitious, but I wondered if his missing the lucky pin made him vulnerable.

I realized the girl was staring at me, so I replied, "He did seem very generous. Are you heading out now?"

"Yes. I guess I'll go home and practice my sales pitch to my dog. He's a very good listener."

I smiled. "I have one of those, too. My name is Maria."

"I'm Jenny. Guess I'll see you tonight or tomorrow."

I figured I would be going home soon, too, so I made a list of what had sold and what I might be able to quickly make again so my booth wouldn't look so empty when I got back.

My mind, of course, was still on the incident. I was sure the police would investigate the accident, as well as officials from the Fiesta. What a travesty.

It wasn't long before I heard voices. Angelica and Marvin entered my booth. He looked sick, and she looked frazzled. She said, "It looks like the police will interview all the passengers here in our booth shortly, but I can't stay. I need to go home and take something to knock me out. Would you mind hanging around until they are finished?" She leaned in and added quietly, "And make sure Marvin is OK? I'm just too upset to think right now."

I said, "Of course. You go take care of yourself. I'll be fine."

"Thank you, Maria. You're an angel." At the mention of Stoney's nickname for her, Angelica started crying again. Marvin walked her out to get an Uber.

When Marvin returned, he looked paler than ever. He sighed and said, "Now the police want to use your space for the passengers to wait until it's their turn to be interviewed." He pointed to my area. "But you really don't have to stay to watch over them - or me. Chris will be here soon. Go on home."

I waved him off. "It's really no problem, Marvin. I have things to do here anyway. I'll go to the check-in booth and ask if they can loan us some chairs."

He said, "I'll help you."

I held up my hands. "No. You go get ready for the interview. I'll take care of everything. I'm so very sorry you lost your friend."

His eyes were red, and he looked as though he might cry when he explained, "I'll never forgive myself. I was in charge. It happened when we flew through that stupid cloud. I didn't have much choice with the helicopter, and all. I shouldn't have listened to Stoney when he begged me to go through it."

I wondered what that meant, but said, "Well, I'm sure the police will understand."

He closed his eyes. "That's not who I'm worried about. It's the Federal Aviation Administration. They'll get me good. I just lost my best friend, AND I'll probably never fly again."

I hadn't even considered he might lose his license. As much as I wanted to comfort the man with a hug, it would have been awkward since I barely knew him.

My thoughts were interrupted when a familiar voice growled, "Okay, Moore, let's get this started." I groaned because the person who spoke to Marvin was the world's grumpiest police sergeant. Oh, brother.

I watched Marvin move toward his booth, and I felt even worse for him now that he had to deal with the annoying Sergeant Barnes.

Chapter 7

The obnoxious detective, Sergeant Barnes, caught sight of me and rolled his eyes. "Olson. Not you again."

There it was, that gravelly voice that grated on me. I studied the man who had bugged the hell out of me last year when he investigated a death near my Upcycled shop. As usual, his gray hair was unkempt, his shirt was wrinkled, and his tie was loosened. I grumbled, "Hello, Barnes."

He shook his head. "Please tell me you weren't a passenger on the balloon in question."

"No, I was not. I was here in my booth."

He looked around and smirked. "Still peddling junk, I see."

This guy was so rude, I couldn't help but say, "And you look like you slept in your clothes." Whenever I'm around the annoying man, we end up sounding like two ten-year-olds.

He looked down at his shirt and scoffed, "I'm a busy man. Now, don't you go sticking your nose into this investigation. This is serious stuff. You just stay here and sell your little trinkets."

I had no intention of getting involved in the investigation, but his command wouldn't make a difference. I mocked a salute and barked, "Sir, yes, Sir!"

Barnes smirked and said, "Good. One less problem for me to deal with." He moved next door just as a young couple from the balloon ride stopped in front of me.

The pretty gal wearing a new Balloon Fiesta sweatshirt with the tag still attached said tentatively, "The pilot's wife said we were to meet here?"

I said, "Yes! Come on in. It's going to be tight with so many people. I'll go find some chairs."

The tall, fit husband said, "I'll help."

He introduced himself as Chad and followed me across the large tent to an area where I checked in daily. My stomach churned when I passed Stoney's booth filled with gorgeous photos. Memories flashed back of him sending out well wishes to the other merchants.

When we arrived at the check-in spot, I informed the woman in charge of the situation and asked to borrow some chairs.

She said, "Well, sure, take all you want, but you could just have the group sit here – we have a lot more room than in your little booth."

"That's true, but I was asked to keep the passengers close by and in my booth, so…" I twisted my mouth.

After Chad and I carried the folding chairs to my booth, I noticed Chris had joined Marvin and Sergeant Barnes. Naturally, they were the first to be questioned since they manned the balloon. We returned for four more chairs and put them in the main aisle. I kinda hoped some of the witnesses might stand and look around at my stuff. Always the salesgirl.

Once the group was all together, I introduced myself and told them my booth was the holding area until they were taken next door to be questioned. I counted the passengers and realized one was missing. Must be that Smith guy. That was weird.

I sat down at my computer and started gluing pennies to another bowling ball. To keep it from rolling, I set the heavy ball on a sturdy plastic bowl.

As the passengers began discussing the accident, I listened in and soaked up as much information as I could. After all, I'd met the guy who died and was concerned for my new friends, the Moores.

An older man said, "Well, this shouldn't take long. We all know the guy was a daredevil and lost his balance."

His wife said, "Yeah, but I didn't see it happen."

Another taller man said, "It happened right when we went through that little cloud. I was so amazed by the magic of the mist that I didn't notice anything. He could have just fallen, or maybe he jumped. It could have been suicide."

I thought no, the Stoney I met was full of life and would never kill himself. He seemed to be optimistic about everything – well, except for whatever was going on with him and the guy named Smith.

The gals in matching balloon shirts had sobered up. The blonde one said, "I didn't think pilots were allowed to go through clouds. He seemed to be avoiding the other ones up there."

Her friend said, "Yeah, but remember, that helicopter came up right above us. I think Marvin descended to try and avoid its draft."

"Yeah, that's what I thought." Chad said, "But did you hear Stoney yell, 'Marv, hit the cloud!'?"

I stopped keeping track of who spoke and just listened.

"I heard it. I looked up to see him leaning out over the edge of the basket with his camera—first facing up in the direction of the helicopter, then down at the cloud below us."

I had so many questions and couldn't help but ask, "Did any of you see him fall out?"

The group gave me a blank stare. Then they came to life when they realized they had someone to tell the story to. They all came at me, talking at once with bits and pieces of what had happened.

"We were all so distracted by the weird, cool mist in the lone cloud. At least that's all I thought about, anyway."

"Yeah. And it only took us about 20 seconds to get back into the bright, clear blue sky."

"When we did, someone yelled 'Where's Stoney?' and we realized we had one less passenger."

A woman said, "That's when someone screamed, and everyone rushed to look over the edge to see if he was hanging on somehow. But there was no sign of him."

My stomach lurched as I visualized the scene. *The tall guy leans over the edge of the basket with his camera in position. As the balloon nears the cloud, Stoney knows he'll get the perfect shot if he angles out just a little bit farther. When the mist disorients him, he loses his balance and falls a thousand feet through the air with nothing to stop him.*

Barnes stepped into my booth, snapping me out of the horrid image. He said, "Okay, folks, please do not talk about the incident with each other or anyone else until the formal investigation is finished."

He glared at me as if I were involved. I wasn't about to tell him I'd already heard a lot. Shoot. Now I couldn't ask any more questions.

Barnes pointed and barked at a lady, "You, come with me."

The woman stood, let go of her husband's hand, and followed Barnes nervously. Why did he have to be such a bully?

The rest of the group was now close-lipped. I tried to lighten things up. "Porta-potties are just outside. I have a few cold drinks in my little ice chest that you are welcome to. Feel free to browse my shop, if you like. I can answer questions about anything I upcycled."

One man took a Coke from my cooler and thanked me. The matching women looked over my jewelry while a man pointed up and said, "Where did you get those piano keys?"

I told him the story of my piano deconstruction, then picked up an ornament and a keychain. "I also made these from the felt hammers that hit the strings."

The guy held up one of the ornaments and raised an eyebrow. So, the hammers come in different sizes to match the thickness of the piano wire?"

"That's right.".

"Wow. I love that. I'll take two of these, two keychains and will think about getting a key rack." He looked at me and added, "You are very clever."

While I processed his payment, Chad, the guy who helped with the chairs, said, "Hey, do you ever need bicycle parts? I have a bike shop, and we use old bikes for spare parts. We can't use many of them on the newer bikes, and I need to clean up the storage room.

I got excited as soon as he started talking, and when he finished, I said, "Oh my gosh, yes."

A woman piped up and said, "Do you need more bowling balls or pins? We used to run an alley, and we have a lot."

Her husband agreed. "We have so many." He rolled his eyes.

"Yes! Please, please, please! I'd love to have anything interesting like that. I also always need books, old clocks, picture frames, light bulbs, toys, or tools. I'm in the Out of the Box shopping center, not far from Montano and Second. Stop by any day except Mondays when we're closed, and I'll take them off your hands. I can pay you for them, of course." I handed business cards to those who seemed interested.

When the detective came back, he traded his first victim for her husband. The woman took her husband's seat and held up a piece of paper. "The 'Up and Away' company is giving us free flight coupons for our trouble."

I was glad she didn't seem upset after being interrogated.

She held up a piece of paper. "The 'Up and Away' company is giving us free flight coupons after this."

Others replied in various ways. "That's the least they can do." "I'm not sure I want to go again after today." "Well, I will, but I'll make sure there isn't a nutcase onboard next time."

I wanted to defend Stoney, but I wasn't sure I could since I knew so little about him.

The group dwindled one by one. Chad and his wife were the last to leave. He said, "I'll bring those bike parts by soon. Can't wait to see what you do with them."

Marvin stopped in and said, "Barnes is talking to Smith now. So, we're almost done. You can go ahead and leave."

I was glad Smith was among those being interviewed. I asked tentatively, "Well, how did it go?"

Marvin sighed. "Everyone corroborated my story, and it was deemed an accident." He looked a little relieved.

"Will you still have to talk to the FAA?"

"Yes. We have an emergency meeting this afternoon at the Air Route Traffic Control Center down on Louisiana Boulevard. The helicopter pilot will be there too." He shook his head. "But right now, Chris, Sergeant Barnes, and I are going to the Balloon Fiesta office to see how to handle things here."

I hated to ask the next question, but I did, "Did Stoney have family here?"

Marvin frowned. "Nope. Angelica and I were the closest thing to a family he had." He backtracked a bit and said, "Well, he has a younger sister in Wyoming, but they've been estranged for years." He shook his head. "She was always trying to get money from him. Then, after she stole the entire inheritance from their parents and bilked him out of his savings, he finally stopped all contact with her."

"Oh, that's too bad." With no family, I wondered what would happen to Stoney's beautiful, framed artwork. His photos weren't my business, but it sure made me wonder what would become of all my belongings if something were to happen to me.

The aggravating detective appeared beside Marvin, holding his crumpled notebook. He growled, "Ready?"

The two turned to leave, but Barnes had to have the last word. He pointed at me. "Someday you're gonna grow up, stop playing with arts and craps, and get a real job."

I frowned—just sure it was his mission in life to make me crazy. I couldn't contain myself and said, "Maybe someday, you'll find joy in your life so you're not such a miserable grump."

The man shook his head as he walked off.

Unsure if I'd be back in the afternoon, I packed up what I could work on at home and left. On the drive, I thought about Stoney's death. Even though I was only 32, healthy, and far from being a daredevil, I realized I should probably get a Will, just in case. Just like Stoney, I had no immediate family nearby. My little sister died of cancer at age ten, and then my parents were in a fatal car accident nine years ago. Aside from my Abuela, who lived in a small town in Mexico, and my Norwegian grandparents in South Dakota, I had no other relatives.

Jill was the closest thing to family I had in New Mexico. We have been best friends since first grade. I decided that my Will would split everything between her and my grandparents, and Zia would go to Jill.

Thinking about who would inherit my assets made me even more depressed as I pulled up to my little old adobe home. I was exhausted. A nap was in order this time, no question about it.

After sleeping for two hours, my alarm rang. It was 12:30. The first thing I did was check the Balloon Fiesta website to see the status of the evening's activities. The official announcement was,

'Due to a freak fatality accident, Sunday evening's Balloon Glow has been canceled. Please check back tonight to get information on tomorrow's events.'

Well, dang. I hated what Marvin must be going through. It was also a shame for the tourists who had come to town for the weekend events, especially after the mass ascension was canceled because of the wind. Then, today, half of the balloons were grounded and weren't permitted to launch due to the accident.

I didn't feel like working, but I had to make more products. While I sat at my dining room table painting lightbulbs, the house was way too quiet without Zia. Of course, she never made any noise, but I talked to her a lot. I needed to hear a friendly voice, and so I called Jill.

"Hey Maria, how are you?"

"Better. I took a much-needed nap. Do you want me to relieve you this afternoon since everything is canceled for tonight?"

"I heard that on the news before I left to come here. And no. You rest or work on products. It's easy here today. Kelly is off, and he took Sophia to the Nambe Pueblo Feast Day to see his family's booth. I only have Zia with me, and she's no problem at all."

"Thanks so much. Oh, Jill, guess which detective is handling the accident case?"

"No. Please don't tell me it's Mr. Grumpy Pants."

"Yes—in all his aggravating glory."

She chuckled. "At least you're not involved in the investigation, so you don't have to deal with him. I tell ya…Kelly was so glad to get moved to administration, so he didn't have to see Barnes every day."

Jill's husband, a big, handsome Native American policeman, worked in IT at the downtown police station. I knew his 6-month stint working with Sergeant Barnes had been torture for him.

After hanging up, I was still in a funky mood and texted Joey. *'Hey, whatcha doin'? I could use a break if you want me to stop by.'*

He wrote back instantly. *'Come on over! We have a crowd, but I'll save a seat for you at the bar.'*

Ah. His words made me feel better. I checked myself in the bathroom mirror. I looked okay, despite the long, hard nap. I took my hair down from its messy bun and ran a brush through it. It was halfway down my back now. Was it time for a haircut? No. That was nothing I needed to worry about this week.

I drove to Out of the Box and walked into the pub, surprised by the number of people. It was a lively scene for a Sunday afternoon. There, behind the bar, stood my gorgeous boyfriend. He was a sight for my sore old eyeballs.

I plopped on the stool that he pointed to, and I yelled above the noise, "Hey, barkeep, give me a tall one of your new brew."

"You can't handle a tall one. You'll fall asleep."

I laughed. "Okay, give me a short. Just hurry. I'm parched." I winked at him.

Once I took a sip of the icy-cold 'Chase Crew Brew,' I relaxed, but when I saw what was further down behind the bar, my jaw dropped open. I yelled, "Joey!"

He came rushing and couldn't keep a straight face. "So, you saw it?"

I nodded numbly. I had seen it. My eyes glistened as I studied the beautiful ghost. It was Granda Finn's incredible piano carcass. The boys had fixed it up, so it was now a cool display cabinet for beer bottles, glasses, growlers, and retro beer signs

I said, "You saved it!"

"We did. Once Jett and I had the thing loaded on the truck, we didn't have the heart to dump it. I told him I wished we could use this at our pub. And the ball started rolling. We love it and are already getting compliments."

I was still so happy and said, "Jill is gonna freak out."

He changed the subject. "So, how's the beer?"

"It's really good. You better watch out, or Jett may take over your brewmaster job."

"Not on my watch. But yeah, it's decent for sure."

I knew it wasn't the best time to discuss my incredible morning, while surrounded by his thirsty patrons, but I told him the gist of what happened.

He frowned. "People have been talking about it since we opened. Sorry to hear it was someone you knew. You ok?"

I sighed. "Yeah. I barely knew the guy, but he was a fun-loving daredevil whose luck ran out."

As Joey left me to settle someone's tab, the words I'd just spoken reverberated in my mind. *His luck ran out.* I pushed my long hair aside and found the horseshoe balloon pin Stoney had given me. It was still pinned on my shirt. Of course, he hadn't fallen because I had his lucky pin. That was ridiculous. Still, I had an uneasy feeling about the accident. Something wasn't right.

Joey was too busy to visit, and besides, a guy was waiting for a seat at the bar. I finished my beer, laid cash on the bar top, and stood to give the man my seat.

I called out, "Joey, I've gotta go. Talk to you later." I pointed to my money so he could see it.

With a sad face, he waved.

On my way out of the pub, I saw his brother talking to the hostess. I stopped by. "Hey, Jett. I love the label on your Chase Crew Brew. And the beer itself is great."

"Thanks. That's good to hear. Man, we haven't seen you for a long time, Maria."

"I know. I'm living in my Fiesta booth."

"Oh, that's right. Did you hear about the accident today?"

I nodded but didn't want to get into it again. Luckily, a cute gal in her twenties ran up and distracted him with a hug. She continued to flirt with him, but that was par for the course. Jett looked like he just stepped out of a Men's Health magazine.

I smirked, waved, and headed to my house. Shoot, I forgot to ask the guys how Burritos and Balloons went.

I had just sat at my dining table/worktable, with my remote in hand, ready to stream reruns of *Gilmore Girls*, when my phone rang with the Mexican country code of 52. It was either a spam call or one of my relatives calling from Mexico. The number didn't belong to my grandmother, but I answered anyway. "Hello?"

A female with a Spanish accent said, "Hey Maria, it's Carmen, your cousin."

Carmen was one of twenty Mexican cousins. If she were the one I pictured, Camen was about five years younger than me, heavyset, and super quiet. I hadn't seen her since my parents took me to Mexico to visit Mom's huge family. I could only think of one reason she would call me.

I aked nervously, "Carmen, is Abuela alright?"

"Oh, si. She's good. She gave me your number. I'm coming to see you in America."

I was surprised that she would come to New Mexico and even more taken aback by how good her English was. I said, "That's great! It will be so good to see you. When are you thinking of coming?"

"Ahh, Thursday."

I put her on speaker so I could look at my calendar for the next few months. "Which Thursday are you thinking?"

"This Thursday. I'm going to fly to see you and the balloons."

I nearly choked. That was not possible during the busiest week of my life and with everything else going on.

I sputtered, "Um…Carmen. I'm very busy this week. I won't be able to show you around because I'm working at the festival and must be there the whole time. Why don't you come in a few weeks or months when I can spend time with you and show you Albuquerque?"

There was a bit of silence, and then she said, "That's ok. I won't get in your way. I just want to see the balloons. I will text you."

Before I could protest further, there was a ding on my phone. I opened the text with her full itinerary. She had already booked her flights! What the hell?

Chapter 8

Oh, my Lord. My Mexican cousin was coming to visit me at the busiest time of my life. The only thing I could think to do, was to call my grandmother. I spoke in rapid Spanish, basically saying, "Abuela, did you know Cousin Carmen is flying here this Thursday? I can't have her here. I have a booth at the Balloon Fiesta."

She replied calmly in broken English, "Nieta, you know how these girls are. They haves the mind of their own. She will do what she want, even if we say noh. So, when you busy, she must make out on her own, si?"

I let out a big sigh, then asked my grandmother how she was doing. I was sorry that the first things out of my mouth sounded like I was frantic.

She assured me that she was fine and healthy, just busy with so many mouths to feed. The poor woman fed and housed family, friends, and even took in folks right off the street. She was a saint.

After the visit, I ended the call with, "I miss you, Abuela. Te amo."

All was well when we hung up – except for the fact that my cousin was coming in three days and I hadn't invited her.

I worked on more products to take to my booth while streaming my show. The mother/daughter relationship in the *Gilmore Girls* made me both happy and sad. I pretended the relationship of Lorelei and Rory might have been ours if my mom hadn't been taken away so early. I sighed and tried to be positive.

At least I would have a blood relative here with me for a few days. Who knew? It might be nice.

Realizing I'd never looked at her schedule to see how long Carmen planned to stay, I studied her itinerary. She wasn't flying out until the following Thursday. She would be here for an entire week? Yikes!

Stop it, Maria. Perhaps Carmen could help in the shop by upcycling with me. It would be like having a sister around. But that thought made me sad, since I had lost my own sister at such a young age. The closest thing to a sister I had now was my crazy friend, Jill. I called her again.

When she answered, I didn't have a chance to speak because she started nonstop. "You won't believe it, but remember that lady who broke the bird from the birdbath and let her awful kids run around the shop? Well, she came back to buy the birdbath. Her boys weren't with her, and this time she wore a ballcap with sunglasses as if incognito. She must have really wanted that birdbath and hoped I wouldn't recognize her."

"What did you do? Did you bring it up?"

"No. I thought, 'What would Maria do?' Instead of making a big thing about it, I sold it to her politely, pretending I didn't notice her disguise. Funny thing was, she left an extra ten-dollar bill on the counter. I guess she felt guilty about the bird she broke."

"Well, that's a very nice ending to the story." I sighed. "I just hope I have as good an ending to my own new story." I told her about Carmen's upcoming visit.

"Oh, goodie! You've met all of my relatives, and I've never met any of yours except your grandparents when they came to town for the...funerals." She said the last word quietly.

"It's fine, Jill. I'm worried she'll be bored sitting around while I'm working. And a whole week? Seriously?"

Jill tried to comfort me. "Oh, you'll get along fine. You always do. Maybe I can take her off your hands a bit. Oh, gee, I should go. My little Sopaipilla is cranky and needs food NOW or she'll go into full tantrum mode."

I laughed. "Sounds just like her mother when she's hangry."

"Ha Ha. I'll see you tomorrow-that is if the show goes on." She hung up.

Her comment reminded me to check the status of the Fiesta. The website now said that the Fiesta would take place tomorrow morning. Good. I texted Jill, '*It's on. See you tomorrow!*'

Since it was only four o'clock, I had time to complete some products. I had been nervous about raising prices, but it hadn't affected my sales, and I was making more profit. Yay Angelica.

As I glued hangers onto my light bulb balloons, I wondered how my new friend was doing. It must be awful to lose a close friend in such a horrific way.

Thinking of the accident, my gut told me something wasn't right. Stoney was daring, but he wouldn't have been so reckless as to fall over the tall side of the basket at that great height. But, since nobody saw what happened, I'd probably never know.

I switched my thoughts to my upcoming guest and vowed that poor, boring Carmen would have a good time if it killed me.

The next morning, I arose way before dawn again, this time with my nerves jangling. I took the pin off yesterday's shirt and stuck it on today's top in honor of Stoney. Maybe the little horseshoe did hold luck.

When I entered the big artisan tent, I encountered Fiesta volunteers erecting a makeshift wall in front of Stoney's booth, essentially cutting it off from shoppers' view. That small action made me feel very sad.

Nobody was in the Moores' booth. There were still a few extra chairs in mine, so I hauled them to the check-in area. As I set the chairs down by the tables, the young gal who had been selling Stoney's photos was there complaining about the booth being closed. Apparently, she hadn't been paid. Oh, great. Another mess to deal with.

The manager of the tent said, "We're really sorry, but we need to find his next of kin to figure out what to do with his stuff."

I piped up and said, "I'm sure Angelica and Marvin Moore from booth 17 can give you some information."

The woman looked at her sheet and said, "Yeah, but they called and won't be coming in today."

"Oh." I got the girl's name and number and told her I'd get back to her if I found out anything.

I turned to the woman in charge and said, "Do you have a sign we could put up, so people don't go into their shop today?"

"I have one that might work." She left and brought back a cute sign that said, 'On a balloon ride. Please stop by later.' This is all we have."

I said, "Thanks. I'll set it up."

I put the sign in the opening of my neighbors' booth, then scrounged around until I found Marvin and Angelica's business cards. I grabbed one of each so I would have their phone numbers.

Once I had set up everything, I texted Angelica to ask how she was doing. I didn't expect an answer anytime soon since it was only 4:45 a.m., but just as the first customers arrived, my phone rang. I stepped into the back corner to answer. "Hello?"

She spoke in her slow, melodic voice. "Hi Maria, I'm glad you texted because I didn't have your number. I'm so sorry I walked out yesterday with hardly a word to you. It was all just too much. Thank you for taking care of the passengers."

"It was fine. I hope you are feeling better. Maybe another day of rest will do you some good."

"Yes. We must take care of business regarding Stoney and his business. And honestly, I wouldn't be good around strangers today, anyway."

"Well, I have a question. Do you know how the girl who worked in Stoney's booth might get paid?"

She gasped. "Oh my gosh…I hadn't thought of that. Can you get her number for me? We'll be glad to send her whatever she is owed."

"I have it right here." I gave her the number and said, "Oh, and we put a sign up in your booth, so people know you are closed today."

Just then, a woman walked up to me carrying a few ornaments and some little paper birds made from old sheet music. I held up my finger for her to wait a second and told Angelica, "Listen, I need to go. People are arriving. I'll call you later."

"That's fine, Hon. Good luck today."

I was glad to hear her sound more like herself than she had sounded yesterday. I took the birds from the lady. "I'm so sorry. It was a pretty important phone call."

She spoke in broken German, "Is gut. I love birds and need small things to take to Deutschland. These are wunderbar."

I smiled as I wrapped each small item carefully so they wouldn't break during travel. "Enjoy the balloons."

"Ya, I vill."

When she left, I felt strangely alone without Angelica next door. I wanted to ask her if we would have a green flag or the dreaded red one today. Since nobody was around, I rushed outside to check the wind. It seemed calm to me, but ground level wasn't the only place where wind speeds were considered.

When I rushed back inside, there were customers in my booth. I sold quite a bit in the first hour.

I saw Jenny bagging up some candy and smiled. Maybe practicing her sales speech with her dog had helped her feel confident. She gave me a friendly wave.

Later, while my booth was packed with people and I was taking a man's credit card, a woman squealed, "Oh, my, these are the cutest things I've ever seen. You are so talented."

Ha. I looked up to see my bestie, Jill, doing her 'hustler' routine. Sometimes she acted like an enthusiastic customer to entice others to buy my products. I rolled my eyes as she pointed at some of the more expensive items and gushed like they were the coolest things ever. It worked. A woman bought a few pairs of blue earrings made from gin bottles. It had taken forever to sand the edges of the broken glass just right, so I was glad to sell them.

Another man bought a piano key rack. When there was only one person left, Jill sidled up next to me and pretended to be interested in the tractor seat I was sitting on. She whispered, "See, what a good salesperson I am?"

"You don't need to do that, silly. I'm doing alright on my own. Where is Kelly?"

"Oh, he and the squirt are in the next booth looking at hats." She looked around. "I like how you have the place set up. It's really cute." Then, she looked around the curtain at the Moores' booth and said, "Aren't they back yet? I wanted to meet your new friends."

"Nope. They're taking another day off. I feel so bad for them."

"Well, their photos are amazing."

Kelly arrived, but he had to duck to get in without hitting the pipe holding up my booth. The man was already tall, but now he was wearing a ridiculous hat shaped like a hot air balloon. The silly hat was the last thing I could imagine the quiet, unassuming man would ever wear. He carried Sophia, who wore a cute bonnet made of hot air balloon fabric, of course.

I hugged Kelly and said, "Are you working undercover? Nobody would ever guess you were a respected police officer in that." I pointed it out.

He pulled something out of a bag and stuck it on my head. It covered my eyes so I couldn't see what it was, or anything, in fact. Jill started laughing, so I pulled up the hat and looked in my mirror framed with bits of costume jewelry. I was wearing a stocking cap with a wild pattern of balloons. "Thanks, Kelly. I love it."

He said, "Actually, this one is for Jill." He took off his big balloon and put it on her head. "And this one is for me." He put on a nice ball cap with a small, inconspicuous balloon on the front.

"Okay, now that makes way more sense."

Jill grinned. "Selfie time," and took a few shots of the four of us in our new hats

Sophia reached her arms out for me to take her, but Jill said, "Not now, pumpkin, we're going outside to see the balloons." She turned to me. "We'll come by later. Want something from Main Street?"

"Yes! Green chile cheese curds, please, or those tiny donuts. Either one sounds great!"

She gave me a thumbs-up as they left.

Other people stopped by; some buying, and others just looking. It was nice to meet people from all over. In one hour, I met people from Norway, South Dakota, Rhode Island, and Italy.

When Pat and Mike showed up, I said, "Hi, guys! I'm glad you could come!"

Mike, who stood a head taller than Pat, said, "Absolutely. We love having Mondays off."

I smiled. "I think it'll be a great day to see balloons."

Pat bounced a little. "Not only that. We get to ride in one." He looked up at his partner with admiration. "Mike surprised me and booked us a flight."

I could feel his excitement. "That's awesome! You're going to love it. I've been a few times, and it's so quiet up there. Just unbelievable. Are you riding in a bit 'Up and Away' balloon?' or a smaller one?"

Mike said, "It's going to just be us, the pilot, and one other person."

Pat added, "We'll be in a striped balloon called, Lollipop."

The two guys looked so happy, but a tiny feeling of dread rushed through me. I tried to dismiss it quickly. After all, balloon travel is very safe. They would be just fine.

Mike said, "After the flight, the chase crew will bring us back here. Want us to stop by and let you know how it went?"

"Yes! Have fun and take lots of pictures."

I watched them leave. The guys still reminded me of Mitch and Cam from *Modern Family*. They are so friendly, and boy, did those two know how to bake!"

When the crowds dispersed to watch the balloons take off, I had time to add up my sales from the weekend. Yay. I was happy to find I had made enough to cover my full booth fee. Everything else would be gravy — well, not really, since I had spent a lot of money on supplies and time upcycling. But still, I was happy.

Since there were so few people in the big tent, I took notice when a man passed by. It was Chris, the handsome Keano look-alike. His straight dark hair swung as he walked past the sign next door and straight into Angelica's booth. I assumed it was fine for him to be there.

I peeked around the corner and said, "Hi, Chris."

The guy was so startled he dropped some papers and stammered, "Oh. Sorry. I didn't know you were there." He picked the papers up and put them in a backpack.

I said, "How are you doing? I can't imagine all you are going through after yesterday's accident."

When he spoke, I half expected him to say, 'Yeah, Dude, it was so gnarly,' ala *Bill and Ted's Excellent Adventure*. Instead, the man said, "I'm okay. I just stopped by to get some papers for Marvin."

I had been afraid to ask Angelica something, but why not ask him? I said, "Was there a decision from the FAA? Will Marvin still be allowed to fly?"

He was distracted, looking around at papers, but answered, "Yeah. They decided it was an accident, even though Stoney caused it by being so reckless. Marvin was fined for flying through the cloud, but the helicopter pilot was fined for getting too close to a balloon. It shouldn't tarnish Marvin's business."

"Oh, good." I walked a step closer. "The whole thing was just terrible. Did you know Stoney well?"

Chris looked a bit irritated at my continued questions, but managed to answer, "Just the few months I've been here." He paused. "He was okay – but a foolhardy show-off."

I thought that was crass considering he was speaking of the dead, but Stoney's antics must have rubbed people the wrong way.

I said, "Well, I'd better get back to work."

I moved back to my booth. Rather than going out to see the balloons, I enjoyed some quiet time. I looked over my merchandise. There was only one hot air balloon made from a book left. I didn't have my jigsaw, so I couldn't make a new one here. I scouted around to see if there was something else I could make today, and ended up cutting strips from New Mexico maps to make cute hanging hot air balloons.

As I sat at my counter, weaving the strips from the maps, I saw another man walk by. He looked familiar. Then I recognized him as that Smith guy who had flown with them on that fateful day.

When I heard raised voices next door, I listened but couldn't decipher their words. I did hear one of them say, "It was an accident. Just leave it alone."

I wish I knew which guy said that. So, someone else thought it might not be an accident? I stood and tiptoed over to my curtain so I could hear better and pretended to hang something up in case one of them saw me.

Unfortunately, all I heard was a loud voice saying, "Can I have a big bag of the Gummy Worms, and ooh, can I try a sample of the freeze-dried green chile?"

Sure enough, across the aisle, an older woman was buying freeze-dried treats from Jenny. Why did she have to choose that moment to be so loud?

Once the woman left, I put my ear to the curtain again, but the only thing I heard was an irritated man say, "Yeah, we'll see."

I watched as Smith walked by in a huff. I considered going over to see if Chris was okay, but customers were moseying back to the tent. Oh well. It was none of my business anyway.

It wasn't long before the Standing Bear family returned, carrying not only a bag of the tiny donuts but the green chile cheese curds I had also been wanting to try. I hopped up and down. "Yay! Thank you." I took a bite of the crunchy, flavorful cheese. "These are amazing. Thank you. So, tell me about the balloons while I chow down."

Sophia was the first to speak. She pointed to my last hanging book balloon and said, "Baboon."

I nearly choked on my last cheese curd. Jill, Kelly, and I snickered at the adorable toddler, but didn't want to embarrass her by laughing out loud. I looked at Sophia. "Were the baboons pretty?" I was sure the three of us would forever call balloons baboons.

She said, "Petty Baboon."

Jill said with a wink, "Maria, have you seen the baboon shaped like Elvis?"

My mouth was full, so I just shook my head, no.

"Well, it's so big and adorable."

I swallowed and asked, "Did you see two baboons shaped like a cop and a robber?"

Kelly said, "Yeah. Those were funny."

I was sure poor Sophia would never live this one down, even once she was grown. I said to her parents, "I'm glad you could come this morning. And thank you for the hat and food. Let me pay you back." I stepped to the back curtain and grabbed my purse, but Kelly said, "You're not paying us. It's our treat, but we need to get her home for a nap."

I leaned in to Sophia, then in a baby voice, I asked, "Is it time to go home and take a nap?"

Kelly laughed. "Not her. Jill is the one who needs a nap. She is nothing but trouble if she doesn't get her eight hours." He winked at me, and they took off. Jill shrugged and followed them.

Chapter 9

I had just popped the last little donut in my mouth when a man asked me how I cut globes in half.

I wiped my mouth and hands on a napkin and grabbed the knob attached to half of a globe. It had been upcycled into a food cover for picnics. I pointed to the edge and swallowed. "It took a long time to score through a half inch of glue. I guess they make it so thick to keep it from coming apart under normal use. I do not, however, use them normally."

He laughed. "Where did you get so many globes to make bowls, candy dishes, lamps, and this cloche? He picked it up."

I was surprised he knew the word cloche. I had recently learned it myself. I said, "Well, I went to the Albuquerque Public School warehouse sale and lucked into buying a pallet of obsolete globes. My whole garage is filled with them, and big pull-down maps just waiting to be upcycled."

The woman with him said, "I like that you kept some of the globes whole on their stands and painted them in different ways." She pointed to one. "Look, John, this one has a slot for cards and is painted with the word, Love! We could get this for Josie's wedding."

He pointed up. "Sure, but I want that globe lamp too." I was glad he was tall so he could get it himself, so I didn't have to drag out my stool. Being so short was a problem, sometimes.

As they left with their repurposed globes, Mike and Pat entered, all out of breath. My booth was like Grand Central Station. Pat especially looked giddy.

Mike winked and said, "Show her."

I squinted at the two, wondering what they were up to. Then Pat held his hand up to my face, where I saw a unique ring with layers of turquoise and copper.

Assuming they had bought it at one of the shops on Main Street, I said, "That's really cool. How was the balloon ride?"

Both of them sported goofy grins as Pat said, "No, Maria. We're engaged!"

When I finally caught on, I gawked at the gorgeous band, jumped up and down, and grabbed Pat's hands. "It's amazing! I'm so excited. So, when? Where? How did this happen?"

Pat waved his arms around. "Ok, so the balloon ride was awesome, and we were having the most amazing time. I was taking a million pictures when I saw we were flying right over our shopping center. I took a picture of our bakery and called out to Mike to look, but he didn't join me. I turned around but didn't see him. For a split second, I thought he had fallen over the edge like that man did. But no, he was down on his knee in the middle of the basket looking up at me, holding this ring!"

Mike said, "I had worked it out so that the pilot's wife would record the whole thing." He looked very proud.

I couldn't stop smiling, myself. "Well, I just can't think of a better couple or a more exciting proposal. Congratulations to both of you! Do you have a date for the big day?"

Mike said, "Not yet. We need to find out when our families can come to town."

"Well, you had better invite me!"

Pat rolled his eyes. "Oh, of course we will. All the Boxcar Adults will be invited, but especially you, Maria. You're our closest friend there – and the first to hear our news!"

Mike nodded. "Pat, we should go call our parents."

I congratulated them again as they rushed off to spread their news to the world. How exciting!

With no evening event, I headed toward my Upcycled shop to work on products. I loved working there when nobody was around on Mondays. As I drove, I realized it would be too lonely without my tiny shadow, so I stopped by Jill and Kelly's house and got my dog back for the afternoon.

Back in my shop, I said, "Did you miss me, Zia?" She was sound asleep, snuggled in my vest, so I knew she had.

As I watched the local news while working on paper projects, a report came on about Stoney's death. I turned up the volume. The reporter stood on the field at Balloon Fiesta Park in a jacket and a stocking cap. It must have been replayed this morning's report, because it was still dark outside.

I listened carefully as she said, "Yesterday, balloons were grounded for the day after a terrible accident in the sky." A photo appeared on the screen. It showed Stoney, standing next to a hot air balloon basket, with his camera in hand. When I saw the excited look on his face, a tear rolled down my face.

The reporter said, "Sam 'Stoney' Stone fell from a balloon in flight and was pronounced dead at the scene. Mr. Stone was 38 years old and was an accomplished photographer. He won many awards with his underwater images, some taken while skydiving, and, of course, his famous hot air balloon photos. He was also quite a philanthropist. The hot air balloon community will greatly miss the Stoney Stone." A different photo appeared, showing Stoney and Marvin standing inside a balloon.

The reporter reappeared and said, "After an in-depth investigation, the incident was deemed an accident. No charges will be filed." She looked directly into the lens. "Accidents are rare. Ballooning is still considered among the safest forms of travel."

The camera cut to several balloons lighting up, ready to take off. The reporter smiled. "As you can see, everything is back on, and according to balloon officials, more than 90,000 visitors are expected here today. Johanna Maxwell reporting from Balloon Fiesta Park. Back to you in the studio, Brian."

As sad as the story was, it was nice to hear more about Stoney.

I worked a bit more until my back started hurting. I took Zia out for a walk around Out of the Box. All the shops were closed, but the Rusty Railroad Brewpub was hopping. Why not stop in and see my friends?

When Joey spotted me, he came out from behind the bar and kissed me. As usual, Zia strained to reach her favorite guy.

Joey touched my shoulder. "What a lucky day for me. I get to see both my favorite girls." He motioned to Jett and pointed upstairs. We followed him up the steps to the pub's new outdoor balcony.

Joey, Zia, and I sat at a table overlooking the forest along the river, which we, New Mexicans, call the Bosque. It was lovely seeing the Sandia Mountains rising above the trees. I could even see the Rio Grande River through the swaying Cottonwoods.

Joey said, "So, did you hear about Mike and Pat?"

Gee, the news had traveled fast, but knowing Pat, he probably called everyone right away. I said, "Yes. I saw them this morning, just after the big proposal. They were so darned cute. And what a fun place to ask someone to marry them."

Joey said, "We're planning to have a surprise engagement party here for them tomorrow evening. Julie's idea, of course. You don't have to work tomorrow night, do you?"

"No. I'm free. The guys will love that. What do you need me to do?"

"Well, you're pretty busy, but if you have any decorations, that would be great. Larry is going to tell Mike and Pat that he's calling an emergency meeting here at seven tomorrow night, and that they need to be here."

I chuckled. "Oh, that should work. How fun." I looked around the new deck. "I've been meaning to ask how your first weekend of 'Balloons and Burritos' went."

"It was packed all three mornings. We sold a lot of breakfast burritos, but the Mimosas and Bloody Marys were the real hit."

"And did the balloons fly overhead?"

"Not yesterday since the winds blew north. But Saturday and today, some flew right overhead."

I nodded, remembering Pat had seen the shopping center as they flew. "Cool. Hey, did any of them land on your X?"

"Nope. Not yet."

I told him everything I knew about the accident. Then, I told him about my cousin who would be arriving in a few days. "I haven't even gotten the house ready for her."

"Well, she's asking a lot of you to come during such a busy week, so I wouldn't go overboard getting ready."

I shrugged. "She probably didn't understand what I was trying to tell her. There's a bit of a language barrier."

"Well, I hope she'll be fun to have around, at least."

"Me too."

Zia and I left, then I worked a few more hours in my shop. When I started fading, I dropped the pup off with her second family and went home to crash.

Tuesday morning, I was relieved to find my neighbor back in her booth. "Welcome back, Angelica." I gave her an empathetic smile.

She sighed. "We had to come back so we didn't void our contract with the Fiesta. Plus, this is our biggest money maker of the year."

That made sense. "Are you doing okay?"

She shrugged. "Even though we've been working on Stoney's stuff, it's just still so hard to believe he's gone. But we're planning a celebration of life this Friday at 12:30, just after the visitors leave. It will be in the pilot's pavilion.

"Oh, that's wonderful. Can I help with it?"

"Maybe. We'll be working with the Fiesta committee. Anyone who knew him is invited, so you should at least stay for it."

"That's sweet, and I definitely will. Oh, and do you happen to have a list of this year's balloon names and their pilots, with phone numbers? My friends got engaged on a balloon ride, and I want to ask their pilot something."

She handed me a directory, and I looked up the green balloon named 'Lollipop'. I jotted down the phone number and handed it back to her. "Thanks. Good luck today!"

After about an hour, when people had started coming into the Artisan tent, Angelica came over, looking frazzled. She said, "Can you watch my booth?"

I jumped up and said, "Of course." Before I could ask what was going on, she bolted for the field. I hoped there hadn't been another balloon accident. I checked my phone to make sure there were no emergencies reported on the news.

While she was gone, I managed to handle all my customers and hers as well. I even sold an expensive 20 x 24 framed photograph of hundreds of balloons taken from high above.

Angelica finally came back and thanked me profusely. "It was just a problem with those knuckleheads, Chris and Smith."

I nodded. "I heard in some sort of skirmish yesterday in your booth, but I didn't hear what they said."

She cocked her head. "They were in my booth together yesterday?"

I scrunched my nose. "I'm sorry, I didn't know they weren't allowed."

"Never mind. It's all okay." She looked at the space on the carpeted display wall and brightened. "You sold one?"

"I did! Surprisingly, the couple had cash. But I didn't know how to wrap it, so they took it as is."

"Great. You deserve a commission."

"No. Please…it's fine."

"Well, let me give you something." She walked over and pulled a small 8x10 photo from the wall. It was of the bumblebee balloons kissing. She handed it to me.

The picture was adorable, but I saw the price tag and said, "Oh, no. I can't take that."

"It's nothing. I have more just like it in that big tub." She pointed to a container under a table. Just take it, unless you want a different photo?"

I took the picture from her and held it to my chest. "No, the bees photo is my favorite! I love it. Thank you."

When I finally left Fiesta Park, I ran some errands for the engagement party and bought food for my cousin's arrival on Thursday. As I left the store, I called Jill. "Hi girl, how's it going? Do I need to stop by the shop?"

"Nope. Everything's under control here. Oh, Maria, this morning a man brought in a shit ton of bowling balls and pins. I wasn't sure where to put them, so I had him stack the boxes behind your shipping container, out by the dumpster. It's not supposed to rain this week, and I doubt anyone will bother them since they're out of sight and super heavy."

"Oh, cool." I explained, "He's one of the people on that awful balloon ride. While the passengers were in my booth, people kept offering to bring me stuff. I'm sorry he came while I was away."

"No biggie. I didn't have to move them. Hey, did you know there is a great big white X between your shop and the brewpub? Is it for baboons to land?"

I laughed at the thought of baboons landing there. "Yeah, I forgot to tell you. Let me know if anyone actually lands on it."

"I will, but most baboons have already landed by the time I get here at 9:45, but who knows? Are you ready for your cousin, Carmen's arrival on Thursday?"

"Not really. I just loaded up on food that I hope she likes. I also got stuff for a surprise engagement party we're having tonight."

"Who is getting married?"

Since I hadn't told her about Mike and Pat, I filled her in.

"That's amazing – I love those guys."

"I'll clean the house tomorrow afternoon. Then Thursday will be crazy since between sessions, I have to go to the airport to get her."

"Want Kelly to pick her up? He might be able to get off early."

I chuckled. "No. I'm pretty sure having a large policeman pick up a Mexican at the airport would freak her out. Besides, we need to get re-acquainted. It's been over ten years since I saw her."

Back at home, I baked two batches of biscochitos – one for Carmen and the other for Mike and Pat's party. I made sure not to overcook the yummy traditional New Mexican cookies because Pat and Mike made the very best ones, and I'd be embarrassed. It felt good to do something other than upcycling merchandise to sell, even though I should have been doing just that.

The only wedding-ish decorations I had on hand were colorful wine bottles with lights inside. To make the décor more personal, I had asked the pilot's wife to text me the video from Pat and Mike's engagement proposal ride. I extracted stills from the video and had 5x7 prints made. I cut slits in some wine corks, inserted them into the bottles, and placed the photos in the slits as a display.

I arrived at Rusty Railroad at 6:15 to help with the setup. When I walked in, all the members of the Boxcar Adults were already there – Louise, Jett, Joey, Julie, the three antique store guys, Larry, and Sally Ann.

My decorations looked nice on top of Julie's pretty tablecloths. There was plenty to eat and drink, since everyone brought food. And of course, there was plenty of beer. I hoped it would be a nice impromptu surprise party.

We had 20 minutes before our "meeting" and when the boys would arrive, so I visited with my friends. Louise reminded me she would be by my booth on Friday with Bart and Lisa.

I said, "You have the cutest and funniest grandkids."

"Don't I know it! They keep me on my toes. I do wish the little buggers lived closer so I could see them more, but my daughter refuses to move here because she doesn't want to dry out her skin. She already wants to get a facelift, and God knows what she might do if she lived here and got even more wrinkles."

I thought about all the lotion I went through. But I much preferred living in a desert to the ridiculous humidity in Texas.

Sally Ann tapped me lightly on my shoulder and said quietly, "I still haven't been to see the balloons. I'm kind of scared after hearing about the accident. Does that happen often?"

I put my hand on her arm. "Oh, no. It was just a freak accident. Actually, the guy who fell was kind of a daredevil and may have been leaning out of the basket too far. It's very safe – and there is definitely no risk in watching them inflate and take off."

The others heard my conversation and listened.

Always ready to get involved, Larry puffed up and said with his whiny voice, "You just don't worry your pretty little head, Sally Ann. It's safer to ride in a hot air balloon than in a car." He put his thumbs in his front pockets and stood taller. "As a matter of fact, I could arrange a flight for the two of us, if you want. I know some really important people." He leaned in and name-dropped a bunch of well-known and influential people in Albuquerque - none of whom she had probably heard of since she was new here.

I waited for the gal's reaction. Oddly enough, she wasn't creeped out by the greasy manager's advances. The mousy girl smiled at him and looked excited at the prospect of going with him in a hot air balloon. Well, good for Larry.

Carl walked up to me. With his head facing the ground, he said, "D d d did you see the man fall?"

"No, Carl. And I'm glad I didn't."

"He was p p p pushed."

Everyone turned to face him. I said, "What?"

"I think h he was p pushed out of that b b balloon."

Joey said, "Why do you think that, Carl?"

"My brother t t told me."

My head swiveled to the only brother there. Danny couldn't be more different from his much younger brother. Due to Carl's autism, he was socially awkward and rarely looked anyone in the eye. Once I got to know Carl, I found he was really sweet. Conversely, Danny was overly confident and intimidating. He was the one antique store owner I didn't know well, and honestly, was a little scared of.

I asked Danny, "Did you say that, and if so, why?"

He made a face at Carl, then started in, "Stoney and I were best friends in high school, and we've met up a lot since. Stoney was really smart - like brilliant. He was also very agile. The guy would do all kinds of stunts that people thought were crazy, but he was in control of everything he did. No way he fell over the edge of a 4-foot-tall basket." He bit his lip. "I just don't believe it."

His theory fascinated me. "Who would have wanted to hurt Stoney?"

He scoffed, "Obviously someone who was in that basket."

I wanted to tell him who was on the flight and ask what he thought, but just then I heard Pat whine to Mike, "I told you we were late to the meeting. Everyone's already here."

We all turned to the door where the guests of honor stood. We yelled out a less-than-enthusiastic, "Surprise!"

Confusion appeared on their faces until they saw the table with food and decorations – something we never had at our meetings. Then they figured it out and brightened.

Louise said, "It's just a little party to celebrate your engagement."

Everyone congratulated the couple as they neared the table. Mike studied a photo displayed above a wine bottle. It was a shot of him kneeling with the ring in his hand. "How did you get these photos from our balloon ride? I thought she was taking a video."

Louise said, "Well, obviously, that would be Maria. She is always on top of everything."

I said, "I just contacted your pilot's wife, who sent me the files, and I captured a few stills. She will send them to you tomorrow."

Pat said, "That's so cool. Ooh, and look at all the food! You guys…this is so special." He wiped away a tear.

The party was fun. I sat between Joey and Louise as Pat described Mike's momentous proposal. Then they told us all about their upcoming plans. The wedding would be held in December with a red and green color scheme. As the excited guys talked, I couldn't help but think of fun gift ideas I could make.

Joey whispered in my ear, "Maria, will you be my plus one at the wedding?"

I smiled. "I was going to have you be my plus one."

We were all having fun, but as time went on, I found myself glancing at the train book clock hanging by the back door. I finally said, "I hate to leave early, but three a.m. will be here very soon."

Larry hollered from the end of the table, "I'm gonna have to bring little Sally Ann over some mornin' to see your booth."

I said, "You do that, Larry."

Before I left, I walked over to Danny. "This Friday at 12:30, they're having a celebration of life for Stoney at Balloon Fiesta Park. I thought you might like to attend."

I gave him the details and he said, "Thanks. I might do that. Stoney was a super cool guy, and I'm really going to miss him."

Wednesday morning was more of the same at my booth, except that I spent most of the day wondering if Danny was right. Had someone pushed Stoney to his death? And if so, who, and what was the motive?

Larry did show up, and Sally Ann acted star-struck around him. "Larry got me a ride on a balloon today. We'll be going in one called "Boots" and it has cowboy boots on the side."

"That's so much fun. I'm glad for you."

Larry puffed up as usual and said, "Sally Ann, why don't you pick something out from Maria's booth as a souvenir?"

She looked around wide-eyed and giggled, "Can I have this?"

The girl held up a picture frame I'd covered in balloon napkins and Modpodged. It was a simple craft anyone could create. I said, "Good choice. If you print a photo from your flight, you can put it in there."

I would have just given it to the girl, but I knew Larry wanted to be a big shot and buy her something. He said, "If you want a picture frame, you get a picture frame. Nothing is too big or small for my pretty date."

Sally Ann blushed at his comment.

Larry whipped out a stack of bills and handed me a ten. He reminded me of Barney Fife when he tried to impress Thelma Lou on the *Andy Griffith Show*. I used to watch reruns with my sister and laugh at the guy.

I noticed Jenny standing alone in her booth across from me. I said in a loud voice, "Oh, Larry, don't forget to check out the delicious, freeze-dried candy across the aisle."

The two walked over, and Larry bought Sally Ann a bag of colorful candy. I couldn't help but smile at the two. Jenny gave me a wave and mouthed thank you.

Once alone, I looked for a pad of paper but only found my pink notebook that Jill and I had used since elementary school. It still had lots of empty pages. Surely, she wouldn't mind if I used it for an important reason. I jotted down names of the people who were on that ill-fated flight and could be suspects in Stoney's death – if it was homicide, that is.

1. Marvin – being the pilot, of course, he was in the balloon that day. I doubted Marvin would harm his good friend, but then again, he was the sole beneficiary in the Will.
    Angelica had said Stoney was Marvin's rival in the photography world, and he also might be jealous of Stoney's attention to her. Still, I doubted he was involved. Besides, he was busy flying the balloon at the time.

2. Chris – I knew little about the guy except he looked like Keanu Reeves and had only worked with the Moore's for a few months. At times, he seemed to be impatient, but no worse than I was sometimes. Besides being indifferent when asked about Stoney, I couldn't think of a motive for him to kill Stoney.

3. Smith –I didn't know much about the man. But he seemed to have ongoing issues with Stoney. I saw firsthand that he

could be very rude. He was unlikable, but did that make him a murderer?

4. The other passengers - Some grumbled about Stoney ruining their flight, but nobody seemed to know him personally.

The whole possible murder mystery bothered me all day, so when I saw Chris and Marvin enter Angelica's booth, I made an impromptu appearance to check them out.

"Hey, guys. How was your flight today?"

They looked up at me. Marvin said, "Well, nobody fell out of the basket."

That made me cringe.

Angelica said, "Marvin. Stop that. Nobody blames you for anything." She turned to me and said, "He's a little bit touchy because a few passengers are refusing to fly in that balloon now."

Marvin interrupted me by saying, "She's right. I didn't mean to take it out on you."

I said, "I just stopped by to ask what I could do or bring for Stoney's celebration of life on Friday."

Marvin said, "Don't worry about it. The Albuquerque Ballooning Club is sponsoring it. Even though Stoney wasn't a pilot, everyone knew the guy and loved him. But do come. The more the merrier."

I remembered that I had invited Danny and said, "I hope it's okay that I invited one of Stoney's high school friends. He's pretty broken up about the whole thing."

This time, Angelica spoke. "Of course, darling. What's his name?"

"Danny Harrison."

She nodded her head slowly. "Marvin, remember Stoney's friend, Danny? We took him up in the balloon not long after his uncle died last year. It will be nice to see him again."

At the mention of his uncle, I had a flashback of stumbling over his body last summer. I felt my stomach flip. I would never forget the death and traumatic events surrounding it. I shook it off and was just glad Danny would be welcome at the celebration.

Marvin agreed with Angelica. "Yes. I remember Danny was pretty intense, but he was more relaxed around Stoney."

As we spoke, I noticed Chris standing silently off to the side. He seemed to be taking it all in.

Without much thought, I said, "So, Chris, how long did you know Stoney?"

His eyes widened as if he wasn't expecting to be spoken to. "Um. I met him when these two hired me to be their assistant. August, I think."

I needed more information. "Are you a Burqueño?"

He narrowed his eyes. "A what?"

Angelica answered for me, "She means, are you originally from Albuquerque? Burqueño is a nickname for locals."

He looked at me. "Oh, no. I just moved here in late July."

I wanted to ask him where he moved from, but he looked so uncomfortable with the attention that I dropped it and said, "Well, someone is in my shop. Better go."

I hadn't unearthed much information today, but maybe I would on Friday when everyone was together at Stoney's ceremony. Wait. Why was I even worrying about it? It was the police's job to find possible killers. For a second, I thought of contacting Sergeant Barnes about it, but dismissed it, considering our history.

After I left the park, I worked on some products at home, then prepared the spare bedroom for Carmen. I cleaned the kitchen and picked up the living room. It wasn't often I had a house guest, and I wanted to get it right. I was actually excited that she was coming.

Thursday morning came early, but I felt refreshed. Angelica made the day even better when she stopped by and gave me a bowl of green chile stew and a donut.

I said, "You didn't have to buy me food."

"I didn't. I got it from the Pilots' Pavilion."

"Oooh, aren't you fancy that you can go in there?"

"Anyone can with one of these." She pulled a lanyard and badge out of her shirt. It must have been hidden in her oversized bosom. "I'd let you borrow mine, but they look at the photos and we're definitely not a match."

"Well, thanks for thinking of me anyway. It smells delicious."

After I ate, a local man came in and bought every single one of my light bulb balloon ornaments as gifts for his staff at the electric company. What an appropriate gift. I was happy about selling out, but I would need to make more of them. Maybe Carmen could help me.

At noon, I hopped into my truck and drove 13 miles south on I-25 to Albuquerque's Sunport. Since I hadn't seen Carmen in so long, I went inside the airport to wait for her rather than pick her up at the curb as I usually do when meeting arrivals.

I sat in the newly recovered seats of the waiting area and watched for my cousin to ride down the escalator.

I loved our medium-sized airport with its beautiful Southwestern architecture and décor. The tall viga beams, the metal clock that hung overhead, and the Native American and Hispanic artwork all gave it a good, homey feeling. I hoped visitors would feel the spirit of the Land of Enchantment upon arrival.

I watched families reunite, couples kiss, and kids holding welcome signs. It was fun to imagine their stories. Maybe it had been years since they had seen each other. Perhaps it was the first time that an older couple was about to meet their grandchild. Watching people arriving always reminded me of the beginning and ending scenes of my favorite movie, *Love Actually*.

A group of three lively girls dressed for a night out partying chattered on their way down the escalator. What was their story? Maybe it was a bachelorette weekend. Just then, one of them pointed to me and squealed, "Maria!"

What? The girl in a short dress looked like a model wearing high heels, styled hair, and a very revealing top. She looked nothing like the homely teenager I met years ago. It couldn't be Carmen, could it? I turned around to see if there was another Maria she was calling out to. Nope. There was only a bald man with a walker standing behind me.

Maybe it was Carmen, but who were the other girls? Did she meet them on the plane, and had they become fast friends?

Once they got to the bottom of the escalator, the girl in question rushed over. It really was Carmen. I recognized her intense dark eyes. She hugged me, but the feathers on her little shrug tickled my nose, making me sneeze. When I pulled back, I noticed she was wearing a pink jewel on the side of her nostril.

The Carmen I remember had been shaped like her father - stocky and short, but now she resembled my mom's side of the family. She looked like me. We were both petite and thin with long dark hair.

I said, "Carmen! You look so different. I didn't recognize you."

"Si, girl…I grew up." She waggled her head in a sassy way. "And you look just the same. You still have bonita azul eyes."

I laughed. "Yes, my eyes are still blue." I couldn't help but notice the other two girls huddled behind her with wide eyes and big smiles. Why didn't they go on?

Carmen said, "Maria, these are mi amigas, Bianca and Coco."

Bianca was a beautiful, tall, thin girl with a wide smile and perfect teeth. Her hair was dyed blonde. It looked unnatural with dark roots, but still looked cool. She could easily pass for a model.

Coco was tiny and looked like she was about 16. Her dark brown hair reached her lower back. She had adorable dimples that made her look even younger.

The girls giggled, waved hi to me, and said in unison, "Hola."

I said, "Hi. Did you girls meet on the airplane?"

Carmen laughed. "Oh, I've known them all my life."

My eyes brightened. "That's so cool. Who are they visiting in Albuquerque?"

She laughed. "No, silly. They will be staying at your house with me."

Chapter 10

Somehow, I kept my mouth from falling open at the news that Carmen had brought two more people with her. I was sure my eyes gave away my shock. "Uh…Carmen, you didn't tell me you had two people coming with you."

"No? Oh well, the more merry for us all."

"But…" I stammered, "I only have one guest room. The third bedroom is now my office."

She turned to the other girls and rattled off the explanation in Spanish. Being fluent myself, I understood their conversation, but Carmen still turned back to me and said, "It's ok, Prima, if you have a sofa, Coco can sleep there."

Dumbfounded, I wondered what I had gotten myself into. I didn't want two strangers and a cousin I barely knew living in my house—especially when I would be gone most of the week. Could I afford to put them up in a motel? That was a definite no.

Then I thought of another problem. I didn't have a back seat in my little truck. How could I even take them home? What a fiasco.

As the four of us walked to baggage claim, I explained in Spanish that I drove a small truck and wasn't sure how we would all fit. They assured me it would be fine.

I watched as they kept pulling luggage from the conveyor belt - two big suitcases each. Oh, brother. My small house was going to be so crowded with the three of them and their stuff.

When we reached my truck, Carmen's two friends started to climb into the bed. I knew it was illegal to have anyone under 18 ride in the back of the truck, and asked quietly, "How old is Coco? She looks young."

"No, no, no. Hermanita is 18 already."

I wasn't sure if Hermanita was a nickname or if Coco was Bianca's little sister. I guess I would find that out later.

I said, "I don't feel comfortable having anyone ride in the back, especially on the interstate."

They shrugged their shoulders and ended up squeezing into the cab. Little Coco sat on Bianca's lap.

I had planned to take Carmen on a little tour of the town, but since there were additional people and so little time, I headed directly home. I exited I-25 onto Central Avenue and told Carmen, "This street is Central. It's the North-South dividing line for Albuquerque, and the railroad tracks divide it East from the West." Why I felt the need to tell her that, I wasn't sure.

As we approached the Downtown Rail Runner Station, I pointed out its beautiful stucco walls and clay tile roof. I explained that besides Amtrak trains and the local Rail Runner train that went north to Santa Fe, the station also served the city buses, which people rode for free." Apparently, architecture and history were not their things, as the girls' eyes glazed over. Duly noted.

Just after we passed the station, Bianca asked in Spanish, "Is that a nightclub?" The other girls sat up and looked out the window.

Sure enough, the building she pointed at was one of the three downtown clubs that hosted late-night raves and parties. I had heard of them but had never visited. I much preferred hanging out at home with Zia, going to a movie, or hiking with Joey.

I looked at the girls again. With their clothes and makeup, they looked as though they were ready to go clubbing right there and then. The bars probably didn't even open until nine p.m., and I knew I'd be fast asleep by then. I sure wouldn't be taking them there. To them, nightclubs were probably just an American curiosity. Besides, Coco was only eighteen. She couldn't even get into one.

I thought about pointing out the cool Kimo Theater on Central, with its awesome mix of Art Deco and Southwest-style architecture. But figured none of the three would be interested.

We continued down Route 66, a famous name for Central Avenue. Just before reaching the iconic Old Town Plaza, I turned onto my street, Old Town Road.

Most of the people I know were impressed that I live in a culturally significant village in the heart of Albuquerque. The small area, founded in 1706, was now a National Historic Site. Tourists from around the world visit it.

Apparently, these girls hadn't heard of Old Town, now filled with museums, restaurants, and shops. I would find time to walk the girls over for lunch and shopping, but not today. I only had another hour before I needed to drive back to Balloon Fiesta Park.

I pulled into the driveway of my old adobe home. I said, "Do you remember when your madre stayed with me here after my parents' funeral?"

She nodded. "She said you had a nice place in the big city. I see what she meant now. I remember how pretty your madre was. It's so sad that she and Tio died so young."

A pang of sorrow hit me, but her comments offered me a deeper connection with my cousin than I had expected. It was so nice to be with somebody who knew my parents. I leaned over, hugged Carmen tight, then said, "Let's go inside, girls!"

We hauled the luggage up the steps, and as usual, I removed some business cards from the screen door-just more realtors trying to buy my house. As soon as we entered, I tossed the cards into the trash. I had no intention of selling my 300-year-old home. After all, it was left to me by my parents.

I showed the girls the spare bedroom, the bathroom, and the kitchen. I showed them how to work the TV controls and asked in Spanish, "Do you want to go see the balloons tomorrow?"

All three girls bounced up and down with excitement. I took that as a yes. In Spanish, I said, "I have to go back to my booth now for the evening event. You should rest from your travels since you'll have a very early morning tomorrow. Decide if you want to catch an Uber at 5:00 in the morning or go with me an hour and a half earlier at 3:30. Here's a key in case you want to walk around a bit. If you do, make sure to lock the door. I'll be back around nine."

I handed Carmen my spare. "I'm so sorry to leave you, but it's my job."

Carmen said, "We'll be fine. Thank you, Maria. Go make the dinero!"

"OK! I will. Call or text me if you have any questions. The fridge has food and drinks. Help yourself."

It may have been awful to leave the girls alone in my home in a new country, but I figured they were probably tired and needed to chill.

When I entered the big white tent, I was surprised to find Stoney's booth empty. Someone had removed the photographs, the display walls, and the curtains. All that was left were the metal poles outlining the booth like a skeleton. I couldn't help feeling depressed at the sight.

My booth was on the other extreme-a packed, bright, cheery space. That didn't help my mood. I hid my purse behind the curtain and laid out some additional products.

Angelica entered wearing a colorful, flowery kaftan. She spoke in her slow, soothing voice. "Hey, how's ma girl doin? I was so busy yesterday morning, I didn't ask what's going on in your life?"

I scoffed, "Well, three strangers just arrived at my house and they are staying a whole week."

Her face scrunched up in confusion, so I told her about my houseguests.

"Oh, that's odd, but kind of cool. Are they coming to Balloon Fiesta tomorrow?"

I shrugged. "Who knows? I'm not sure of anything. I don't know if they brought money or expect me to pay for everything while they are in town. It's all stressful." I frowned. "And I'm bummed because I just saw Stoney's bare booth."

"Oh, yeah. Management had us take it down." She went on to say, "It's our responsibility since Stoney listed Marvin as the sole beneficiary of his Will a few years ago."

She saw the surprise on my face and shrugged. "We were the closest things he had to family. He had his Last Will and Testament drawn up about a month after he almost died in a deep-sea diving accident."

I was even more surprised to hear that, so she explained. "Stoney was on an underwater photo shoot, but his equipment malfunctioned when the inflator valve was stuck open. He ran out of air and ascended too quickly. The rapid pressure changes caused him to get the bends. It was touch-and-go since once he surfaced, he was in pain and even paralyzed. For a while we thought we might lose him, but after he recovered fully, he decided to make a Will."

"Oh. That's terrible. I guess he really was quite an adventurer."

"That's an understatement." She was wistful for a moment and then said, "I never met anyone so full of life."

I said, "Marvin mentioned that Stoney had a sister in Wyoming? Will she come to the celebration of life?"

"I hope not. Scarlett is a nightmare. We met her years ago, but they've been estranged for at least five years. He was so relieved when she moved away and went to Wyoming. But there's a chance she could make a stink about the Will."

I had trouble understanding family discourse. I couldn't imagine shunning any blood relative and would give anything to have my parents or little sister back. This Wyoming Scarlett girl sounded awful, having stolen money from Stoney. But still, I wondered if she regretted how things went down, now that her brother was gone for good.

This all made me realize I should be happy my cousin came to visit, and I decided not to complain about Carmen anymore, even though she did bring two additional people to stay at my house. Family first!

When Angelica said something, I snapped back to the conversation. "I'm sorry, what did you say?"

She pushed a fluff of dark curls back under her scarf and said, "Oh, just that we're going to donate some of Stoney's award-winning prints to the Balloon Museum and will add some for sale here and at the event as a fundraiser for the ballooning club. I'm having a special sign made to explain his adventurous spirit."

"Awe. That's so nice."

Angelica perked up. "Hey, if you and your houseguests want to ride in Marvin's balloon tomorrow, he has some open spots. A family from Minnesota had to cancel their trip here."

"Wow. If I didn't have to run my booth, I would jump right on that."

"You go if you want. I know someone who could watch your shop." She winked.

"No, really, it's fine. I've flown before and need to stay here, but I'll tell the girls about it. They will be so excited!"

"Good."

Since there was a little time before people started to arrive, I asked, "So, can you tell me about the issues between this Smith guy and Stoney?"

She sighed. "Well, remember the deep-sea-diving accident I mentioned?"

I said, "Sure." Having just heard it ten minutes earlier, it would be hard to forget.

"Well, they were on that trip together, but had a blowout because Smith was the one who set up the equipment that failed. Stoney accused Smith of sabotaging it on purpose and considered filing charges for attempted murder. Smith denied it and said he would sue him for defamation of character.

Marvin managed to quell all their threats, since all turned out fine. But their animosity continued. My Marvin never believed Smith could sabotage Stoney's tank…but I always wondered."

My face must have shown my horror. "Really?"

"Well, I believe Smith was jealous of our golden boy. Most guys were. Stoney won at everything he did, girls, sports, photography…well, until this time." A tear trickled down her cheek, and I knew I should stop asking questions, but just couldn't.

"Why was this Smith guy arguing with Chris the other day?"

She rolled her eyes. "Oh, Smith is aggravating. He can't seem to keep his mouth shut. He's always making rude comments and kicking up dust wherever he goes. Chris didn't like him the minute he met him, and that was just another time they clashed."

"Then, why are you and Marvin still friends with him?"

She gave a deep sigh. "Unfortunately, Smith is married to Marvin's little sister, so we sort of have to tolerate the guy."

That explained a lot. I changed the subject. "I sure hope you sell a lot today!"

She brightened. "You and me both, girl. Have your higher prices turned people off?"

I smiled. "Nope. No sticker shock."

She lifted her head triumphantly and said, "I knew it." The woman floated out of my booth like a big, beautiful butterfly.

The evening went well with the highly anticipated Special Shape Glowdeo. Many people came by on their way to see the enormous objects and funny characters coming to life on the field.

During the lull when I only had a few customers, questions swirled around my mind. First and foremost was the fight between Stoney and Smith. Was it possible that Smith had actually tampered with Stoney's air supply? If he was that angry with Stoney before, could he have tried again and succeeded in the hot air balloon? I shuddered at the thought.

But nobody saw anything, and none of the investigators suspected foul play. Why was I getting so worked up? Just leave it alone, Maria.

When the fireworks show finally ended, the visitors moseyed back to their cars or shuttle buses. The other artisans started closing up shop. I grabbed my purse and peeked into the Moores' booth. "Angelica, I'm heading home to see what's up with the three girls. Carmen never called me today, so I'm hoping no news is good news."

"They probably went to bed early. See ya in the morning, Hon."

The good thing about being the last to leave and the earliest to arrive at the park was avoiding the horrible traffic getting in and out of the enormous parking area. Unfortunately, tonight, for some reason, the traffic was at a standstill. I sat for a ridiculously long time worrying that by the time I got home, I'd only get five hours of sleep, if that.

Upon arrival at my house, the lights were on, and the door was locked. Good, I was glad they were being cautious. I unlocked the door and tiptoed into the living room in case one of them was asleep on the couch. No one was there. I tapped lightly on the door of the guestroom, but nobody answered. I opened it a crack only to find it empty except for clothes strewn across the room. Had someone dumped out a suitcase on the floor? And where were those girls?

I thought maybe they were probably sitting out on the back patio and headed that way. But, no, they weren't there either. How had I lost three people? Surely, they hadn't been kidnapped. My anxiety hit, and I started the breathing techniques a therapist taught me years ago, just after my parents had died.

I went to the kitchen and drank a glass of water, which usually helped to calm me. On the counter, I found a note, reading, 'We went to the nightclub. To return later – Carmen.'

I wasn't sure if this news was much better than the thought of them getting kidnapped. The nightclubs were about two miles away. How had they gotten there? Had they walked? That might be a long trek with those heels they were wearing earlier.

I called Carmen's cell phone and waited while it rang. Her voice came on, asking me to leave a message, which I did. "Which club are you at? Are you okay? Do you need a ride home? Ok, well call me back or text me."

I waited another ten minutes, but there was no reply. Should I go look for them? No. They were adults and could figure it out on their own. But what about Coco? She was too young to be admitted into a club. Anything could happen to those girls, especially since two of them spoke no English. Besides, a few areas of downtown are sketchy. I am a local and still wouldn't want to be there after dark.

I knew I couldn't sleep, so I grabbed my purse and jumped into my truck to search for my three Mexicans. As I drove, I watched for them, but nobody was walking.

I found a parking spot on Central, only a block from the three nightclubs that I was familiar with. I put my keys between my fingers in case I needed a weapon and walked along the dimly lit street.

When I reached the first club, the music was so loud I could feel the vibrations of the bass pounding in my chest. I showed my ID to the bouncer at the door and paid the $10 cover charge.

The place wasn't very crowded, but then again, it was a Thursday night. I figured it would be easy to spot the three girls if I picked the right club. They weren't on the dance floor, so I walked among the bar top tables along the edge. Noisy clubbers tried to talk above the music. None of this seemed like fun to me, but it wasn't my vibe.

I checked the bathroom just in case they were in there, but still no Carmen and friends.

I thanked the guy at the door and moved to the next club. As I walked down the sidewalk, I had to step around a rather dirty guy sitting on a blanket and asking for money. Like every city, we have a problem with unhoused people, despite the city's many shelters. I empathized with him but didn't want to engage and kept moving.

The next stop had a ridiculously high cover charge of $25. The big bouncer, covered with tattoos on his neck, was intimidating. I told him I would only be a minute because I was just looking for someone.

He lifted an eyebrow. "Yep. Everyone here is looking for someone."

I rolled my eyes. "No. I'm not looking for a hookup – my three friends just arrived from another country and I'm trying to find them. Have you seen three cute girls? One tall, one short like me, and the other tiny?"

"I don't keep track of who comes in or out. Give me $25 and you can check for yourself."

"If I come right back out, can I get my money back?"

He just gave a big laugh at that. "No."

I reached into my purse. There goes the money I just made from selling a lampshade covered in slides. Exactly why did I think hunting for the girls was a good idea?

I handed the jerk my cash, and he stamped my hand - this time with a big, black skull and crossbones. The first place had a red star. If I kept this up, I'd be out of cash, and my hand would resemble the tattooed guy at the door.

I wove my way through the large crowd and continued my search, wishing I had brought my concert earplugs to save my poor eardrums. Everyone seemed to be having fun. I looked for Bianca's bleach-blonde hair since she was the only one tall enough whom I might be able to see.

I scanned the room and there she was! Bianca was standing by a table, drink in hand, and talking to a tall guy. Wow! Had Bianca found someone who spoke Spanish? Or maybe he didn't care what language she spoke. She was so striking. Where were Carmen and Coco? As I inched closer, the guy talking to Bianca moved aside to grab his drink from a nearby table, and I spotted Carmen.

I pushed my way past people on the dance floor and somehow ended up in the middle of four guys encouraging me to dance. I said, "No. I'm going over there." I pointed.

"Not before you dance with us."

One guy grabbed my hand and raised it with his to wave in the air. I tried to pull it down, but he was strong. I said, "Give me my hand back."

"It's just a dance!" He spun me around effortlessly, as if I were a puppet.

My heart started beating faster. Like most people, I wasn't fond of being pinned down or forced to do something against my will. In response to his unwanted grip, I kneed him in the groin. Well, that did it. He dropped my hand immediately, doubled over, and I escaped. Out of breath, I rushed over to Carmen.

She laughed. "Maria, I didn't know you liked to dance! We would have waited for you to come with us."

I growled. "I don't like to dance. That guy was a jerk and grabbed me."

She made a face. "Then, why are you here?"

"I came to find you and make sure you were okay."

"Si. We're good. This place is awesome."

"How did you get here?"

"We took the bus. You said it was free, so I found the schedule online. It took us right down the street. So easy."

Wow. She had listened to something I told her on the drive. I said, "Well, that was pretty smart. I tried calling you."

"Oh. I'm so sorry. It's so loud here, I didn't hear my phone."

I looked at Coco, who was guzzling a beer. "How did you get her in? She isn't 21."

Carmen looked surprised. "She had a fake ID made before we came here. We learned it from American movies. Didn't you get one at that age?"

I shook my head vehemently. "No. I did not. Does her mom know she drinks?"

"Sure. It is okay to drink at 18 in Mexico. Her mother put Bianca in charge of her little sister."

I sighed and shouted to be heard above the increasing volume of the new song. "How long are you planning to stay here?" I waved my hand at the place. "Tomorrow morning is coming very early. I'm not sure you'll be able to get up at 3 or 4 if you stay out late."

"The bus only goes until 12:30, so we'll go back then. We may wait until Saturday to go to the balloons." She shrugged. "We'll see how tonight goes."

A short guy walked up to Carmen and handed her a beer. He looked at me as if I were in the wrong place, probably due to my frumpy cardigan and jeans. Gosh, I must look boring.

I gave an even more anxious sigh and said, "Ok. As long as you know what you are doing." I didn't even want to tell them about the offer to ride in a balloon since partying seemed to be all that was on their minds.

I waved at Coco and Bianca, then left, thankful to be back on the quiet sidewalk. I turned to the big dude at the door and said, "I found my friends. I didn't drink or do anything fun, so can I have my money back?"

"Ha! You are hilarious. I saw you dancing in there."

At that, I turned away and stomped back down the street. This time, when I passed the smelly man, I dropped a dollar in his rusted bowl and said, "Have a good evening."

He said, "Thank you."

Chapter 11

After a very long day of work and "clubbing", I fell asleep by 11:30. Unfortunately, at one a.m., a big ruckus in my living room woke me. The girls had returned and were giggling and sounded drunk. This was NOT the quiet, mousy girl I had expected as my houseguest. At that late hour, I had no desire to talk to them, so I covered my head with a pillow to drown out their noise, and after a while, I drifted back to sleep.

My eyes felt glued shut when my alarm went off. I pried them open with my fingers and managed to get dressed. Three hours of sleep was not enough for anyone to fully function. I crept into the living room, hoping not to wake whoever was on the couch. As I tiptoed, I stopped and watched little Coco sleep. She looked so young, curled up in a fetal position. These girls might end up sleeping all day after their big day and late night.

I made a pot of coffee, drank a cup, and took one with me as I drove to the park for another busy day.

When arriving at my booth, Angelica raised her eyebrows. "Rough night?"

"Yes, ma'am." I rubbed my eyes and described last night's mess.

She asked, "Do you think the girls will come today?"

"No way. They had less sleep than I did. I'm sorry if Marvin held the open spots for them."

"Oh, it's fine. He'll have extra room tomorrow, too." She sighed. "When his bosses weren't sure if he'd be back, they called in another pilot and balloon, so his basket will be practically empty."

"Oh, well, maybe they can try to go tomorrow, then. I'm just gonna rest my eyes for a minute."

"Ok, honey. Don't forget this afternoon is Stoney's memorial. I'll wake you when the crowds roll in."

I sat down on my tractor seat, leaned my head on my table, and started to think about Stoney's celebration of life, but within seconds, I was sound asleep.

"Excuse me. Is anyone working in this shop?"

I jerked my head up, wiped a little drool from my mouth, and saw a man standing with his hands on his hips. As I focused, I realized it was Joey smirking at me. I sat up straight and tried to wake up. "Joey, what are you doing here?"

"To think I was worried you were working too hard, and here you are sleeping on the job. Don't worry. I won't tell the owner." He winked.

I rolled my shoulders, trying to wake up. "You better not. I promise I'm usually a little more animated." I stood and kissed him. "Can you just take me away somewhere so I can forget that I'm babysitting three girls from Mexico?"

He narrowed his eyes and said, "I'm gonna need a little more information before I answer that."

I explained the situation.

His eyes were wide when I finished. "And you went clubbing with them?" He pointed to my hand with the stamps still visible, even after I tried scrubbing them.

I rubbed them again. "I did not. I tracked them down to make sure they were okay."

"Oh, I see. Well, as much as I'd love to take you to a warm beach somewhere to escape, my siblings would kill me if I skipped out on work during the busiest week of the year. We're just gonna have to wait."

I leaned my head on his chest. "So, how did you get out of working the Balloons and Burritos shift this morning?"

"Several of the staff love working it. Jett got to sleep in yesterday, so today it was my turn. I thought I'd come here instead of sleeping in."

"Ahh." With my head still leaning on his strong, warm chest, I almost fell asleep again.

Just before I nodded off, a sultry voice said, "Well, who do we have here?"

Startled, I pushed away from Joey. I cleared my throat and said, "Angelica, this is my boyfriend, Joey Roth. He and his brother own the Rusty Railroad Brewpub next door to my shipping container in the Out of the Box center."

"Nice to meet you, Joey. So, is your brewpub made of shipping containers, too?"

"Yep. All the businesses are. We used six red boxes to make Rusty Railroad." Joey continued. "It's nice to meet you, Angelica. Maria told me how much she enjoys your friendship."

She turned to me. "Maria, why don't you and Joey go up in the balloon today? Marvin plans to take advantage of the Albuquerque Box and land right back where he took off, so it would be a short flight. And I will watch your booth."

"Oh, I don't know. I'd feel guilty having you watch it again."

"It's really fine. Marvin can call me when he's ready to lift off, and you two can pop into the basket. It probably won't take more than an hour altogether."

I looked up to see Joey's eyes sparkle. Flying above the city with Joey really would be romantic. I asked him, "What do you think?"

"I would love to go. It's something I've always wanted to do."

I was surprised he had never been in a hot air balloon, but he and Jett had only moved here from Denver a few years ago.

Joey looked at Angelica, "Are you sure it's alright with your husband?"

"I wouldn't offer if it wasn't." She looked between the two of us and gave a knowing smile.

I hugged Angelica and said, "Thank you so much." When I released her, she picked up her phone as she left my booth. We could hear her telling Marvin he had two more passengers.

Joey's eyes twinkled. "Looks like we get an escape after all, huh?" This time, his kiss was so intense that I was now wide awake.

I couldn't help but grin about our impromptu adventure. I said, "Why don't you go enjoy the Fiesta. After all, you paid to get in. There is a lot to see. The food is amazing, and the Dawn Patrol launches soon. I'll call and tell you where we're meeting, so keep your phone handy."

"Will do!"

I had never seen Joey so excited, well, except maybe when he was selected as a volunteer for Doctors Without Borders.

An hour later, the sun rose behind the Sandia Mountains, and the green flag was up. Angelica came over and said, "Marvin is in Row P, launch site 6. They'll be ready for you in about ten minutes.

I thanked her, called Joey with the news, then grabbed my jacket and new hat. I met Joey at the site. As soon as I saw him, I said, "Ooh, someone did some shopping. Don't you look fancy?"

He spun around and showed off his new purple jacket emblazoned with big, embroidered balloons on the back. "I'm commemorating my first balloon ride with an official Fiesta jacket."

Joey was just too cute wearing his new purchase. I grabbed his hand and pulled him over to the basket. A couple and an older woman were already inside. I called Marvin over and introduced the men. "This is the pilot I told you about, Marvin Moore. And this…" I patted Joey's arm. "…is my boyfriend, Joey Roth."

The two shook hands over the basket ledge, then Marvin pointed to Keanu and said, "That's my assistant, Chris." Joey and Chris gave each other the sup nod that guys do. Marvin continued, "We have a few chase crew members on the ride this morning in exchange for their help this week."

I smiled at a familiar-looking guy and girl I'd seen working before the fateful ride. Then I pointed to the footholds and told Joey, "Hop in."

Once inside, Joey asked Marvin a few questions about the burner. He was like a little kid, as he watched in wonder each time the flame shot up. Meanwhile, I studied the interior of the basket. If I were to guess, it was about the width and length of a king-sized bed, which was good since it sometimes held a dozen people and equipment.

The sides were so tall, I couldn't fathom anyone falling out. Maybe a tall guy like Stoney's center of balance would be above the edge, but Joey was about the same height, and it was above his waist. Stoney just had to be doing something audacious – or someone had helped him go over.

Marvin cleared his throat and introduced himself as the pilot. "Before we take off, I need to give a safety briefing. This flight should last approximately 50 minutes. Expect to hear a loud sound each time the burner is lit. The flame is safe as long as you don't touch the burner or control lines during the flight. Smoking is prohibited anywhere in or around the balloon. Under no circumstances should you lean over the edge of the basket."

I grimaced, hoping everyone was listening carefully.

Marvin smiled at everyone. "Now, what you CAN do is relax, enjoy the scenery, and take lots of photos. Just keep a good hold of your phones and cameras. Dropping something overboard can be a hazard for people below."

When Marvin pointed to Chris, he added, "During the landing, Marvin will ask you to assume the proper landing position. You are to bend your knees and hold onto the inside handles. Avoid grabbing the edges of the basket. Once the balloon has landed, do not leave the gondola until we direct you to do so. A sudden change in load may cause the balloon to lift unexpectedly."

Marvin smiled again. "Is everybody ready?"

We all cheered, and he shouted, "Up and Away!"

The flame whooshed, and our basket rocked a little before lifting smoothly upward. People who stood on the ground cheered, as well. Joey's eyes were wide open, and he grabbed my hand.

Once we rose high enough that all sounds from below had dissipated, I looked at Joey and could tell he experienced the same peace I felt. He dropped my hand, grabbed his phone, and started taking photos. I did the same, marveling at the other balloons flying above, below, and beside us.

As we floated along, I noticed Marvin taking photos with his 35 mm professional camera. He'd bend and swivel with fluid movements as he captured just the scenes he wanted. I was amazed by how fast he switched out lenses. Meanwhile, Chris was manning the controls.

The temperature was a perfect blend of cold and hot. While drifting in the quiet air, a chill would set in, then a stream of fire would warm us up again. Lovely!

I kept an eye on Marvin and Chris to see if they were doing anything unusual or suspicious, but I didn't notice a thing.

The other passengers in the balloon were excited and snapped selfies to capture memories. Putting my phone down, I put my head on Joey's shoulder as we hovered high above Albuquerque.

"Look, Joey, there is the Rio Grande!" He immediately started taking photos of the trees and the river.

Marvin said, "Anyone want to try a Splash and Dash?"

We all yelled, "Yes!"

'Splash and Dash' was a maneuver where the balloonist briefly touches the basket to the water, before immediately ascending again. I had never experienced it before, so I was very excited.

He said, "Let's give it a try! I see a spot where we can touch down and get this big thing back up quickly."

Joey asked the question I was formulating. He said, "I understand the heat makes it rise, but how do you make the balloon go down?"

Marvin said, "It's just the opposite. I must release some of the hot air in the envelope. See that circular opening at the top? That's the parachute vent. When I open it, heat is expelled. Once the air is cooler, the balloon becomes heavier than the outside air, and we descend."

He pulled a cord, and sure enough, we began to drop slowly downward. All the passengers leaned over the edge, watching the river as we neared it. We glided over the trees and came close to hitting some, as he aimed our basket at the water.

"Eeeeek." I heard myself squeal when we touched the Rio Grande. I reached over the basket to see if I could feel the water, but my arm wasn't nearly long enough.

Within seconds, the flame ignited, and we popped back up. Everyone cheered.

Joey said, "That was so cool!"

I agreed and looked over at Chris. Surprisingly, his face was lit up as if it were his first Splash and Dash, too.

After that, everyone was in a festive mood. Marvin expertly maneuvered us up and back toward the field to utilize the 'Albuquerque Box' phenomenon. Named the Albuquerque Box because a skilled pilot can catch the wind blowing in the preferred directions, ultimately taking off from one spot, then navigating the wind patterns to land back in the same place.

The more I watched the jovial pilot, the more I was certain he had nothing to do with Stoney's death. I focused on Chris more carefully. He was quiet and a bit mysterious, but followed Marvin's directions to a T.

As we returned to the field, we drifted past other balloons flying just above or below ours. A woman's voice yelled, "Maria!"

No woman in our basket knew my name. Then I heard, "Maria! Up here!"

I looked up at the balloon that had just passed by us. There, standing in the basket of a red, white, and green balloon, was my cousin, Carmen. What the heck? As I watched in disbelief, two other girls started waving. Both Bianca and Coco were on the flight, too? How had they managed that? With my mouth wide open, I lifted my hand and gave a little wave as they floated farther away.

Joey asked me, "Do you know those girls?"

I shut my mouth. "Yes. They are my houseguests."

"I thought you said they weren't coming today."

"Well, they were dead to the world when I left. I have no idea how they managed to wake up, get a ride here, and get into a balloon. I'm so confused."

"It sounds like they are very resourceful girls."

"I'll say." I rolled my eyes in disbelief.

We were nearing the field when Marvin said, "Chris, wanna take it in?"

Chris jumped at the chance and said, "Sure." I watched him open the vent just as Marvin had done. Chris grabbed the burner control and vent cord, but it was obvious he was not an expert. We seemed to be approaching land too fast.

Marvin told him to shut the vent and ignite the flame, but Chris didn't listen.

Marvin yelled to us, "Hold on, everyone, we're coming in fast!"

I grabbed the rope attached to the inside the basket as we hit the ground hard and bumped along. The landing was certainly not as smooth as the other flights I'd gone on. In fact, the basket turned on its side, dumping me right on top of Joey. We slid along the grass a few more feet and eventually came to a stop.

Marvin asked, "Is everyone alright?"

The others said, "Yes, sort of," but I watched one older man adjust his toupee.

I was discombobulated but not injured. I said, "I'm ok. How about you, Joey?"

He looked up at me and smiled. "Yeah. I'm fine – I got my girl right here."

It was funny to be lying face-first on top of Joey, surrounded by the other passengers. When he reached up and kissed me, I started to laugh.

We climbed out of the overturned basket and righted ourselves. Joey helped an older lady to stand, saying, "What an adventure!"

She agreed, then turned to Marvin. "Maybe you should do the landings from now on."

Just as the chase truck drove up to meet us, Marvin told all of us, "Sorry, that was kind of rough."

Chris said nonchalantly, "Yeah. I'm not that good at landing the balloon yet."

Ya think? I thought about all that still had to be done with the balloon and frowned. "Marvin, I'm so sorry I can't help pack up. I need to get back to my booth."

He raised an eyebrow. "Not before the ceremony."

Oh yeah. I'd forgotten about the first-time flier's ceremony. I stayed and took pictures as Joey and three other newbies were given certificates commemorating their first flight. Then, when every passenger and crew member had a cup of champagne in hand, Marvin recited the Balloonist's Blessing:

"The winds have welcomed you with softness
The sun has blessed you with its warm hands.
We have flown so high and so well that God
Has joined you in laughter and set you gently
Back into the loving arms of Mother Earth."

After the toast, we drank our bubbly, except the older woman, who said she never touched a drop of liquor in her life.

Joey hugged me and said, "That was amazing. Thanks for knowing the right people so I could fly today. I'm going to help them roll up the 'envelope' before heading back to work. Maybe I'll see you tonight." He seemed so proud that he knew the word envelope.

I said, "Sounds good, but I may just crash tonight. I didn't get much sleep last night, you know."

I gave him a quick kiss and hollered to Marvin and Chris, "That was lots of fun. Thank you. See you two at Stoney's thing later." I rushed back to the tent.

When I reached my booth, I almost tripped over my feet in shock when I saw a child sitting behind my counter, taking money from a customer. It was Bart, Louise's grandson. What, in the *Twilight Zone,* was going on?

Chapter 12

Little Bart looked up and told the woman in front of him, "Ma'am. You are in luck. This is the proprietor of Upcycled. You can meet her right now. Mildred, meet Maria Olson."

Why the heck was an eight-year-old working in my shop? I was flummoxed by the whole thing and wasn't sure how to react, but assumed a more professional demeanor and said, "Hi. Mildred. Thanks for stopping by."

The woman, who had to be in her late 80s, said, "What a nice boy you have here. He's just delightful and such a good salesman."

"Oh, thank you. I'm glad to hear that." Despite my words, I was sure my face showed my confusion."

When she left, I ran next door and found Angelica wrapping up a large, framed photograph for a customer. Well, that explained why she was missing, but why was Bart here?

I walked back to find him neatly stacking bills and coins in my cashbox. I spoke quietly to him, so I didn't bother the other two shoppers in my booth. "Bart, where is your grandma?"

"Grandmother Louise took my sibling, Lisa, to use the facilities. Ms. Angelica was in a bind and needed to work in her booth, so she asked me to stay here temporarily. I had no other commitments, so it wasn't an inconvenience."

I squinted at the wonderkid and said, "Well, thank you?"

He grinned. "I was able to sell three of your necktie glasses cases and two Scrabble tile bracelets."

"Wow! You are a good salesman."

He nodded. "Yes, I believe I could excel in the sales industry if I chose to make it my vocation. Unfortunately, I'm not familiar with your credit card processing program, so I was forced to ask the customers for cash."

This boy was something. He handed me a piece of paper that had the list of items he had sold printed in a messy, kid's scrawl. I was glad to see that something about him, besides his short stature, was still childlike. What surprised me the most was the letterhead with Bartholemew Jones printed at the top of the paper.

"Bart, since when do eight-year-olds have their own stationery?"

He answered, "I'm not eight anymore. Mother asked what I wanted for my birthday, and I told her I wanted office supplies and this." The boy held up a small briefcase.

That made sense for this kid, but why the heck had he brought a briefcase along to see balloons? Before I could ask him about it, Louise entered in all her sequined ballooning glory. She held the hand of little Lisa, who had her face painted with glittery hot air balloons.

Louise boomed, "There's my little Norwexican. How was your balloon ride? I heard Joey went with you. How romantic. There wasn't another proposal up there, was there?" Her eyebrow was raised.

I couldn't help but laugh at the silly woman. "No. Good grief, Louise, we've only dated a year, and he was gone four months of that."

"Well, where is that boy?" She looked around as if I had Joey stashed on a shelf.

"He's helping the crew pack up the balloon." I raised my own eyebrows. "So, it seems that Bart, here, took care of my shop? Your grandson is quite the businessman."

"Oh, you don't know the half of it. He wanted to wear a suit today because, now that he's nine, he wants to look more professional."

I turned to Bart and asked, "When was your birthday?"

"Yesterday."

That explained the obsession with his new briefcase. I said, "Why don't you pick something out from my store as payment for being such a good salesman. Or if you prefer, I can give you a cash commission."

His eyes grew wide as he scanned the store, but finally he said, "I believe I would like to be compensated with monetary payment so I can start to save for a stock portfolio."

I was dumbfounded that a kid so young would know anything about stocks. Then I had to hold my ears when Louise barked, "You'll do no such thing. You only helped my friend out for fifteen minutes, and you don't need to be paid."

I turned to her and said, "No, Louise. He worked and should be paid for his time." I took a twenty from the stack of bills and handed it to him. "Now, Bart, if you are going to be a real businessman, you need to keep in mind that there are taxes on income, so make sure to always set some money aside for that."

He said earnestly, "Thank you, Miss Maria. I will keep that in mind."

Louise shook her head and said, "Well, kids, the show's over. Time to get back to the shop."

Lisa said, "Loulou, you said I could get someping at her shop, today."

Her grandma twisted her mouth and said, "You have the memory like an elephant, don't you, Lisa?"

Lisa giggled and held her hand out like a trunk, then began shopping. She took her time studying every little thing. Louise rolled her eyes while Bart sat on the floor cross-legged, with his briefcase open. I felt sure he was writing something important that would benefit his entire future, and possibly that of mankind.

Eventually, Lisa chose a pink polka-dotted coin purse made from a baby sock. I slipped some coins inside it before handing it to the child. She was ecstatic and hugged my legs.

I looked down at the girl who wiped glitter from her face onto my jeans. I asked, "Did you like the balloons?"

"Oh yes, they were bootiful. I wiked the wabbit."

Of course she did. Louise managed to get her to release me, and she skipped out of my booth holding the new purse, followed by Bart and her Loulou.

Shortly after the adorably odd crew left, and while I was in the middle of a customer's transaction, Angelica re-emerged.

She walked around the store picking things up and putting them on my counter. I wondered if she was really going to buy them.

Once the shoppers left, Angelica said, "Darlin, I'm so sorry I skipped out, but those people were buying several of Stoney's framed photographs. They love them. Apparently have big bucks, and want to help with the fundraiser for the ballooning club."

"It's fine. I was just surprised to find an eight-year-old…I mean nine-year-old selling my stuff."

"I'm so sorry. I didn't know it would take me so long. I had no other option."

She looked upset, so I quickly said, "No. He was amazing. He even kept track of everything he sold. I'm thinking of hiring the kid." I laughed at my own joke. After all, there were child labor laws.

I added, "And thank you so very much for the balloon ride. It was incredible, and Joey was in heaven. Marvin even did the Splash and Dash."

"Yeah. He told me, but I heard about your crash landing, too. Why he let Chris take over, I'll never know."

"Yeah, it was pretty bumpy. So, Chris isn't a pilot?"

"Oh, heaven's no. He's just a very hard-working assistant. I mean, Marv lets him take over while he takes photos sometimes, but never for takeoff or landing." She shook her head and continued to pick up items.

I sat on my stool and asked, "How did you two meet Chris?"

"Oh gosh, let's see…I was helping Marvin during a full flight one morning in August. You know, one of those unusually cool mornings when we could fly that time of year? Well, Chris was a paid passenger, and after the flight, he volunteered to help us. We told him he could join our crew, and he jumped at the opportunity."

I listened but wondered why she kept piling more things on my counter.

She continued, "He became a consistent part of our team, never missing a flight. He's been a hard worker and dependable. As a matter of fact, since he started here, he's only taken two weekends off, to visit back home. We're his second family now."

"That's so cool. So, did he and Stoney get along?"

She picked up one of the little sock purses. "They never hung out together as far as I know, but I never heard cross words, either. Some guys got annoyed by Stoney's showboating, but Chris just thought he was foolish."

When she finished, I asked, "So why are you bringing me all this stuff? Are you really interested in baby sock purses?"

"Up these prices, Maria."

"Oh, come on. There are only two more days after today."

"Yes, and they may be the biggest sales days. Now, I should get over and help set up for the memorial event."

"Can I do anything to help?"

"I don't think so. See you in about an hour."

I submitted to her by changing the prices on a few items. Since I wanted to have some inexpensive things, I kept the sock purse prices the same.

A few minutes later, I heard familiar giggles coming from the hat booth next door. I walked out and found my Mexicans trying on hats. I was glad to see the girls were not wearing clubbing clothes and were appropriately dressed for the cool weather.

Coco saw me first and said, "Maria! Te gusa mi sombrero?"

I looked at her funny purple bucket hat with balloons on it and answered, "Si, Coco. Tu sombrero es muy bueno."

The girls put the hats down and came into my booth. It was fun to watch them oohing and aahing over my products. They chattered and asked questions. When Bianca asked me about the earrings made from little, round metal letters, I realized my Spanish had become rusty over the years when I tried to couldn't remember the word for typewriter.

Carmen helped me out by saying, "maquina de scriber." Then she said, "The girls are trying to learn more English while they are here."

"Wonderful." I turned to Bianca and said, "Typewriter."

Marvin walked past my shop and into his. He was only there a few moments before he stopped by, holding a few framed prints. "Oh, I see you have customers. I'll talk to you later."

I caught him before he walked off. "No. These are just my houseguests visiting from Mexico."

He brightened. "Oh, the girls we thought might ride today?" He turned to them and said, "Hi. I'm Marvin."

Carmen introduced herself, and Bianca slowly said, "Hi, my name is Bianca."

She motioned for her little sister to speak. Coco said, "Me llamo..." She corrected herself. "My name is Coco."

Good. They were doing their best trying out English.

Noticing the prints in his hand, I asked, "Marvin, do you need help?"

"Actually, yes. We want all of Stoney's framed photos at the event to sell for charity. Chris is busy setting up the display walls. If you and your friends want to help, that would be great."

I said, "Sure! Just show us which ones you want."

I followed him to his booth, where he pointed out several to take. "Ok. We'll be right there."

"I appreciate it. Just come when all your customers are gone."

I did my best to explain to the girls in Spanish what was going on. I told them about Stoney's death, his memorial, and the photos. All three were saddened to hear someone had died that way and were more than happy to help.

For a while, Carmen, Bianca, and Coco continued to shop, but stopped to watch me sell some silverware jewelry to a couple of teen girls. When the teens left, I looked out into the aisle and saw that the tent had emptied of most of the visitors.

In English, I said, "You sure surprised me this morning. How in the world did you get to ride in a hot air balloon?"

Carmen, the only one who understood my question, answered with enthusiasm. "At the club, we met a chico who owns a balloon. He is from Mexico City and asked us to ride! And so today we took Uber to get here.

I knew it was common for balloonists to travel from all over the world to attend the International Fiesta. For many years, I have watched the Flight of the Nations Mass Ascension, where the foreign balloons were highlighted, but this Wednesday, I was busy in my booth and missed it. What were the chances these girls would meet up with the pilot of a Mexican balloon on their first night in America? Unbelievable.

Speaking in Spanish this time, so I didn't leave Bianca and Coco out, I asked if they enjoyed the balloon ride.

"Oh Si!"

All three rattled off with their favorite parts. Carmen liked how quiet it was in the sky. Bianca enjoyed the champagne afterwards. And Coco was enthralled with the Darth Vader and Yoda balloons she saw. I wondered if Coco had listened to *Star Wars* in English or Spanish. The thought of Darth saying "Lucas, yo soy tu padre" made me chuckle.

The girls put a few things they were interested in on my counter. Then, I closed up shop and collected the items Marvin needed. As we headed down Main Street, the sun was bright, and the temperature was 70 degrees with no wind – perfect for a walk.

When we got to the center stage, we turned East toward the Pilots' Pavilion. The Pavilion was an event center at other times of year, and I had only been in it once for a wedding reception. During the Fiesta, it was only accessible to pilots, so I felt special entering it today.

The place was huge, with tables and chairs set up mainly for the pilots and crew to have a warm place to have food and drinks before the sessions started.

I saw a buffet table set up with food on one side and a makeshift photography gallery on the other side. Rows of chairs were in the middle. As I continued to look over the place, a man walked to a microphone and tapped it to test the sound system.

We made our way to Marvin, who stood by the walls of framed prints. I handed him the photo I carried. He said, "Thanks. This will make a good display, don't you think?" He pointed to the walls.

I said, "It will be lovely."

When Chris appeared from the other side of a partition, the girls made a collective gasp.

Biance blurted out, "Keanu Reeves?"

Chris froze in place and stared at Bianca as if in shock. Why was he so surprised? Surely, a lot of people must mistake him for the famous actor. Or maybe he was just awestruck by Bianca's beauty.

He finally smiled and said, "No. I'm Chris." He held out his hand and shook hers. "I probably should at least cut my hair." When he reached up and pushed the long black hair away from his face, he was still handsome, but it was obvious he wasn't Keanu.

The girls seemed a tad disappointed, but I was pretty sure it wouldn't stop them from trying to get to know the look-alike better. I explained to Chris who they were, as the girls handed the hottie the framed pictures they were holding.

I turned to Marvin, "Where is Angelica?"

"Oh, I'm sure she's setting up the food and wine table. That's where she feels most at home – did you know she used to be a chef?"

My eyes widened. "No. I did not."

"Yep. There are many layers to my girl. Everything she does is extraordinary."

"She isn't a jazz singer, too, is she?"

He laughed. "No, but she could be. Her singing voice is as smooth as butter."

I laughed. "I knew it would be! The first time I met her, I thought she might be a sexy, sultry, soul singer."

"She's sexy, alright." He winked. I could tell that Marvin was crazy about his wife.

I headed over to see if Angelica needed my help. "Hey, Chef, can I be of any assistance?"

She turned and arched her eyebrows. "Mmmhum. Marvin's been boasting about me again, hasn't he?"

"I find it very sweet that he's so in love with you."

"It can be a bit much at times. He's a wonderful husband, when he's not jealous."

That struck me as odd, but I didn't respond. A woman in a black apron handed Angelica a platter of hors d'oeuvres and walked away. Angelica added little sprigs of lettuce around the edges of the tray, making it a gorgeous display.

She looked at me and said, "Are you good at opening wine bottles?"

"I sure am."

She smiled, handed me a bottle opener, and pointed at the next table. "Just open a couple of whites and reds for now."

Now this was a job I could handle. I had bartended when I was first out of college and had no trouble opening the bottles. I set them next to the balloon-themed plastic cups. Since the event was being catered, everything was especially nice and looked beautiful.

It was 20 minutes before the celebration was to start, and I looked around for the girls. I spotted them standing around laughing with Chris. His whole demeanor was different from when I'd seen him last. He was smiling. Why wouldn't he be? Three adorable young girls were falling all over the 30-something guy.

Carmen noticed me and came over. "Is it ok if we stay for the celebration? Chris said we can."

I thought about it. "I guess it's okay, but please be respectful. It may be a solemn event." I felt like a mother telling her children to behave at church. Heck, I really didn't know these girls at all, and I sure didn't want them to make a scene by giggling during a eulogy or while someone paid tribute to Stoney.

When Marvin placed a large photograph of Stoney on an easel, my throat tightened, and tears started to form. The picture showed his infectious smile and the adorable dimple in his chin. He was so full of life, and now he was gone.

I noticed something on Stoney's shirt and walked up to the print. I got so close, my nose practically touched the glass. He was wearing the horseshoe balloon pin that he had given me.

"Looking at his pin?"

I jumped back at the sound so near my ear. It was Marvin. He said, "That guy never did anything without his lucky charm pin. Said it saved his life several times."

I could barely speak. Stoney had given me his lucky pin. In fact, it was pinned to my shirt right now, but my long hair was covering it. I wasn't a superstitious person, but after what Marvin just said, I had to wonder if Stoney might still be here if he had worn his lucky pin.

Chapter 13

Did I dare tell Marvin that Stoney wasn't wearing his lucky pin when he died? And if so, would he be angry or even more emotional if he knew that I had the sacred pin? I decided I would tell him, but not right before the event.

I turned around when I heard Carmen and Coco coming up behind me. Still a little anxious because of the pin situation, I forced a smile and said, "Hey, girls. Having fun?"

Carmen leaned in and said, "I think Bianca and Chris like each other."

My eyes widened as I looked behind her at the couple. They were giving each other googly eyes. Bianca hung onto his arm as he stood puffed up and proud. Coco watched them – probably trying to learn flirting tactics from her big sister.

I whispered to my cousin, "So, have you met anyone you like in America?"

"Oh. I'm not looking. Javier is waiting for me at home." She pulled up her phone camera and showed me a photo of a nice-looking young man standing behind Carmen with his hands around her waist.

"He looks really nice."

She raised her eyebrows. "Do you have a lover?"

I almost choked at the question, but chalked it up to a language difference. "Well, here is my boyfriend, Joey." I showed her a pic.

She said, "He is so tall and cute. Was he in the balloon with you today?"

I turned to her and held her hands. "Yes. I'm so sorry we haven't visited at all since you arrived. After Sunday, I'll have much more time to spend with you to catch up. I promise."

"And I can give you the gossip on your other cousins."

Over her shoulder, I saw Smith enter the building with a pale, thin woman. I thought she must be his wife, Marvin's sister. I saw a resemblance in her face, but without her brother's white hair, she looked considerably younger. What didn't make her seem so young was her wobbly gait.

When Chris caught sight of Smith, he looked disgusted. He quickly told Bianca to find something to eat and find a seat, then he walked away. As they headed to the buffet line, the other two girls teased Bianca about her "amor."

Marvin greeted his sister with a peck on the cheek and Smith with a handshake. I figured I should be polite and say hello, so I made my way to join them.

Marvin patted my shoulder and said, "Mary, this is our new friend, Maria. She makes treasures from trash."

I held out my hand and took hers, surprised it felt so thin. I was worried I might break the frail bones, so I held her hand gently. I said, "Hello, Mary. Hi, Smith." That sounded odd since I assumed Mary's last name was also Smith, but I'd never heard the man's given name. I faced him. "So, do you have a first name?"

Mary and Marvin chuckled, but Smith seemed to have been born without a funny bone. He growled, "Of course, I have a name. It's Barry."

As he spoke, his stupid dangly hot air balloon swayed back and forth from his ear. I did think the names Mary and Barry were kind of cute, but I didn't mention it.

Speaking of jerks, my nemesis walked into the pavilion. Sergeant Barnes was wearing his typical attire – a wrinkled suit. Great. I was sure I was in store for more harassment by the obnoxious detective.

Barnes headed towards a man on the other side of the room rather than to me, I was relieved. I felt bad for the guy when the detective started up a conversation.

I turned back to Mary. "So, have you been to see any of the balloons this year?"

She gave a little frown. "Oh, no. I've been ill and can't stand up for very long, but Barry took photos on his last flight and showed them to me. They were beautiful."

There was an awkward silence when we realized that the flight she meant was also Stoney's very last flight. Here I was, standing with two of my suspects. Surely, I could think of something to get more information. I perked up. "I got to fly this morning, but I didn't take many photos. Barry, can I see yours?"

Smith scrunched his nose and mouth as if I might try to steal his phone if he handed it to me. He sneered, "I'd rather not. This isn't the time nor place to be on a phone."

Gee, this guy could be annoying, but he was probably right. I noticed Danny standing inside the door and was glad I could get away from Smith. I excused myself and made my way over to Danny. As I walked, I considered the normally confident man, who now looked nervous as he fidgeted while scanning the area of strangers.

I smiled as I neared him. "I'm so glad you could get away from the antique store."

"Arnie and Carl are watching it. I just hope they don't burn the place down or get robbed while I'm gone. God help me. He rolled his eyes.

I said, "Want to get some food and a drink?"

He nodded. "Yeah, I'm pretty hungry."

We joined the line and picked up some plastic plates. I hadn't had anything today except coffee at three a.m., so I was starving.

Danny pointed at the display walls. "Are all those photographs, Stoney's?"

"Yes, and the sales today will go to the charities he supported."

"I only have a few of his shots that he e-mailed me, but I never had a chance to print any."

I perked up. "They're having a drawing over there to win a framed print. Why don't you fill out a ticket? His stuff is amazing."

He left, and when he got back, I figured I had time to do the same. "You know what? I'll enter too." I ran across the space to the table and jotted my name and phone number onto a ticket, and put the stub in the basket.

Back in the buffet line, I put a pile of green salad on my plate — something I'd eaten far too little of this week. Then I served myself creamed corn, beans, smoked turkey breast, and beef brisket—all catered by Rudy's Barbecue. Yum.

At the end of the line, Angelica was serving the wine. "Hello, Maria." She raised her eyebrow seductively and said, "And if I recall, this is that sweet boy, Danny, whom I met a few years back. Right?"

He smiled at her and said, "Hello, Mrs. Moore. Nice to see you again."

Danny must have been working on his public relations skills, since calling her Mrs. Moore was pretty formal.

Angelica must have thought the same thing, because she said, "Oh, just call me Angelica."

He laughed and quipped, "I almost said Angel. That's what Stoney always called you. He thought you were the best. Always said he wished he had met you earlier before Marvin did."

Hmm. Angelica was in her mid-fifties, Marvin was about seventy, and Stoney was in his early forties. She was smack in between the two men. It wouldn't have been weirder for her to date a younger man than an older one, at least before she married.

Marvin walked up in the middle of Danny's comment, not looking very pleased with what he heard. His reaction made me wonder if he had been jealous of the attention Stoney gave to his wife over the years.

Angelica defused the situation by saying, "Oh, you know Stoney was harmless. He flirted with everyone. She took Marvin's arm and said, "Honey, do you remember Danny?"

He gave Danny a polite smile and said, "Sure."

Before they could speak further, a man tapped the microphone. He was dressed in a suit coat with the Balloon Fiesta logo on the pocket. He announced in a loud voice, "Hi everyone, thank you for coming today. I'm Al Barkley, member of the Board of Directors of the Albuquerque International Balloon Fiesta. WE along with the Albuquerque Ballooning Club, the Balloon Federation of America, and the Moore family, want to welcome you today to celebrate the life of our own, Sam "Stoney" Stone. If you never got to know Stoney personally, I'm sorry. He was quite a corker. You'll hear more about the man shortly. But for now, we invite you to enjoy Stoney's favorite meal. Then, have a seat for our brief program. Thank you so much for coming to celebrate a brief life well lived."

I grabbed a cup of red wine and scooted over to find a seat behind my three Mexican girls. I patted the seat next to me, and Danny joined me.

Carmen turned around and said, "This food is really good."

I said, "Glad you like it. It's an all-American meal."

It was difficult to hold my cup while trying to cut the brisket, so I put my wine cup on the seat next to me. I turned back to talk to Danny, but just as I did, Smith sat right down on my cup of red wine. As burgundy liquid dripped onto the floor, he jumped up and started screaming at me.

"You imbecile. Look at what you've done. You've ruined my new pants."

I wasn't sure what to do. I was trapped in the middle of a row. I apologized and handed him my napkins, but he swatted my hand away. His wife, Mary, tried to calm him down, but that didn't work. Honestly. It wasn't my fault that he didn't look at the seat before he sat down.

After Smith pushed his way out of the row, I used the napkins to wipe off the seat. There wasn't much wine on it, since most of it had soaked into his khakis. I turned and watched him stomp away with a big red spot on his butt.

Danny bit his lower lip as he tried to keep from laughing aloud. He asked, "Did you do that on purpose?"

"Of course not!"

"Well, from what Stoney told me about Smith, he deserved that and more."

I finished wiping the seat and said, "So, he used to talk about Smith?"

He raised his eyebrows and gave a big nod. "All the time. Couldn't stand the guy. Even before the scuba-diving accident, he said the guy was a jerk."

"Then why did he have Smith take him out diving that day?"

"The other diver was sick, and Stoney really wanted to get a great underwater photo for a contest deadline. It didn't work out very well, but thankfully, he survived."

"So, I understand why Stoney hated Smith, but why the other way around?" I finally started eating my brisket.

Danny licked barbeque sauce from his finger, leaned his head back and let out a sigh. "Oh, a few months before the scuba incident, Stoney was being Stoney and jokingly said Smith couldn't beat him at any race. Smith, who touted himself as being very athletic, took it as a dare and said, "Wanna bet?""

"Stoney acted nonchalant and said, 'Sure. You choose the sport, the day, and time, and I'll be there.'"

Danny paused to take a swig of wine. I wanted him to hurry, so I could hear what happened before the ceremony began. I kept eating as I listened.

"Smith's face got all red, and he said, 'I'll bet 100 dollars I can beat you in a bike ride down the other side of Sandia Mountain. We'll do it this Friday, at 10 a.m.'"

I said, "That sounds difficult on a bike. It's pretty steep, right?"

He said, "Yeah, it is. We were all surprised by his choice. You're basically riding down the ski run, so you need to be an avid mountain biker to try riding the four miles of switchbacks. Stoney shook his hand, and the bet was on."

"When the day came, Mary drove Smith and Stoney and their bikes to the top of the Sandias. She tried to get her husband to back off the bet, but he refused. After shooting the starting gun, they took off. Another buddy and I waited at the bottom to declare the winner."

"Mary texted me when the two took off, and we waited for them to ride in. I knew it was about four miles long and descended over 4,000 feet. I didn't think it would take very long.

A few other riders asked what was going on. We told them about the bet, so a small crowd began to form.

At 20 minutes, Stoney came flying down the trail and skidded sideways on the gravel and came to a halt. We cheered for him, then waited for Smith to arrive. After ten minutes passed, we started to worry.

I was about to call for help, but just then, another cyclist walked down carrying two bicycles. He was out of breath when he said, 'Is that your friend up there? He slid off the trail and broke his leg. Here's his bike.'"

When I realized my mouth was open in anticipation, I quickly shut it and wished I had my wine back.

He continued, "We thanked him, and before anyone could discuss what to do, Stoney raced up the mountain on foot while I called for an ambulance."

I shook my head at the wild story.

He continued his story. "Stoney practically carried Smith a mile down the mountain while I waited with EMTs. Once they arrived, Smith was taken to the hospital and had his leg set."

"Gee, I hope Smith appreciated Stoney's help."

He scoffed. "You might think so, but no. He was so mad about losing the race that it was a month before he spoke to him again."

I found that hard to believe. "Wow."

Danny leaned closer and said, "It's a good thing Smith wasn't in the balloon on Sunday, or I'd think he had something to do with Stoney's death."

I froze, realizing Danny didn't know who was in that basket. With wide eyes, I turned to him and said, "Barry Smith was on that balloon flight Sunday."

Danny practically jumped out of his chair, and his face turned red. I grabbed his arm and said, "Wait. This isn't the time. Let's hold off until after the celebration."

His breathing was deep and rapid, but he finally calmed down and sat again. He said, "I had no idea he was anywhere near Stoney that day."

I said, "Let me change the subject for a second. Did Stoney ever tell you anything about the new guy, Chris?"

Danny looked at me and said, "Yeah. He said he's okay, he just thought it was weird that he glommed onto Angelica and Marvin so quickly."

Hmm. That was interesting. When the man who spoke earlier stood to make his way to the microphone, I whispered to Danny. "I'm going for more wine since mine is on Smith's pants."

At the drink station, I found myself face-to-face with Detective Barnes.

He snarled, "How's the crafty little princess?"

Why did this man have so many dumb names for me? I answered, "Doing well. Thank you for asking. I have a question for you, Sherlock. Did you ever consider that Stoney may have been, "helped", out of the basket?"

"Oh, give me a break. Don't tell me the town snoop is back at it again."

"Only because the town grump isn't doing his job."

The man at the microphone began to talk about the man of honor. We turned to listen.

"Stoney was known by all of the pilots, mainly because he kept mooching rides."

Everyone laughed.

He continued. "When he was on a flight, you could guarantee a good time for your other passengers. He was friendly, happy, and made everyone feel better about life. Most importantly, Stoney was quite a philanthropist. He donated photos and money to all of our organizations, and he was always first to volunteer at every …"

Barnes leaned over to me and said quietly, "We exhausted all angles and talked to everyone in the basket. Nobody saw anything."

"And that all means zip since there were 20 seconds with no visibility when they went through the cloud."

"Give it up, Olson. You have no evidence, no suspects, or motives to kill him."

I closed my lips and looked up and away, then said, "Maybe I don't, but maybe I do."

The man at the mic announced that anyone who had something to say about Stoney was welcome to come to the microphone and say a few words.

Angelica was first to speak, so I grabbed a replacement cup of wine and rushed back to my seat to listen.

"He was like a little brother to me…" Angelica said, with an uncharacteristic wobble in her voice.

She described Stoney and how he had become a part of her and Marvin's family. She went on to give examples of how everyone's needs came before his own. After she finished her emotional tribute, I wiped my eyes.

Marvin was next. He seemed genuinely distraught about losing his friend but told stories about Stoney's lighter side and his daring nature.

Then a few people I didn't know told funny stories about Stoney. They also touted his kindness and infectious personality.

I was surprised when Danny got up and walked to the front. He stood erect and spoke comfortably into the mic as though he had made public speeches all his life. "Stoney and I grew up together, here in Albuquerque. He was my very best friend." Danny detailed some of the silly things the growing boys did.

He added another one. "And one time when we were twelve, neither of us had money to buy a skateboard, but we wanted to try out the new skate park. Stoney found an old Coke crate in his dad's shed. We disassembled it and glued the slats together to form two boards. We still needed wheels, so I removed four from a rusty wagon, and Stoney took apart one of his sister's roller skates. We attached them to the boards."

He continued, "On our very first try going down the concrete ramp at the park, both of our boards broke apart and we crashed. I shattered my wrist, and he broke a leg. Our parents were upset, but his little sister, Scarlett, was furious because she only had one working roller skate." Danny shook his head and said, "Stoney was a special guy who I'll miss deeply."

That was a cute story. It was also the first time I'd heard much mention of Stoney's little sister, besides her having stolen his parents' inheritance.

I wasn't sure anyone else noticed that before Danny stood down, he gave a menacing glare aimed at someone behind me. I turned to see Smith with wide, frantic eyes, so he must have noticed. I hoped Danny wouldn't take action on what he thought might have happened in the balloon.

When Danny returned to our row, another woman took the microphone.

I whispered, "Great job, Danny. Sounds like you two had a lot of adventures. So, what do you think of Stoney's sister?"

He looked annoyed, and I wasn't sure if it was due to my question or if he didn't like the sister. I soon found my answer when he said, "Scarlett was a pain in his ass. She was always conniving and lying to their parents, just to get him in trouble. When she grew up, she was even worse. Stoney's world became much nicer when she took off for Wyoming. I heard she hooked up with a guy and finally left Stoney alone."

Wow, Scarlett must be a piece of work. I said, "I thought she might come for this." I motioned around the place.

He laughed. "She better not ever step back in New Mexico, or I'll find a way to destroy her."

Yikes. That was a strong statement. The look on his face could kill. No wonder I had been intimidated by this guy since I'd met him last year.

The man with the booming voice returned to the microphone and announced, "Stoney's framed prints are available for purchase today. All proceeds will be divided among the three charities listed on the sign." He pointed at a poster. "But one lucky guest here today will receive their choice of paintings. Let's draw a name and see who wins."

Angelica carried the ticket basket to him, and he turned his head away to pull out a stub. He read the name aloud. "Danny Harrison."

Danny's face brightened, then crumpled a bit. I thought he might actually cry. I was happy for the guy, despite his recent outburst. He loved Stoney and probably couldn't afford to buy one of the framed prints. I turned to him and said, "Now, you'll have a special memory of your friend."

He grinned and walked over to the wall of photos, where Marvin told him to choose one. How cool that he got to choose even one of the most expensive ones if he wanted. We all watched as the big guy stepped around the display, studying the prints. He finally pointed to one, and Marvin reached up and removed it from the carpeted wall.

Out of all the choices, Danny picked a small photo – maybe only 8 x 10 inches. Everyone cheered as he held it up. He stopped by my row and said, "Thanks, Maria, for letting me know about this. I've gotta go back to the store, before my brothers ruin the business, somehow."

I watched as he moved toward the exit. Smith saw him coming toward him and instantly moved Mary in front of him, basically using his sick wife as a shield. Weirdo.

Danny walked past Smith without stopping, but I was fairly sure he gave him a dirty look.

With only an hour and a half before I needed to return to my booth for the evening session, I hoped I had time for a catnap at home.

I cornered Angelica and asked if she minded if I took the empty wine bottles for a project I had in mind. She said, "Sure." When I asked if she needed me to do anything, she gently turned me around and pushed me. "Go rest a while. We've got it covered."

I found Carmen and her crew. Before I could speak, Carmen said, "We're taking an Uber and are going shopping. There are two malls in town!" She sounded amazed, which was weird. Guadalajara was a much bigger city than Albuquerque and only a few hours from their home.

I said, "Okay. Have fun." How did these girls find the energy to keep going after a very late night and super early morning?

Carmen added, "Chris said we can fly with him on Sunday morning. You want to come too?"

"Uhh. No. I still have to watch my booth, but thanks." I wondered if Chris had gotten permission from Marvin to invite three people, but it wasn't my business. I just hoped Smith wasn't on that flight with them.

Since the girls would be out shopping, I went straight home for a catnap. I called Jill on my way to check on her.

She told me everything was fine at the shop and that Sophia had been asking about me all morning.

"Awe. I miss her too. After Sunday, I'll be around to play with my Godchild, I promise. And I'll retrieve my dog-unless she prefers the Standing Bear family now to little old me."

"Nah. Every time a truck drives up, Zia thinks it's you."

I filled Jill in on my incredibly long night and morning. It all seemed like it had happened days ago rather than today. "These girls are like Energizer bunnies. They don't slow down."

"You better get some sleep, girl. Those muchacas might just run you ragged."

"Truer words were never spoken."

Chapter 14

I was groggy as I made my way back to the park. One hour of sleep wasn't nearly long enough, but it was all the time I had.

The evening session went well, and I sold so much that my booth looked bare. I just hoped I had enough for three more sessions.

Chris stopped by to ask me for Bianca's phone number. He still surprised me every time he spoke. I kept wanting him to call me 'dude' or say 'excellent' or 'bogus', but this version of Keanu never did anything fun.

I said, "I don't have Bianca's number, but I can give you Carmen's." He seemed fine with that. He probably wanted to tell her the time they should meet for the balloon ride on Sunday.

Before I left for the night, I gathered the items the girls were interested in and put them in a large bag.

When I arrived home, Carmen and Coco were on the couch, eating from a bag of Cheetos. I don't have white carpet or white furniture, but still, seeing their orange fingers made me nervous.

Shopping bags were lined up on the floor. Where had they gotten so much money for an extravagant vacation?

"Maria! You are back." I was surprised it was Coco who spoke.

I said, "Nice, Coco. Your English is getting so good."

"I try."

I asked Carmen, "Did Chris contact you? He was trying to get in touch with Bianca."

"Yes. He wanted her to go out tonight and he picked her up a few hours ago."

Well, that was interesting. "Are you two staying home this evening?"

"Yes. How you say, we shopped 'til we dropped. Do you mind if we watch your television?"

I laughed. "Go for it."

I grabbed a Biscochito and ate it with a glass of milk, then went to bed. I made a quick call to Joey and told him about the celebration of life. I turned off the light, but unfortunately, I couldn't fall asleep. I kept thinking of all I'd learned today:

1. Chris doesn't know how to land a hot air balloon
2. Marvin is nice and patient, but he may have been more jealous of Stoney than I realized.
3. Joey is adorable
4. Angelica had been a chef
5. Chris and Bianca like each other and are now dating.
6. Danny suspects Smith as I do.
7. Danny hates Stoney's sister. I can't remember her name, but it starts with an S.
8. Barnes is still a jerk and doesn't think there was any foul play in Stoney's death.
9. My cousin and her friends rarely sleep
10. Always check your seat before sitting down

I still had no concrete evidence on any of my suspects, but my instinct told me it might have been Smith.

Saturday morning, after a good night's sleep, I found Coco curled up on the living room couch. I looked around, hoping Bianca made it back safely from her date.

I made coffee and was surprised to hear Carmen say in a sleepy voice, "Buenos días."

Not bothering to speak English, I returned the greeting and handed her a cup of coffee.

Blowing on my hot drink, I asked, "Did Bianca get home safely?"

She shook her head. "No. She's still gone. Must have slept over with Chris."

I wasn't too concerned. They were both adults. I only worried about the language difference. I said, "I brought home the things you girls wanted. I dug in my bag and put them out on the counter.

"Oh, how much do we owe you?"

"Don't worry about it. It's my treat."

"No. That's too nice. We can pay you. We have savings to spend."

"It's fine. I haven't spent any money on my guests. Let me do this for you."

"Gracias Prima." She reached out and hugged me.

I said, "Oh, and before I forget, I have something for you to take to Abuela." I hurried to my workroom and picked up the clock I had meant to mail her. It was made from a copy of my grandmother's favorite book, *100 Years of Solitude*. I couldn't find the book in Spanish, so I used the English translated version for the clock. I said, "I already wrapped it up, so it would be easy to transport home."

She took the package from me. "She'll love it, whatever it is."

I looked around at all the shopping bags and said, "I hope this isn't too much for you to carry."

"No. It's fine. We brought empty bags for extra things."

"Well, I had better get to work again. Let me know if you need anything or have questions about getting around." That was probably a dumb thing to say, since they had already proven they were capable of getting anywhere they wanted to go.

The morning was so busy, I didn't even have a chance to check on Angelica. I did hear her voice, so I knew she was there.

I looked around my booth, surprised at how many things I had sold out of. If I ever did this again, which is a big if, I would be much more prepared. I certainly wasn't complaining. I had made much more money than I expected to make.

Between sessions, when I had my normal break, I zipped over to my shop so Jill could run some errands. It was like old times hanging out with Zia in my shop. She seemed to miss me and wouldn't let me put her down. Each time I tried, she just scrabbled her way back into my jacket as if she were a baby kangaroo who belonged in her mom's pouch.

I switched back and forth between helping customers and working on a project until the husband, who had been in the fateful balloon, came in. I recognized him once. "Hi, Chad."

He waved. "Nice place here. Your store really is inside an old shipping container, just like you said." He looked around the place. "I wasn't sure you would have much room in it, but this is great!"

"Yeah. I had to get the 40-foot container because, well, no way I would have room for all this stuff in half this size.

"I'm finally getting around to bringing the bike parts to you. They're in my truck."

"Cool! I'll help you." I told Zia to stay as I put her down. I joined him outside and found he'd brought me an amazing number of bikes and parts. Some were rusty but still had potential. Gosh, I could use almost every part for something. As I carried some bike seats to add to the pile, I said, "This is like Christmas! I can't wait to make some cool things from them. Can I pay you for this?"

"No. I needed to get rid of them, so you did me a favor."

After we stashed everything behind my container, I took him inside and said, "Hey, pick something out as a thank you. It's the least I can do for all the free bikes."

He looked around and said, "How about this?"

He held a bird feeder made from a New Mexico license plate.

"Great!" I took the feeder from him and began to wrap it in newspaper. "Thank you so much, Chad. So, how are you and your wife doing after the event on Sunday?" I made a face.

"We're okay. It was just a weird fluke. Cindy isn't too excited about going up again, but I want to. But you know…I felt a weird vibe from several of the men in the balloon that day."

I perked up and asked casually, "Oh? Which ones?"

"Well, the pilot, and another guy in an 'Up and Away' shirt that my wife swears looks like Keanu Reeves, then the one who died, and some rude man with an earring."

I nodded. "Yeah. I know a couple of those guys didn't get along very well. Do you remember anything else? Like what they said, or who they were standing next to?"

He shook his head. "Didn't hear anything specific. But there was some bickering with the guy who wore the earring. He seemed to antagonize the others just by his attitude. I really wasn't paying attention to anything but the view."

I had no proof of anything except that nobody liked Smith. Big shock. I needed to stop trying to figure out what happened. Stoney had just done something dumb and had fallen out.

I handed Chad the package and said, "Thanks again, Chad. Come by and see what else I make with your bike parts — but don't expect anything anytime soon."

"We'll come back. My wife, Cindy, will love your store. By the way, I really like your sign out front with the bike wheel and the name, Upcycled. I should have thought of it for my bike shop. I did take a picture of it to show my staff."

Since there were no customers at the time, I went out to organize the bikes behind my shipping container and found the bowling balls and pins Jill had told me about. Wow. So many of them! I couldn't help but smile with anticipation of what I could make from the things in my new treasure trove.

While I was still out back, Jill and Sophia returned. I hollered, "Need anything made from bicycle parts?"

When they came around back, I took Sophia from her mom, cuddled her, and showed off my new haul to Jill.

"Gee. It's starting to look like Smitty's junkyard back here."

I chuckled. "I know. I hope nobody throws it all in the dumpster since it's so close by." I pointed to the big metal container only 10 feet away.

Jill chuckled. "I think you are safe. Who would lift that heavy stuff over the sides of a dumpster unless they had to?" As we started back toward my front door, she looked at me. "How was the celebration of life yesterday?"

"It was very nice. Carl's brother, Danny, from the antique store, came. I heard he was close friends with Stoney, so I invited him. He's nicer than I realized, but he does have a temper."

She smirked, "Like Father, like son."

"Ha!" That was true. His dad, who used to own the antique store, was grumpier even than Sergeant Barnes. I thought back to my involvement with the old man a year ago, when I found a dead body just outside of my shop. A chill went down my spine as I passed the spot where the murder happened. Returning to the topic, I said, "Oh, and my three houseguests were at the memorial, too."

I opened the door, surprised to find a woman shopping. Oops. I hadn't seen her arrive.

Jill picked up Zia and said quietly, "Why were Carmen and her crew at Stoney's thing? They couldn't have met him."

"I'll explain it all in a bit." I walked up to the tall woman who was holding a teapot sewing kit. "Let me know if I can help you find something or answer any questions."

"Thanks. I'm just browsing."

I went back behind my counter and spoke softly to Jill, "After their late night and their ride in a hot air balloon, they helped me take framed prints to the event where Bianca fell for Chris. She even went out with him last night!"

Jill turned to me, confused. "Wait. Is Chris the jerky guy with the balloon earring or the one who looks like Keanu Reeves?"

I laughed at the thought of beautiful Bianca with frumpy Smith and said, "No. Smith is married, and he's gross. She had a date with Chris – the cute Keanu guy." I looked around as if I were gossiping, and the woman might overhear us. I whispered, "She didn't even come home last night."

Jill waggled her eyebrows. "Must have been some date!" She let out a sigh. "Ahh, those were the days."

I made a face at her. "What do you mean? You have a gorgeous, sweet husband. How could you possibly miss dating?"

She gave a little shrug. "It was just more exciting back then."

I guessed that might be true for her. She was always a big party girl and had so many boyfriends that I couldn't keep track. I was the opposite – a stick in the mud, at least according to Jill. Everyone was shocked when Jill settled down and got married.

She said, "Look, you had better get going or you'll be late."

"Thanks again, Jill. You are a lifesaver."

I kissed Sophia and tried to hand her back to her mom, but the toddler held on tight and cried out, "No. I go Mia baboons."

I pushed my lower lip out at the adorable child. "Sophia, I can't take you with me today. I have to work. Maybe mommy can bring you back to see the baboons?"

Jill made a face at me and said, "Um…I wasn't planning to see the baboons again, Maria. Thank you very much."

Oops. I whispered to Jill, "Well, maybe she'll forget what I just said."

"Ha! This child has the same memory I have when it comes to food, shopping, or something she wants. I promise she won't forget."

"I did say MAYBE you could take her…"

"Yeah, like that helps." She sighed. "Oh well, Granda wants to go to the Fiesta tomorrow. His friend, Seamus, from Dublin, brought his balloon from Ireland, and Granda hasn't seen him yet. Maybe we'll go with him for a while in the morning. I could be back by ten to open the shop, right?"

"Unless you start shopping. Then you'll surely be late."

She stuck her tongue out at me, playfully, and took Sophia back. I doubted my friend would ever grow up, but she was the best friend ever. I kissed Zia and Sophia goodbye, grabbed some merchandise to fill in blank spots at the booth, and left.

I didn't have time to stop by the house to check on the girls, so I called Carmen. "Hey, girl. How are my three Mexicans?"

"Oh, Coco and I are at the aquarium. She wanted to see the fish." She said more softly, "Sometimes I think she's still a child."

I said, "Well, she did just turn 18, so…. While you are there, make sure to look around the amazing Botanic Gardens."

I loved to visit Albuquerque's Bio Park, which included the Zoo, Aquarium, and Botanic Gardens. They were all close to my house, and with my annual membership, I went as often as I wanted.

I asked, "Isn't Bianca with you?"

"No. She never came home."

"Wait. And you haven't heard from her?"

"No. She didn't answer her phone. I will worry if I don't hear from her tonight."

I started to worry right then. I didn't know the first thing about Chris. What if he were a sex trafficker and was holding the beautiful girl against her will? Bianco spoke so little English that she may not have understood what was happening. I should have been better at protecting the girl.

Chapter 15

I was worried sick about Bianca and seriously considered making a missing person's report. I felt responsible since I was the one who introduced the two.

However, my cousin didn't seem very concerned. Bianca was an adult, and I wasn't her guardian. I gripped the phone tight, took a deep breath, and told Carmen, "Please let me know if you hear from her," then I hung up.

I parked and hurried to my booth. After dropping off my big bag, I looked over to Angelica's booth and saw her bent over her computer, working on something. Her scarf today was a gorgeous mixture of reds and oranges.

I said in a rush, "Angelica, has Chris been in today?"

She spoke so slowly that it made me anxious. "No. He called this morning and said he'd be here this evening. Said he had stuff to do, so another guy on the crew helped Marvin during this morning's flight." She looked up at me and said, "Why do you look so harried, girl?"

"It's probably nothing, but one of my Mexican friends went out with Chris last night and never came back. I'm just worried since I feel responsible for them while they are here."

She narrowed her eyes. "That's the first time I've heard of him dating. They probably just got caught up doing something fun. Let's wait and see if he shows up. We'll ask him about it then."

I've never been good at waiting and felt antsy. I paced, put things on shelves, and straightened other merchandise. Once customers started to arrive, I welcomed the distraction.

About an hour later, I heard a female's accented voice. "Maria, your shirt is good."

I whipped around to find Bianca standing there. I rushed to her and blurted, "Are you ok? We were so worried about you. Why didn't you call Carmen?" I realized I rattled it off too quickly for her to understand, and so I repeated the phrase in Spanish, but a little less frantically.

She scrunched her nose and gave me a guilty look, then she explained in Spanish that her phone had died. Chris didn't have the right charger.

I let out a big sigh and rolled my head around my shoulders. I grabbed my phone, called Carmen's phone number, and handed it to her. "Talk to Carmen, please."

I listened as she explained the situation to Carmen. She told her she would be back after the balloon glow, or better yet, that Carmen and Coco should meet her here. When she hung up, she handed the phone back to me.

I finally relaxed and asked nicely, "Well, did you have fun?"

"Si." Her head bobbed up and down.

Chris walked in and asked Bianca in perfect Spanish if she wanted to go shopping before the balloons went up.

I was surprised to say the least. "Chris, I didn't know you spoke Spanish?"

He winked and said, "There's a lot you don't know about me."

"Well, next time you run off with an out-of-country guest, please remember people might be concerned about her. Her phone was dead, and you could have called Anglica to let us know she was alright. I suddenly remembered something, and my mouth dropped open. "Wait a minute. I gave you Carmen's phone number. You could have called her yourself."

He closed his eyes and gave a little shake of his head. "Gee. Chill out. She's an adult, and I didn't kidnap her. I was just showing her Albuquerque."

Now, I was really upset. I hated to be told to chill out. It was akin to having someone say, 'calm down.' Nobody ever calmed down after hearing those words.

After they left, I did manage to calm down on my own. I took a deep breath and exhaled slowly. Everything was okay. I hadn't lost a Mexican – not yet anyway. But the three were causing me more stress than I could have imagined.

Angelica entered and said, "See. There was nothing to worry about, Darlin'."

"I know. It turned out all right, but those girls are going to put me in an early grave." As soon as I said it, I realized it wasn't an appropriate thing to say after Stoney's sudden death.

Luckily, it didn't seem to bother Angelica. She looked at what remained on my shelves and said, "Can you believe we only have one morning left here?" She motioned around the place. "I'll bet you are ready to go back to your normal life."

"I am."

"Do you think you'll rent a booth here next year?"

"Right now, I'm so tired I think not, but give me a few months and I may say something different. I'm glad I did it this year, though. I would never have met you if I hadn't."

She tipped her head to the side and said, in her soft, kind voice, "That's what I'm thankful for, too. You are a little jewel. I hope we can keep in touch. You know, Marvin and I love having parties. I'll make sure to put you on our guest list."

"Oh, I would love that."

"You can bring your adorable boyfriend, too. We live in Foothills North, in the Skyline Estates neighborhood. Do you know the area?"

I almost choked. That was a very exclusive area in Albuquerque, with huge luxury homes on big lots overlooking the city. I had been to a house near there once for a fundraising event for the Children's Cancer Fund. It was the most beautiful place I'd ever seen. I said, "Wow. I'll bet it's a gorgeous home."

She chuckled. "Oh, hon, it's just a house."

A man in my booth, who looked to be in his sixties, held up one of my last remaining necklaces. He joined in, "I'm sure you have a great view of the city."

She nodded. "Yes. We are fortunate."

Angelica was so nice and non-assuming. I couldn't imagine her ever bragging about anything.

"Well…I live in a little two-bedroom house with no view, but it is in Old Town."

Both Angelica and the shopper man said, "That's really cool," simultaneously.

A bit later, I was surprised when Jill appeared. I said, "What are you doing here? Aren't you coming here tomorrow?"

"I closed up your store, stopped by Blake's, and bought my bestie a snack." She handed me a small foil-wrapped burrito. "Thought you might be hungry."

"You are an angel." I unwrapped the burrito and took a bite. After swallowing, I said, "But the admission and parking aren't cheap, especially just to drop off a burrito. Did you win the lottery?"

"Nope." She fanned herself and acted fancy. "I'm the daughter of the famous Grass Man who got free tickets and parking passes." She explained, "Dad was holding out on me. The newspaper gave him a bunch of tickets since he has bought ads there for years."

The O'Brien family had a very successful synthetic turf business. Jill and her brothers had worked in the family business since they graduated from college.

"Ahh. That's sweet. So, where's our little squirt? Didn't Sophia want to see the baboons?"

"Kelly took her to his folks for the afternoon, and they are staying for dinner."

"Nice."

She sat on my tractor seat. "So, what's going on here?"

I said, "I'm pretty exhausted, and so ready to be done and go home to a nice, quiet space. But of course, I can't do that, because I have three other people living at my house."

Jill took a bite of her burrito. With her mouth full, she said, "They'll be gone on Thursday, and you can have your life back."

I looked at my funny friend and realized I was being a big baby. I said, "Why am I whining? Your life has been turned upside down, too, and that's all because of me! Aren't you ready to go back home so you can play with Sophia all day?"

"Well, actually… the time I spent in your shop made me realize I need to be around adult-type people. I have decided to go back to work part-time at the Grass Man. That way, I can take her with me, and Mom and Dad can see her there every day. Plus, I'll have more spending money. It's a win-win-win."

"That's awesome, girl. But I am proud of you for taking more than a year off to bond with your pipsqueak. I didn't think you would last a month at home."

"Oh, ye of little faith."

Just then, there was a burst of squeals and shrill, fast-talking Spanish. We turned around and found Carmen and Coco. Bianca and Chris stood right behind them.

Jill, who always spoke her mind, blurted, "Wow, you do look like a young Keanu Reeves."

I worried Chris might get angry with everyone comparing him to the actor, but he didn't seem upset. He just shook his head and turned back to kiss Bianca. Wow. PDA much?

Behind the group, a woman with long, light-brown hair, wearing a ball cap, stood at the freeze-dried candy booth talking to Jenny. I wouldn't have noticed her, but she kept looking over at me. When Jenny gave her a few samples of candy, the girl chewed but kept her eyes turned my way as she crunched. Maybe the woman was waiting for the noisy group to leave so she could shop here. She was probably interested in my last few of the hanging book balloons. It would be nice to sell them before the show ended.

Carmen said, "We are going to see the balloons light up."

Coco agreed with an enthusiastic nod, and said, "Jes."

I said, "Are you all still planning to go up in a balloon in the morning?"

Carmen looked at Chris with a smile. "Yes. We're going in Chris's big balloon."

Chris lifted his chin a bit as if he were enjoying the attention.

I almost corrected Carmen by saying Chris didn't have a balloon and that the pilot was Marvin, but kept my mouth shut. The girls would find out for themselves in the morning. "So, tonight you might want to get a good night's sleep because the morning will come early."

Carmen waved me off. "No! After this, we will eat at the Frontier Restaurant, then we'll go to two clubs. Chris hasn't been here long, so we're going to show him around."

Jill and I looked at each other. How in the world did these foreigners, who have only been here two days, already know more about Albuquerque's nightlife than he did?

I stammered, "Well, okay, but stay safe."

"We will." She turned and gave her friends a forward-ho signal. "Vamos!"

The four of them left us there. I began to wonder what just happened. I said, "They know more about the current nightlife than we do, and we've lived here all our lives."

Jill said, "See? Another reason it's fun to be single and dating."

"Not for me. I'm still a homebody." I looked across to see if the candy-shopper wanted to come in and look at my stuff, but she was gone. Whatever. I said, "At any rate, those girls are sure confident. I could never party like that in another country."

She looked up. "Boy, that Chris and the tall girl sure seem to be hitting it off."

I nodded. "I know. Not sure how it will go anywhere when she's leaving in five days, but it's none of my business."

The crowds shifted to the field when it was dark enough to see the glow of the balloons. Jill surveyed my area. "It looks like you sold almost everything."

"I did. I made good money, and I have a lot less to pack tomorrow afternoon. That reminds me, I need to ask if Joey might be free tomorrow to help me."

As if by magic, my phone watch buzzed. It was Joey. I held up my finger and walked out into the aisle. I grabbed my phone from my pocket. "Hey, Joey. It's so weird, but I was just talking about you when you called."

"I hope you weren't saying something bad about me."

"I sure was." I lowered my voice and said, "I told Jill that you were a real bad boy."

"Oh, yeah? Well, this bad boy wants to invite you to a special dinner at the pub. We have a cool giveaway going on tonight. Can you join me?"

"What is the giveaway?"

"You'll see when you get here. Invite Jill if you want."

"Ok, but I can't be there until around 9:30. Will they still be serving dinner?"

"I'll arrange for it to happen. See you then."

Jill's eyebrows lifted when I returned.

I said, "You want to go to Rusty Railroad tonight? They're giving something away with a special dinner."

"Yes. Yes, I do. But I can't. I need to do some laundry and console Kelly after dealing with a toddler for three hours." She laughed. She threw away her burrito wrapper in my trash can.

I put my hand on her shoulder. "I'm sorry you haven't spent much time at home lately. You've been a lifesaver to work in my shop so much."

"Well, I'm not doing it for charity. I'm making some money too – you know. Besides, you know I like to stay busy. Oh, and heads up. Tomorrow, when Granda and I come here, I may leave Sophia with Mom. We'll bring her back next year when she's older and will appreciate it even more."

I said, "I just hope she still calls the balloons baboons."

Jill snickered and started to say something silly, but we heard raised voices next door. I peeked through the slit between the curtains. Marvin and Smith were facing off with each other in what looked like a standoff. Smith, sporting his weird combover, growled, "Exactly why can't I fly with you tomorrow on the last day?"

By this time, Jill had come up behind me and put her chin on my shoulder as we spied on my neighbor. I could feel her hot breath on my chin. The girl has never had boundaries.

Marvin answered in a more forceful voice than I'd heard him use before, "Because I said so, Barry. I'm in charge of the balloon, and you have done enough damage. I don't need you ordering people around anyway. Just go home and take care of my sister.

She needs you to be with her during chemo while I'm working this week."

Smith said, "Mary's fine. Her friend is there with her. She told me to go have fun."

I started to wonder if his wife wanted the jerk out of the house.

Marvin said, "Even if I wanted to let you ride, I'm at capacity. I got a last-minute booking, and Maria's three friends rounded out the group. Just go home, Smith."

Barry Smith looked as though he might explode. "So, your new friend, Maria, and her friends take precedence over family? After all I've done for your sister, you should have saved a spot for me."

Gee! I was sure glad Smith wouldn't be in the basket with my friends tomorrow. If he were, I'd have to convince them not to go. He was the only one unstable enough to have killed Stoney. He could do it again.

When Smith stomped away, we scooted back by my counter and tried to look busy. Jill said, "Well, that guy was a jerk."

I scoffed. "And that's why I think he might have killed Stoney."

Her mouth dropped open. "What? You never told me that! Wait. You don't think it was an accident?"

My face flattened. Oh, brother, why didn't I keep my mouth shut? Jill was the last person who needed to hear about my suspicions. I looked at her wide eyes and gave in. "Okay, I am probably wrong, and Stoney just did something crazy and fell out, but from everything I've heard, he was very agile and much smarter than just a crazy guy. It's just too coincidental that it happened right when the balloon went through a cloud. Something doesn't seem right to me."

Jill said a breathy "Unbelievable."

"So, this is where my mind was the other day." I pulled out my pink spiral notebook and turned to the page marked 'Suspects.'

Jill gasped. "You used our Pro/Con notebook to make a suspects list? How dare you!"

I knew she was only kidding, but she had a right to be surprised. The notebook, covered in Lisa Frank stickers, had been used by the two of us since we were in fifth grade. Whenever we had a big decision to make, we wrote a list of Pros and Cons. After much deliberation, we made the best choice.

I shrugged. "Sorry. It was the only thing I could find at the time."

She reviewed what I wrote. "So, Marvin is Stoney's sole beneficiary?" She looked at me to confirm. After I nodded, she said, "That is a good motive. Wait. And he may have been jealous of Stoney's relationship with his wife? Hmmm."

"Yeah, but I'm sure he knew it was just innocent flirting. Marvin is so sweet. I just can't imagine him hurting his best friend."

Looking down, she said, "So Chris is on this list, but he has no real motive, huh?"

"No. But he's always acting aloof and odd. And Chris was in the basket."

She wiggled her eyebrows. "Apparently, Bianca doesn't think he's aloof or odd. She is all over him."

I said, "That's true."

She looked back at the page. "And the last one is Smith, the earring guy we just saw? It says here he is rude, a terrible husband, and had beef with Stoney. Do you know what that was all about?"

I told her the whole scuba disaster story. Her eyes widened, and she speculated, "So, you think he may have tried to get rid of Stoney back then? That's really creepy." Her face sagged at the thought. Then she said, "And what does your best buddy, Detective Barnes, say about your suspicions?"

"He's sure it was an accident. He just made fun of me for bringing it up." I rolled my eyes.

"Of course he did. What a bozo."

I laughed.

Jill stood up. "Well, I'd better get home. See ya in the morning."

"Right. Very early in the morning!"

This was my last evening session at Balloon Fiesta, and I was relieved. I didn't have many customers, but most of those who came bought something, so that was good.

Just as I finished up in my booth, Angelica stopped by. She looked a bit frazzled.

"What's wrong?"

"Oh, Marvin is upset about Smith. He worries about his sister, Mary, living with him. I'm not sure if you know, but she's been diagnosed with cancer and is going through a tough treatment process."

I didn't tell her I'd overheard the conversation earlier, and just said, "I'm very sorry to hear that. So, I take it Smith isn't very helpful?"

"Ha. That's an understatement. He ditches her whenever he can. We spend more time with her than he does."

"Ooh, that's awful."

"Yeah. So, today Marvin lied and told Smith his basket would be full tomorrow, but he has one spot open. In case Smith shows up, would you mind riding with your cousin and her friends?"

I held up my hands, knowing it was a bad idea to leave my shop again, but she jumped in before I could say no. "I can handle both booths for a while."

"Really? Are you sure you don't mind?"

"I'm too tired to find someone else to take the spot on such short notice. Marvin prefers not to be near Smith right now. He doesn't like him or trust him anymore."

I totally understood his feelings and said, "Well, sure. I can't pass up a free balloon ride. Thank you so much."

I hurried home, took a quick shower, then met Joey at the Rusty Railroad Brewpub. It was pretty late for me to go out, but I needed to decompress. Besides, I was hungry. That burrito Jill brought me was small, and I ate it five hours ago.

He kissed me at the door when I entered.

"Do you greet all your guests this way?"

"Only beautiful Norwegian Mexicans. Come this way, my dear."

The place was packed as Joey led me to a table for two. It was my favorite spot, right by the window. I waggled my eyebrows. "Wow, I guess owning a bar comes with perks. You got us the primo table!" When he pulled out my chair, I sat down and smiled. "Thank you kindly, Sir."

Since it was dark outside, I couldn't see the Sandia Mountains, but it was still a treat to sit at the cozy table.

He sat across from me and smiled. "I hope you are hungry because I ordered us a big meal."

"I'm famished."

Amy, my favorite server, who always gave a treat for Zia when I brought her in, brought us wine glasses and showed me a bottle of Cabernet Sauvignon. I turned to Joey, amazed. "When did you get your full liquor license?"

His eyes sparkled. "It was approved on Monday. It took us over a year."

Amy smiled as she poured each of us a glass of rich red wine, then left the bottle on the table and went back to the kitchen.

We clinked glasses before taking a sip. Joey beamed as he told me the details of getting the permit, then said seriously, "You know, there are people who don't like beer, so this may be really good for business."

I couldn't help but grin at his exuberance. "I'm sure it will be." So cute. How did I find such an awesome boyfriend?

He held his glass up to the light. "Did you look at the glass?"

I held mine up and saw the Rusty Railroad logo etched beautifully into the glass. "Oh, this is so cool."

He said, "You get to keep it. We're giving them away tonight." He leaned in and said, "You can take mine and give it to Jill."

"Oh, she will love it."

The meal was lovely. We ate grilled Alaskan salmon, jasmine rice, and grilled asparagus as we discussed all that had happened since we rode in the balloon together yesterday morning.

While we were deciding whether to get dessert or not, my phone rang. Carmen rattled off a whole lot of Spanish. "Slow down, Carmen. Tell me again what happened."

As I listened, Joey watched my eyes grow wider. I said, "Okay. I'll be right over," and hung up.

I said, "Well, it looks like I will be skipping dessert, for I'm going on an adventure." I explained, "Marvin's assistant, Chris, who landed our balloon so badly, drove the girls to a nightclub. It turns out he couldn't keep up with their drinking and passed out. Carmen asked if I could come and get them, since they don't have American driver's licenses." I frowned. "Do you mind going with me, so we can get Chris and his car, too?" I raised my eyebrows at Joey, hoping he would go along.

He immediately stood up and flagged down Amy. He told her, "We need to fly. I'll take care of your tip later. And can you put these two glasses aside for me?"

"No problem, Joey."

I stood, grabbed a twenty from my purse, and threw it on the table for Amy, and we rushed outside.

Joey said, "Let's take my Jeep, since it has a back seat."

I climbed in and we were off - heading to rescue four stranded partiers.

Chapter 16

When we pulled up to the address Carmen had given me, I wondered if I had understood her correctly. There were no signs, and the building didn't look at all like a club. There were no flashy lights, and no bouncer standing outside the door. However, plenty of cars were parked along the quiet street.

Joey and I looked at each other, confused. I said, "Stay here. I'll check it out." I hopped out and walked to the only visible door. I tried the handle, but it was locked. What the? I pulled my phone from my pocket and called Carmen. She answered on the first ring.

"Carmen, we're at the address you gave me, but the place is closed. Where are you?"

"Oh, I forgot to tell you. You have to knock, then give them a password. Just say, 'Wiley Coyote."

"Are you serious?"

"Yes, Prima."

Wondering if this was all some elaborate prank, I decided to go with it. I shrugged my shoulders at Joey and knocked on the door. A guy opened it a crack, and I said, "Wiley Coyote."

He swung open the door, easy as pie. What was this place? A speakeasy from the Prohibition era? Before I entered, I held up a finger for Joey to wait. I walked into a dark hallway lit by neon signs hanging on both walls. The music wasn't too loud, but as I moved forward, it became much stronger. What was this place?

I turned a corner and entered a large room that looked like a regular club, with a bar. People were drinking and dancing. I was quickly met by Carmen, who led me to a round booth in the corner. Bianca leaned over the slumped body of Chris. He was breathing, but looked really out of it. "How many drinks did he have?"

Carmen shrugged. "Same as us."

I sighed. "We will definitely need Joey's help to take him outside. I called him and explained how to get in.

He seemed confused. "Seriously? A hidden bar in Albuquerque? How did they even know about it?" He paused and said, "Oh, never mind. I'll park and be right there."

When Joey came inside, I introduced him to my cousin and her friends. With some effort, the five of us managed to get the comatose dude to his car. We leaned him up against the door.

Joey said, "Anyone know where he lives?"

I asked Bianca if she remembered how to get to his place, but she shook her head, no.

Joey got the car keys and wallet from Chris's pockets and checked his driver's license. "It's out of state, so there is no Albuquerque address."

That made sense since I had noticed the Montana plates when Biance pointed the car out.

Joey sighed and said, "Well, I don't know where to take him, so I guess he's staying with me."

I said, "But, Joey, he needs to be up early to work at the Balloon Fiesta. Maybe he should stay at my place, or you'll have to get him up really early. Coco can sleep with me tonight, and he can have the couch."

"If you're sure."

We loaded Chris up in the passenger seat of his car, and Joey drove him to my place. The girls and I took Joey's Jeep.

Once Chris was situated on my couch, I walked Joey outside. I leaned my head on Joey's arm and said, "I'm sorry the evening didn't end up like you planned."

"My only plan was to spend the evening with you, and I did - just with a bunch of other people." He chuckled. "I just hope the guy still wants to go to the final Mass Ascension after this."

"Me too." I kissed him goodbye and was asleep in my bed next to Coco by midnight.

The next morning, my alarm went off at the same ungodly hour it had for the last ten days. I sighed with relief that it was my last early morning. The Fiesta booth had been a great money maker, and I made several new friends, but I probably would never do it again. Early mornings were not my thing. It was a once-in-a-lifetime experience, but I liked a more boring life.

On my way to the kitchen, I peeked at the couch, but Chris was gone. I looked outside, and his car was also missing. I assumed he had gone home. It was on him, now, to get to the park on time. That was a relief.

When I went into the kitchen, I found a note from Coco by the coffee maker. The note, written in English, read, "Thank you Maria to let me stay." She had drawn a beautiful picture of a hot air balloon on the bottom of the paper. This girl had real artistic talent. I would have to comment on it later.

Just like every morning, I put Stoney's horseshoe pin on my shirt. Then I grabbed a light jacket, since today's temperature was to be the warmest of the week.

Before any customers arrived, I ran out to get a cup of coffee, since I'd accidentally left my freshly brewed cup on my kitchen counter. I also bought a pack of tiny donuts to go with my java. I enjoyed walking along the dark "Main Street," lit only by the glow of the food vendors' booths. They would turn on the other lights shortly to welcome the visitors. The only sounds I heard were the vendors as they prepared for another busy day. Main Street was eerily calm, without crowds of people.

On my way back to the tent, I dodged a colorful cart full of balloon toys being pushed by a woman wearing a glowing necklace. As I jumped back, I bumped into a short man, and worse yet, I spilled my hot coffee on him.

"What the hell?" The man grabbed his shirt and brushed off the hot liquid. I cringed when I saw who it was. I had just spilled coffee on Smith.

When he recognized me, his eyes narrowed and he yelled, "You? First a cup of wine, now coffee? What is with you ruining my clothes?"

"I'm very sorry. I was dodging the woman with that cart…" I pointed at the blinking toys. "I didn't see you dressed in all black."

His arms flailed. "Sure. Blame it on me because of what I'm wearing. Everyone blames everything on good old Barry Smith."

"I certainly didn't do it on purpose." I continued to defend myself to the touchy man. "No. I didn't mean it was your fault. Here, have some napkins." While reaching in the dark to grab some, I accidentally flung one of my hot sugary donuts at his face.

He growled, "Oh My God! Get away from me." He huffed, "Your friends took my place in Marvin's balloon today, and now you're throwing food at me. I should sue."

I shrank back and opted not to tell him I'd be on the flight too. Instead, I said, "I've gotta get back to work. I'm really sorry."

Carrying what was left of my coffee and donuts, I stopped by Angelica's booth. I told her what just happened and about the wine incident earlier.

She erupted in a deep, hearty laugh, and tears streamed down her face. I couldn't help but join in. She caught her breath and managed to say, "I'm sorry, but that is just too good. And you didn't do either one on purpose?"

I shook my head earnestly. "No, of course not. Do you think he can sue me, like he said?"

Angelica wiped tears from her eyes and caught her breath. "No. Smith is always threatening to sue someone for something, but he never does. Well, I'm sorry you felt bad, but it was pretty funny." She asked, "Are you ready for your last day?"

"Yes. But I don't think it's a good idea for me to go on the balloon today. If Smith sees me, he will really have a fit. And besides, you can't watch both shops."

She raised a defiant eyebrow. "Oh, yes, I can. I'll just do what I should have done last time. I'll push our dividing curtain back so I can see both booths. Most of the shoppers will be out on the field anyway, so I shouldn't need the services of the little boy again."

I took a deep breath and let it out. I knew I couldn't change her mind, so I said, "You have been way too kind." I started to leave, but turned back. "Have you seen Chris this morning?"

"Not yet. Why? Did he kidnap your friend again?"

I chuckled. "No, but he's probably going to have quite the hangover after last night's binge drinking."

"I see. Well, let's hope he arrives on time. Marvin will need help today with a full balloon."

When the gates opened, people streamed into our tent as usual to shop. The only other options besides shopping that early in the morning were to stand in line for food or wait for the Dawn Patrol to light up.

A woman with a heavy Swedish accent was overjoyed to find a clock made from her favorite book, *Pippi Longstocking.* I had taken old, ragged paperback copies of all four Pippi books and made a collage before Modpodgeing it and turning it into a clock.

She introduced herself as Elin. "I live in Stockholm. Pippi is our national heroine. I have been looking for the books in English, but this is much better. I can't believe I found this at the Balloon Show."

Her enthusiasm touched me so much that I offered to ship the bulky clock to her. I'd never done that for a customer from another country.

I took down her address and put the clock in a large box to pack up and mail on Monday. To my surprise, she handed me a tiny little bluebird carved from wood. I cocked my head. "What's this?"

In her thick Swedish accent, she said, "It's a good luck bluebird. Everybody needs good luck, yes?"

I nodded and said, "Thank you so much." I waved as the sweet woman left and slipped the bluebird into my pocket.

Sunday, the final morning, was very busy until the balloons began to inflate out on the field. I thought Carmen and crew might stop by, but they didn't. However, Jill and Granda did.

"Hey, my little Maria." There was sweet Granda, wearing an Irish sweater and little green hat, followed by Jill, sporting a green jacket with leprechauns on it.

She shimmied up to me and sang, "I'm magically delicious!"

I'd never seen the jacket before and asked, "Where did you get that?"

"Granda has a whole closet full of Irish clothes. I chose this one for today's ride."

"You two are so cute. Let me get a picture!"

I made them pose together and snapped a photo. Their red hair really stood out in the image. "So, are you ready to fly this morning?"

He answered, "I've been ready for years. I do miss the sky."

"Where are you meeting your friend?"

"Row J. Can't miss it because it's big and green."

"Cool. Jill, did I tell you I get to ride in Marvin's Up and Away balloon again?"

"No. That's fun. Who else is going?" She squinted, probably worried Smith might also be a passenger.

"Some strangers, Marvin, Chris, my three señoritas, and me, I think. Smith isn't going, thankfully, but do remind me to tell you what happened this morning." I shuddered as I remembered the coffee incident.

She raised an eyebrow. "Sounds interesting. I think it's just the three of us on ours."

I said, "Nice. We're meeting at Row L. Keep your phone handy, and I'll call if I see you near us in the sky!"

"Okay. Have fun, girl."

"I will. Granda, I hope your friend lets you take the controls while you are up."

"Me too." He gave his infectious giggle as they turned to go onto the field.

A bit later, Angelica pulled back the curtain and said, "Showtime. Get your little butt over to Marvin's balloon."

I handed her my iPad and said, "Good luck and thank you again!"

I wasn't sure I even needed my jacket, but I had it and my purse just in case. I headed to the balloon but stopped by Granda's friends' spot on the way. The envelope was just a lump of green on the ground, waiting to be inflated.

When Jill saw me, her upper lip twitched. "Granda's friend isn't here. His crew said he wasn't feeling well and went into the Pilot's Pavilion to lie down."

"Oh, that's not good. Hope he gets better in a hurry."

"I know. Granda is really looking forward to going up."

"Does he want to take my place? I don't need to go again."

She hollered, "Granda. Do you want to take Maria's place on an Up and Away balloon?"

He said, "Oh, no, my dears. I'll wait for Seamus. He's a tough bird. I'm sure he'll be here soon."

I felt bad about the situation and told Jill, "Let me know what happens."

She gave me a solemn nod. "Hope he's not too late." She looked at her watch. "I'm supposed to be at your shop by 9:45."

"Oh, that's right. It's not the end of the world if you open late." Then, I joked, "Or…maybe I could ask Louise's grandson to open up for us. Bart is quite the salesman."

She put her hand on her hip. "So now you're replacing me with an eight-year-old?"

"No. Because he's actually nine now." I winked and headed to Marvin's balloon.

A few rows ahead, I saw Marvin's familiar crew hard at work. Carmen, Bianca, and Coco stood away from the balloon, near the other passengers. I came up behind them as they watched the balloon fill with hot air. I asked, "Are we ready to fly?"

Carmen turned around and smiled. "Yes! We're ready to go in the bigger basket this time. Chris is excited to take us up."

I looked at Chris standing there alive as could be. He said, "Josh and Emma," as he checked a couple of teenagers' names off the passenger list. I was glad Chris was none the worse after the poor state he was in last night. His long black hair hung down in front of his face, but I definitely saw him wink at Bianca.

I looked at Carmen, "You do know Chris isn't the pilot, right? Marvin is. He's the one with white hair."

"It's okay. We don't care who takes us, as long as we're all together. Why are you here?" She brightened. "Do you get to go on the balloon with us, Maria?"

I smiled. "Yes. It looks that way!"

"Que, bueno." She jumped up and down as she told the other girls. They looked equally happy that I was joining them.

Chris approached someone behind us and read off the names, "Chad and Cindy Johnson?"

Did he say Chad and Cindy? My head whipped around. Sure enough, the guy who gave me the bike parts was there with his wife, Cindy. I walked over and said, "Fancy meeting you two here. Remember me? Maria?"

Cindy smiled, and Chad said, "Of course. So, we decided to use our free 'Up and Away' trip, after all. It's gotta be a better ride than last week, right?"

"Absolutely"

Cindy asked, "Are you on the flight too?"

"I am."

Next to us, Chris checked off a fit woman in her 60s, then he got us. Afterward, he called out to Marvin. "Just one missing, a Sarah Stevens."

He replied, "Well, let's load everyone else up while we wait."

Chris and another crew member helped the passengers climb into the basket, one by one. When it was my turn, I hopped up and over the edge, being a near expert, since I did it just two days before.

Once we were all inside the huge basket, I found a spot near Carmen and we took a selfie. I immediately texted it to our abuela. Why hadn't I taken a picture as soon as we got together? Oh well, better late than never.

Marvin went through his safety briefing and even pointed out the instrument panel, asking us to stay clear of the gizmos.

After he finished, the tight area became noisy. Passengers visited while Marvin adjusted the propane, keeping the air inside the envelope just the right temperature. Each time the flame went up, people squealed.

The loudest sound was the obnoxious voice of Smith, who had just walked up to the balloon. He barked, "Wait a minute, Marvin. You are letting her ride today?" He pointed at me. Even in the dim morning light, I could see that his face was full of rage.

Marvin replied sarcastically, "Oh, golly, I'm so sorry I didn't send you copies of the passenger list, Barry. It must have slipped my mind. Now, if you don't mind, we need to take off."

Smith wasn't having it and started counting heads in the basket. "Aha! You only have eleven! You have room for twelve."

Was this guy for real? All the other guests stared at the manic man, as I worried Smith might jump on board and try to hurt me. After all, I had made him angry twice in two days…well, three if you count me being in the basket now. I also noticed Cindy grabbing Chad's arm as she looked at Smith. She didn't want the guy on board any more than I did.

Marvin addressed our group loud enough for Smith to hear him. "We're still waiting for one more paid passenger. She must be running late."

I crossed my fingers that the girl would arrive so Smith wouldn't manage to take her spot. The zebra next to the balloon blew his whistle, signaling that it was our turn to take off. The scene was a little tense as we waited for the last passenger to arrive.

Just then, a gal ran up wearing a hoodie and sunglasses. She called out, "Wait. I'm Sarah." She was out of breath. A crew member quickly helped her to climb on board.

Smith crossed his arms and scrunched his nose. He knew his chance to board was over. And he began to sulk like a little kid.

As soon as the girl was situated and given a brief safety talk, Marvin said the company's slogan, "Up and Away!"

Coco pointed her finger in the air and shouted, "Hasta el infinito…y mas alla!"

I laughed at the little cutie.

The older woman asked me, 'What did she say?"

I snorted. "It's shouted Buzz Lightyear's favorite phrase, 'To Infinity and Beyond!'"

The lady grinned. "That's adorable."

Coco was really cute. I looked at all three of my house guests, amazed by how they constantly surprised me.

Whew! The balloon slowly rose just as it had a few days earlier - nice and smooth. I giggled at the sight of Smith fuming below us. I'd never seen a full-grown man be such a baby. I felt certain we were safe, now that we were high above him. He couldn't hurt anyone now.

Ahhh, this was the life! We floated south, among a sea of balloons below us, beside us, and above.

Carmen interrupted my reverie. "Maria, can you find someone to take a picture of the four of us?" She pointed to her two friends.

I asked the woman standing next to me, "Excuse me, could you take a photo of our group? Then I'll take one of you."

"Oh, of course!"

We settled ourselves against the padded edge and smiled. The woman with her cropped gray hair really knew how to take photos. She zoomed in, took landscape and vertical shots. Then she kneeled down, snapping all the while. Then she said, "Make silly faces," which we did.

Before she handed the phone back to me, Bianca said, "Chris, come here!"

Carmen said, "Yes. Let's get one with Chris."

He left his post beside Marvin, and put his arm around Bianca's tiny waist, making her giggle when he squeezed. Just as the nice woman held up my phone, the girl named Sarah, who had arrived late, said, "I'll take this one." She yanked my phone from the woman.

Gee. That was a weird and rude thing to do. The adept photographer woman thought so too as she made a face at the girl. That's when things started to go a different kind of South.

After snatching the phone, Sarah didn't lift it to take our photo, but just stood, staring at us.

I glanced at our group. Carmen, Coco, and Bianca posed with big smiles as expected. But when Chris looked up at the gal, his big grin disappeared, and his eyes widened in horror. He dropped his hand from Bianca's waist and held it down to his side.

I studied Sarah, wondering what could cause his odd reaction. She wasn't holding a weapon and didn't look scary to me. Oooh, maybe she was a jealous girlfriend. This was going to be interesting.

When Sarah took off her hood, something about her looked familiar. It was in the way she stared at Chris. That was it! She was the one who had stood in Jenny's freeze-dried candy booth staring across at my stuff yesterday. Then it clicked. She wasn't looking at my hanging book balloons; she was watching Chris cozying up with Bianca. Oh, this was not cool.

Breaking the awkward silence, I asked, "Do you two know each other?"

Sarah never took her eyes from Chris, but answered, "Why don't you answer that, Chris?"

He came to life and cleared his throat. "Uh. Yeah, we do." His face reddened as he told her, "You just surprised me." He stepped forward and grabbed her arm. "Can we talk?" He took my phone away from her, and handed it back to me.

I watched as the two moved to the middle of the balloon, barely out of earshot from other riders, since it was such a small space. They spoke in soft tones, but anyone could tell it was an intense conversation.

Carmen whispered to me, "I think she might be his girlfriend."

I nodded. "Looks like he's been caught cheating. How is Bianca?"

Carmen then turned to Bianca, who was wiping her eyes.

I certainly hadn't planned to spend the flight watching people argue, and I swiveled around to soak up the beauty surrounding me. The sun had finally popped above the mountain and was so bright that I had to get my sunglasses from my purse. As I put my sunglasses on, I realized why Sarah wore them indoors yesterday and this morning. She obviously didn't want Chris to recognize her. That had worked, but now I wondered about her name. He had read it off from the list. Why wasn't he freaked out then? Glancing at the couple, I was thankful I couldn't hear their bickering. It was none of my business anyway.

I carefully moved across to the other side to see the sunlight hitting the balloons to the west of us. The lighting was amazing, so I snapped some pictures. I took a deep breath and smiled. There was nothing else like this.

My watch buzzed, alerting me to a phone call. I swiped to answer. "Hey, Joey. I'm flying high now. Whatcha doing?"

"Just wanted to make sure that drunk guy woke up."

"Oh yeah, he did. He's here on the flight, but…" I lowered my voice and whispered, "he's in the middle of a lover's quarrel."

"With Bianca?"

"No. Someone else. It's so odd. This gal confronted him right on the flight. Not sure how he knew her – maybe from Montana?"

"You mean, Wyoming."

I said, "No. He's from Montana. That's what his license plate says."

"Well, his driver's license is from Wyoming."

I thought about it. The states are right next to each other. Maybe he had lived in each place for a while. I said, "Well, anyway, it sure made for an interesting start to the ride. I feel bad for Bianca, though. She seems pretty upset."

Joey said, "Oh, that's sad. Look, I didn't mean to interrupt your flight. I'll let you go, but I'll come by to help you pack up this afternoon. Just text when you are ready."

"Oh, awesome. Thank you! See you soon."

After hanging up, I made my way through the group to Marvin, who asked, "What's up with Chris?"

"I don't know. I guess that girl who was late for the flight might be Chris's girlfriend. She seems jealous that he was with Bianca."

Marvin turned to look at Chris. He chuckled. "Didn't know we had a Don Juan on board. Just then, Sarah took off her sunglasses, and Marvin's face froze. He stammered, "No. No. Not Scarlett. Why is she here?"

Chapter 17

Marvin was staring straight at Sarah.

I said, "Scarlett? Stoney's sister? But she said her name was Sarah."

"No. That's Scarlett. I'd stake my life on it."

I studied the woman in question. Without her dark glasses, I could see the similarities, despite her being younger than Stoney. She was tall with a wide nose, light brown hair, and green eyes. She was just missing the dimple in her chin.

Marvin nodded, but his lips tightened in anger, "I can't believe she's showing her face around here."

"Maybe she came to show her respects?" I offered.

He scoffed. "More likely she came to try to check out his inheritance."

I didn't think that was right and asked Marvin, "But how does she know Chris?"

He shook his head. "I have absolutely no idea."

Someone yelled, "Uhh, Mr. Pilot, there's a power line over there."

When Marvin realized we were heading downward towards the wires, he jumped into action by igniting the burner. We quickly rose out of danger's way. Everyone steadied themselves from the sudden movement. Marvin shook his head and said to me. "See? She's already causing me problems."

As we moved steadily upward, I said, "Marvin, if they are both from Wyoming, maybe Chris knew Scarlett there."

He shook his head. "Chris didn't live in Wyoming. He's from Montana."

"Oh." Hmm. Guess we were confused about those states.

As I made my way back to Carmen, I overheard Chris say, "I'm not your property. I've done what you wanted and don't owe you anything else. Leave me alone."

I glanced at Sarah, actually Scarlett. Her face was red as her name, as she watched Chris go to Bianca and console her.

This was nothing like the relaxing balloon ride I had experienced with Joey. I rolled my head around on my shoulders, trying to forget the drama and enjoy the scenery below. As we flew over Paseo del Norte, I was amazed at how small the cars looked on the busy road. They looked like ants marching in perfect rows.

When raised voices interrupted my ant-watching, I turned to find Marvin and Scarlett in quite a kerfuffle. It was impossible to ignore their fight due to the close quarters.

Marvin growled, "How dare you come back here after all the terrible things you did to Stoney. You never cared for him. Go back to Wyoming and leave us alone."

She gave the eeriest expression as she gritted her teeth. "I'm not going anywhere, old man."

The two garnered everyone's attention as several beautiful balloons floated past us.

Scarlett said, "You are so gullible. Did you really believe that Chris wanted to learn the ballooning business?" She scoffed. "He had no interest whatsoever. I just sent him here to check out your relationship with my brother."

Marvin closed his eyes in confusion and said, "What?"

Scarlett laughed. "Yeah. Chris and I worked together at the gaming store in Cheyenne. I was running out of money. Once we started dating, I realized he would do anything for me."

Chris's demeanor turned from nervous to livid, but Scarlett went on. "When I told him about how you turned my brother against me, he asked what he could do to help. So, he came here to watch you and Stoney."

I was surprised at the twist in the story. So, Chris was just here as a spy for Scarlett?

Marvin looked at Chris, who closed his eyes, apparently wishing she would shut up.

Scarlett leaned up against an empty spot on the basket's edge. With her elbows on the padding, she said, "I had no idea you and your woman would fall in love with Chris. You had no idea that he reported back to me every day..." She glared at Chris and Bianca and added, "Until three days ago, when he got distracted. I can just hear you and Angelica…" She continued to mock them. "I can just hear Marvin say, 'That Chris is such a hard worker. He learns so quickly. What a nice guy, Angelica. We should adopt him and make him part of our family.'" Scarlett's face darkened as she added fuel to the fire. "You treated Chris the same way you did Stoney."

Scarlett twisted her mouth and growled, "Then, after Stoney died, I found out that I was not named as his beneficiary. You were!" She looked manic. "You weaseled your way into his heart. That's why my brother chose you over me. You and your wife have no right to Stoney's money and artwork. It's mine, and I deserve every bit of it. I'm his real family."

Marvin finally found his voice. "I did no such thing. Stoney was like family, and we loved him. I never manipulated him. As a matter of fact, I tried to talk him out of putting me in the Will, but he refused to change it. And let me tell you something else about that. Stoney…"

Scarlett interrupted and scoffed. "Right. And how convenient that he died so young in YOUR balloon when you are in his Will."

Was she suggesting that Marvin killed Stoney? My stomach twisted, and I began to feel sick.

At that point, Marvin's face paled to a sickly ash color. He stammered, "I couldn't hurt Stoney, or anyone for that matter. You take that back!"

I looked over at Chris, who stood with wide eyes as he watched his former girlfriend go crazy.

Scarlett let out a laugh and said, "Well, I will feel much better once you pay for everything you did to my brother." She gave him a demented look and pulled out a knife.

At that, Chris bolted forward and yelled, "You are not killing Marvin, too."

He took the knife from Scarlett's hand and threw it overboard. This just angered the woman even more. She poked Chris in the chest and said, "What's the matter, don't want the truth to come out?" She poked him again. "You are the weakest of the weak — just following directions from anyone who gives you attention. You are so pathetic, Chris, but I know you'll take care of Marvin, too, because I own you. Remember how I was your alibi when you stole that car and I lied to the police. I can always change my story, you know."

"It was your idea to steal the car." In a fit of rage, Chris picked Scarlett up and held her against the basket. "Nobody owns me, and I'll prove it!"

Scarlett's face was contorted. She reached out to grab something, but it was too late. Chris heaved her body out of the basket, and she disappeared over the edge.

Everything turned silent. Once the reality of the horrifying moment set in, several people began to scream.

I gulped and ran past Chris to the edge, where Scarlett had fallen. I looked over the side, desperately hoping she was hanging on to the side somehow, but there was no sign of her. She must have fallen into the Bosque or maybe the river. My heart sank as I realized nobody could survive a fall from that distance. Chris had just killed a woman right in front of us!

Everyone was in shock as they watched Chris stalk around the basket like a crazed monster. He hissed like a snake, and then he ranted, "She made me do it. I didn't want to kill him, but she made me."

I gasped. Was Chris admitting to killing Stoney? Had he shoved two people over the edge of a basket? He was a certified murderer.

What in the world were we to do? Everyone was upset. The two teenagers suddenly looked even younger. Cindy, who had already seen a man being thrown overboard, cowered and shook in Chad's arms. Who could blame her? When I saw Marvin's pale face, I was afraid he might faint.

I carefully took my phone from my pocket and dialed 9-1-1. Just as I lifted it to my ear, Chris stood in front of me. He was so close, I could smell the liquor from last night on his breath. He snarled, "Put it down!"

I did what he said, but felt around behind me until I grabbed hold of the frame pole. I held on tight in case I was to be his next victim. He scanned all the passengers and then ran to the controls. He pushed Marvin aside and said, "I'm taking control of this balloon."

At this point, Marvin was gulping air. I wondered if he was having a medical episode, so I helped him sit down on the floor.

Chris ignited the flames, and we moved upward. He was hijacking our balloon? Where in the world would he take us?

Meanwhile, on the other side of the basket, Chad must have thought the same thing. He slowly picked up a fire extinguisher. Without showing any reaction, I kept my eyes on both men.

Chad showed the extinguisher to Josh. The high school boy nodded and stepped away from his girlfriend to join him. Chad lifted the heavy red canister and clobbered Chris hard on the head. The teen caught him as he crumpled at my feet. Then, the two young men tied him up with a loose rope and moved him to an open spot.

I blew out a long breath and released my grip on the pole, thankful the madman was out of commission-at least temporarily.

The rest of us clapped for our two heroes, then talked all at once about what had just occurred.

I heard the lone woman say into her phone, "Yes, we've had a crime committed on an Up and Away hot air balloon." She continued to describe to the police what had happened and asked them for help. I was glad that the police were now aware and would look for Scarlett's body.

Marvin didn't look good. He was trying to catch his breath after all the excitement.

I put my hand on his back. "You okay, Marvin?"

When he didn't answer or sit up straight, I started to worry. Just then, he fell over onto the floor, grabbing his chest.

I screamed. "Help! Is anyone a doctor?" That got everyone's attention.

Within seconds, the woman who had just called 9-1-1 came to me and kneeled next to us. "I'm not a doctor, but I'm a nurse at Presbyterian Hospital. He needs to lie still and remain calm."

I stood and stepped back to give them room. Coco rushed forward and wadded up her jacket to use as his pillow. She kneeled down, then pulled out a water bottle covered with Hello Kitty stickers from her bag, and handed it to the woman

The teenage girl, Emma, asked quietly, "Um, who's flying the balloon?"

My mouth dropped open. Both Marvin and Chris were obviously indisposed, so I made another announcement, "Does anyone have experience flying a hot air balloon?" This time, all faces were blank, so I added, "Or flying anything, for that matter?"

Still nothing. I looked at Chad. He was probably the most mechanical, but he had his hands full with a hysterical wife. Cindy was bent over trying to catch her breath as he patted her back.

Josh and Emma shrugged helplessly, and Carmen and Bianca shook their heads.

Angelica would know what to do. She needed to know about Marvin, anyway. I called her with the grim news about her husband collapsing on the floor of the balloon.

"How can that be? He just had his annual aviation medical evaluation two weeks ago and passed beautifully. What happened?"

I didn't want to alarm her, so I said, "First of all, Marvin is resting. There is a nurse on board who is tending to him. But, Angelica, one thing you need to know is that Chris admitted to killing Stoney."

When the line went silent, I waited a few more seconds and said, "Angelica? Angelica? Are you there?" I worried the news might put her over the edge, too.

Her voice was weak when she said, "That can't be. We've trusted him and had him at our house many times."

My heart sank for her, but I told the rest of the story. "I think when Chris threw Scarlett out of the basket, it was way too much for Marvin, and he collapsed."

She said with force, "Wait, Scarlett was there? Why? Oh, this can't be happening. Poor Marvin."

Since Angelica had been so upset over Stoney's death, I felt so bad being the bearer of bad news and said, "I'm so sorry, Angelica. We need to land the plane, but unfortunately, we don't have a pilot capable at the moment. I need to know how to fly this balloon, so we don't crash."

I heard Angelica take in a deep breath and let it out. She told herself, "Get a grip, Angelica."

Then, in a much stronger tone, she said, "Even though Chris caused the problems, can't you have him land the balloon?"

"No. He can't. He was out of control, planning to hijack the balloon, and another passenger knocked him out and tied him up. Nobody here knows how to pilot this thing."

She calmly said, "Okay…Maria, get Marvin's walkie-talkie and tell the ground crew what is going on. I will call an ambulance, Fiesta management, and the FAA to report the emergency. Someone should be able to assist you soon. Keep your phone on."

"I will. Thank you so much. I really didn't know what to do."

"You're fine, Love. Stay strong."

After I hung up, I found the walkie-talkie lying next to Marvin. Not knowing the first thing about how to use it, I asked Carmen to help me figure it out.

She said, "Cousin Pedro and I used them when he lived next door. I can do it."

"Great. Can you contact the crew and explain what just happened? Tell them we have no pilot and need help."

While she moved to the side and spoke into the device, I looked out and found we were crossing the river. It brought back memories of Friday's exciting Splash and Dash. That seemed like ages ago. But now, that excitement was replaced by anxiety. We were losing altitude fast. I was afraid we might hit the grove of trees on the other side of the Bosque.

I grabbed my phone and called my friend. "Jill, are you and Granda up in the sky yet?"

"No. Seamus still hasn't arrived yet. Apparently, he ate a bad burrito this morning and has tummy problems. We've been waiting forever, and I'm ready to fly."

"I need to talk to Granda now. We have an emergency. There is no pilot on board. I need to know how to fly this thing and, more importantly, how to land it."

"Oh, OK."

I heard some rustling, then Granda was on the line. "You say you have no pilot?"

"Right. He's incapacitated, and we're getting really close to some trees."

"Okay, darlin', now take it easy. Go to the controls and follow my directions. Find the blast valve. It's a trigger up just under the burner. You need to squeeze it pretty hard, so a lot more propane flows. Let me know when you find it."

I lifted my hand up to the red pipe I'd seen Marvin hold onto, but I couldn't reach it. I stood on my tiptoes but couldn't feel anything to pull. That was a problem with being short. I called Bianca over since she was a good six inches taller than me. In Spanish, I asked, "Can you feel a lever like a trigger to pull?

She felt upward. "Si. I have it."

"OK, now squeeze it hard." I pantomimed how to do it.

When she did, big flames shot upward, causing us to rise. Whew. I put the phone to my mouth. "We got it. We're ascending again."

He said, "That's good. Hold on a sec." Then he hollered to his friend's crew something about taking off immediately. After some back-and-forth arguing, he was back on the line. "We're gonna come find you and guide you down. Does Jilly know what your balloon looks like?"

"Yes, but there are nineteen more like this."

"Oh. Well, there should be a number on the side of the basket. Can someone read it?"

I asked the teenage girl who stood nearby, "Can you carefully lean over and tell me the number on the side of the basket?"

As she rushed over to the side, Granda deftly walked me through more about the controls. The girl returned and said the number was 358. I thanked her and relayed the number to Granda.

"Thanks again, Granda. I'm just glad we didn't crash into anything while the pilots were distracted."

He said, "Your balloon probably has a metering valve that keeps a continuous flame. Without attention, it just started to drift downward. Now, can you tell me where you are?"

I looked over the edge. "I'm not sure, but we just crossed the Rio Grande. I saw the river as we flew over, so we're on the East side now." East and West directions were easy for local Burqueños. We knew the mountains stood to the East and the volcanoes were to the West.

"Okay, just don't go so far that you land on I-25."

I thought that was a no-brainer. Who would want to land on a busy interstate? I said, "I'll avoid that if I can figure out how to change directions."

Granda said, "The only way to control horizontal movement is to follow the wind patterns. Once we have our balloon in the air, I'll give you advice on that. Are there any other balloons around you?"

I looked about but didn't see even one. "No. Where did they all go?"

"Can you tell me what the propane gauge says? The gauge is attached to the tank on the floor of the basket. I need to know how much longer you can stay in the air."

It never occurred to me that we could run out of fuel. That made me even more anxious. I knelt and said, "It is at 40 percent."

"Good. You have enough to make it somewhere safely."

I tried to figure out where we were by scouting the area for familiar landmarks. It was odd to be above so many buildings, none of which were recognizable. Then I pointed, as if he could see. "Oh, Granda. I can see the movie theater by Jefferson."

"Okay, good. Now we know where you are. We're taking off now, and we'll be there as fast as we can."

Jill's voice came next. "I know you are worried and maybe even scared, but how does it feel to fly a hot air balloon?"

"Terrible. I have ten people depending on me to get them to the ground."

"I thought it held twelve."

"It did, but one got tossed overboard."

"What?"

"Listen, I need to concentrate. I'll give all the grisly details once I land."

"OK. Be careful. I need you to be safe. You're Sophia's Fairy Godmother."

"I am not her Fairy Godmother. I'm just her regular Godmother." I shook my head then added, "I promise I'll be as safe as I can be. Call me as soon as you can see our balloon."

When I hung up, I checked my phone battery. Good. It was at 52 percent. I looked at Carmen, who held the walkie-talkie to her ear. I whispered, "Did you reach the ground crew?" She nodded and held up a finger for me to wait.

I looked down and realized our balloon was now directly over the movie theater. Unfortunately, that theater was right beside the interstate. There was no steering wheel on this thing. How, the heck, could I find the wind patterns to change directions and move Westward?

My phone rang, and I was happy to hear it was a man from the Federal Aviation Administration. He spoke matter-of-factly, like dispatchers do on TV. "I understand you have an emergency."

"Yes! Both the pilot and his assistant are incapacitated. We're currently near I-25 and Jefferson. Another balloon is just leaving Balloon Fiesta Park and heading our way to try to help guide me. But can you tell me how to make the balloon go West? I don't want to go over the Interstate but don't know how to turn."

"Right. You don't want to cross I-25. Can you tell me the number on the Altimeter?"

"What is that?"

He calmly said, "Look at the instrument panel. Look for the letters A.L.T. and turn the dial to those letters. The numbers below ALT tell you how far you are from the ground. We need to know your precise altitude.

It all sounded like mumbo jumbo to me, but I did find a dial with the letters ALT, and I read off the number to him.

"You are at a good height, now. There are layers of wind, which move in different directions. To move to the West, vertically, you need to try moving up a tiny bit by gently pulling the trigger on the blast valve."

I brightened. "Oh, oh, I know which one that is." I pointed up and directed Bianca to squeeze the trigger lightly. Right away, we rose a little bit. Then, like magic, we shifted and started moving gently to the West. I gave a sigh of relief and said, "It's working. Thank you so much."

"Are you in touch with your ground crew?"

"Yes."

"Good. Do you have much propane?"

I looked at the gauge and saw that the percentage had gone down. "It's at 29 percent. Is that Okay?"

"You should be fine. We'll stay with you until you land.

"Ahh. That's so good. Thank you."

Carmen signaled me, so I asked the FAA man to hold on a second. I turned to Carmen. "What do you know?"

"The crew can see us and will follow our balloon. They suggest we go South to a more open area." I nodded my head to her that I understood.

"I got back on the phone and said, "Okay, now how do we move South?"

"It's the same thing. You have to find the current that took you South in the first place. It's either higher or lower. Just don't go too high or too low."

Argh. So confusing. At this point, I wanted to hand the reins over to anyone else, but everyone was depending on me. I needed to land this puppy soon.

"Um. How do we move lower again?"

"See the cord hanging down? It is called a vent or valve cord. If you pull it, hot air is released from a vent at the top."

"I said, "Okay. We'll try that. Thank you."

When I reached for the cord, I knocked my arm into one of the load supports, and fumbled my phone. As if in slow motion, it slipped from my hand. I tried to grab it, but my iPhone slid over the padded edge of the basket into the blue sky.

How could I have been so clumsy? My phone was gone. How could that FAA walk me through the landing? Jill was supposed to call me, too. Could this day get any worse?

Chapter 18

I couldn't believe I dropped my phone overboard. I needed it now more than ever. The local FAA man only had my phone number, so he couldn't contact anyone else on board. And what if it had fallen on some unsuspecting person and hurt them?

I was about ready to give up and cry, but I heard Carmen say into the walkie-talkie, "Looks like she lost her phone. Can you help us land?"

Yes, that was a good idea. Surely, they could help.

Carmen moved close enough for me to hear the crackly reply, "Uh. We're not pilots and don't know how to do that. We just help direct Marvin to a safe place to land and then help pack up the balloon."

Dang. Everyone around me was paying close attention since their lives depended on me getting them down safely.

The woman helping Marvin said, "At least the police know that we've gone rogue."

I wasn't sure how the police could help us land, but I did wonder if they had found Scarlett's body yet. Ick. I looked around frantically, wondering what to do.

Behind us in the distance, I saw a green balloon. Maybe that was Jill and Granda! I yelled, "Keep an eye on that green balloon. I think my friends are in it. Maybe they can help us."

My goal was to head south to find a safe place to land, but I also wanted to wait for Granda. What to do? Bianca was already a pro at managing the blast valve. This time, when I directed her, she raised the balloon. Unfortunately, we started floating East toward I-25 again. I quickly tried the vent cord to move back down to the layer of wind that would take us West.

The balloon jolted from the rapid up-and-down direction changes. Thankfully, it did move us away from I-25.

I watched as the percentage changed on the propane gauge. It was now at 23. Hopefully, we could get down slowly before we ran out and started to fall. While we slowly inched Westward, I surveyed our group. Everyone seemed stable.

I looked behind us and realized the oncoming green balloon had to be my best friend. Oh, how funny. It was a big shamrock! It wasn't too far away now. I just hoped Granda could help us land safely.

When the giant clover was closer, Jill shouted, "Pick up your phone, dummy!"

I yelled as loud as I could, "I can't. I dropped it somewhere between the Cinemark 24 and the Bosque."

"Well, why the heck did you do that?"

From that distance, she couldn't see my eyes roll, but I'm sure my annoyed posture was pretty telling.

My Irish hero's voice came through the air loud and clear. "Maria, find somebody good at throwing to toss me the drop line."

It was fair that he asked for someone else to throw, since he had coached my softball team when Jill and I were ten. I was a pretty good batter, but I sucked at throwing a ball.

Josh stepped forward and said, "I can do it. I pitch for Rio Rancho High's baseball team."

"Great!" How lucky were we to have a nurse and a baseball player on the flight? A pilot would have been better, but beggars…

I yelled to Granda Finn, "What is a drop line?"

"A big, long rope. It should be coiled on the floor or wrapped around somethin'."

Emma leaned down and started unwrapping a rope hanging on a hook. She said, "Is this it?" Everyone agreed that it probably was.

The boy yelled to Granda, "Tell me when, and I'll throw it."

While we waited for the balloons to reach throwing distance, Jill shouted. "Where are you headed, Maria? To your house?"

I scoffed. "No. I was just trying to stay afloat until someone helped us land."

When their balloon was about 20 feet from us, Jill squealed, "How about we land by your shop on Joey's big X? Looks like we're only about a half mile away."

I looked down. She was right. I recognized the neighborhood. The space was big enough, and there was plenty of parking for the ground crew and emergency vehicles. "Great idea, Jill!"

Granda shouted, "Okay, Laddie, throw it now!"

The lanky kid grabbed the end of the rope like a lasso and swung it around a few times in his right hand while his other one held onto the rest. When he threw it, he released the length. Granda caught it on the first try. Everyone cheered. That was amazing.

After the older man tied the rope to his basket, Granda smiled and hollered, "Now we're suckin' diesel."

What the heck did that mean? I looked at Jill. She must have wondered the same thing, because she shrugged. Who cared? We were attached to them, so we weren't on our own anymore.

I asked Carmen if I could speak to someone on the ground. She handed me the radio, and I spoke into the device, "Can you meet us at the Out of the Box Shopping Center? The address is…"

Carmen tapped me on the shoulder and said, "Maria, you have to push the button to talk."

"Oh." I felt stupid and started over, talking into the walkie-talkie with the button depressed. I gave the address and added, "It's close to Montano and Second."

The walkie-talkie crackled, and I heard, "Copy. The EMT's are with us, we'll let them know, too. Over."

I handed the device back to her and made my way to Chad and Cindy. It worried me that she was sitting on the ground, rocking with her hands on her knees. I mouthed, "How is she?" to him.

He said quietly, "She's not doing well at all. We thought we were safe when that jerk with the earring didn't get on the flight, but no…this was even worse than the last ride." He shook his head. "I mean, what are the chances a second person would go over the edge?"

I frowned. "I know. It's awful. I'm so sorry you had to experience that." I put my hand on his shoulder. "I wish there was something I could do."

He looked up and pleaded, "Just get us down safely."

After seeing Cindy's reaction to the deaths, I realized I hadn't cried or internalized the events at all. It would probably all sink in later. But, with all that was going on, it was a good thing I didn't break down. Someone needed to take charge.

Thinking of Marvin, I grabbed Anglica's card from my purse, glad I'd picked one up a few days ago so I had her number. I handed it to Carmen. "Can you please call Angelica and ask her to meet us at the Out of the Box shopping center?"

Once I had a chance to breathe, I smiled to think we were being pulled through the air by the big shamrock. I wanted so badly to take photos of the two envelopes bouncing off each other as we were being pulled across Albuquerque, but alas, I had no phone or camera. At least my nerves had calmed down considerably since our flight was in Granda's hands.

The nurse called from several feet away. "Maria, Marvin wants to know if you contacted his wife."

I nodded yes and moved closer. "I'm sorry. I never got your name."

"I'm Janet."

"Hi, Janet. Was it his heart?"

"I'm not sure. I'm actually an obstetrics nurse, so I don't have a lot of experience with older people in the labor and delivery department. But he is stable now."

I smiled at Coco, then kneeled beside the trio. While pushing my long hair back so it wouldn't blow in Marvin's face, my finger touched the horseshoe pin that Stoney had given me on my second day of Balloon Fiesta. Marvin needed any luck it might provide more than I did. I took it off and gently pinned it to his shirt. I said softly, "Marvin, Angelica, and an ambulance will meet us when we land. It shouldn't be much longer. Oh, and your balloon is being towed by a big shamrock."

Although his eyes were shut, they squeezed tighter when he heard that. Hopefully, he thought it was funny.

I stood and looked out to see our progress. We were getting closer to my .shop. Good. My best friend and her grandpa were leading us home. What a weird day.

I held up an imaginary camera and yelled, "Jill!" When she saw my "air camera," she made a ridiculous pose, leaning her head back like a supermodel. I clicked and clicked my fake camera. We needed to do something to ease the tension of the day.

I noticed Emma taking real photos of Jill with her phone. I hoped someone also snapped pictures of the tethered balloons.

Then Jill took a picture of me standing by the instrument panel.

I was just so glad that we were being taken care of by an expert balloonist – even if he hadn't flown in almost 50 years. That thought reminded me that Granda didn't have a valid pilot's license. What if his friend, Seamus, reported his balloon stolen, and Granda was put in jail? That would be another disaster. I should have thought of that before I asked him to help us.

My anxiety came back full throttle, and it got worse when Bianca yelled, "Chris!"

I whipped my head over to the guy slumped on the floor of the basket. His eyes were now open, and he tried to get his hands loose in vain. Chris stopped moving, blinked a few times, and squinted at the scene. I could only imagine his thoughts as he tried to make sense of what he saw: Marvin was clearly in bad shape, I stood at the controls, and we were tethered to another basket, being towed by a towering clover. No wonder Chris looked confused.

He croaked, "What the hell?"

Cindy came to life and answered him in an emotional rant. "Well, let's see; you killed someone again, the pilot suffered a medical episode, and we may crash land. That's what's going on. I'll be scarred for life, you monster!" Wow. She sure told it like it was.

Chris stared at the fallen pilot and said, "Marvin, are you okay? Oh my gosh! I never wanted anything to happen to you."

Chad stood over Chris, looking as if he could kill. He said, "That's really touching, but it's too late, buddy. We're all living with the consequences of your actions."

Chris blew his long black hair out of his eyes and said, "Well, if you untie me, I can land the balloon."

I couldn't help but laugh. I said, "Oh, I was on a balloon that you landed – and it was not a great experience. We'll take our chances. Nobody is untying you, except the police when they trade the ropes for handcuffs."

Chris tried another tactic. "Bianca, you know I'll help you."

I was proud of the girl as she scowled at him and said, "No way, Pendajo."

Nurse Janet said, "Yeah, you're barking up the wrong tree asking for mercy from this group."

When Chris realized he wouldn't get empathy from anyone, he gave up and slumped with a sour expression.

I looked over the edge. We were approaching our shopping center, so I called out, "Granda, what do we need to do?"

"I need you to pull the vent cord gently and try to stay level with me as we descend. Lighten up if you start to go faster than us."

I said, "Okay." I was happy to have practiced opening the vent.

He said, "Get your passengers to assume landing position."

Everyone heard him. Those who were standing did as directed and held onto the inside of the basket with their knees bent slightly.

My heart started pounding so hard I was afraid I'd miss his cues with all my internal racket, but the calm old man spoke clearly and said, "Okay, darlin', pull."

I pulled the cord and looked up to see the flaps at the top open. As we moved downward, our envelopes continued to bounce off each other.

"Now, close it."

Starting to get the hang of it, I released the cord and adjusted the vent to match the balloon next to us. When it was higher, I pulled. When our balloon was lower, I let up. This was working! The two giant balloons were moving in tandem.

Carmen said, "I can see where we're going. Over by the police cars, right?"

I peeked down and was shocked to see all the commotion less than a block away. An ambulance and several police cars with lights flashing surrounded Out of the Box. The two chase crew trucks and balloon trailers were also there. A crowd of spectators had formed, but we were too far away to see individual people. I hoped Angelica had arrived and that Joey would be there. I hoped we would land safely because I could sure use his warm hug now.

When Granda yelled, "Open!" I realized he was five feet below us, so I pulled the cord, releasing more hot air. I had to pay better attention as he steered us in.

We were descending quickly now. My balloon was getting really close to some of the businesses. I could hear Granda talking to the crew on the ground, asking for assistance in guiding the two balloons.

I yelled, "Granda – we are going to hit that dollar store sign!"

He looked over and said, "Give it some gas."

I said, "Bianca, hit the burner."

She turned the lever, but there was just a little sputter of flames, then it stopped.

I yelled, "I think we're out of propane!"

He nodded and hit his own burner so hard that a huge flame shot upward. I closed my eyes. It made sense that his smaller balloon could help us go down because of gravity, but did his smaller balloon have the power to lift our heavy basket full of people?"

Suddenly, our balloon lifted. We narrowly missed the sign by mere inches. That was close. We had no big obstacles in the way now, except the second story of Joey and Jett's brewery.

Granda deftly took us around their new upper patio. I was glad because there were people there watching us. It would have been bad for business if we hit them.

He said, "Pull the cord. We're here."

Thankfully, the wind was almost non-existent, and so we came in slowly towards the giant white X. I braced myself, as did all the other passengers.

Bump, bump, bump. We skidded along the open space, but who cared? Several people were there to grab the baskets and keep them upright, so we didn't tumble over on top of each other as we had two days, prior.

When our balloons came to a complete stop, everyone cheered. I checked to make sure everyone was okay, then looked over to find Jill giving me a thumbs up. She reached up and kissed her Granda. What a hero.

What made me even happier was the sight of Joey holding onto our basket to help keep it from lifting off again. Of course, he had come to help out. He was always there for me.

He said, "Looks like you had quite an adventure."

"You don't know the half of it. I've never been so happy to be on the ground in my life."

"Well, let's get you out of there."

I leaned over the basket and gave him a big kiss. I said, "The captain never leaves the ship until all passengers are off safely." I smirked, but I truly wanted to make sure they got off first.

Angelica rushed forward and yelled from the ground, "I'm here, Love!"

He was in no shape to answer, but his eyes opened at the sound of her voice, and his face relaxed.

Within seconds, a man from the FAA, who identified himself as the one who had spoken to me, climbed on board. He started doing whatever pilots did to keep the balloon from taking off again. I was just happy nobody expected me to do anything else.

When crew members set out some steps, a few EMTs climbed up to assess Marvin's situation.

One of the medical crew members thanked Janet and Coco, then told them they would take over.

The basket was getting crowded, and the medics needed to tend to Marvin before they could take him out, so I said, "All healthy passengers, go ahead and disembark."

That was all it took for Cindy to jump up and be first to leave. I really couldn't blame her. Chad followed, of course. He stopped by me and said, "Sorry if we caused even more drama."

I shook my head vehemently. "No. I totally get it. Just take care of her."

Next to climb off were Janet, Coco, Bianca, and Carmen.

Before Josh and Emma climbed over, he said, "Thank you so much for all you did."

For anyone to complain that teens are rude these days, I would highly object. Josh and Emma were sweet and helpful. I said, "Thank you both so much. I may have to go to one of your games, just to see you pitch."

He smiled and she nodded.

That left Marvin, the medics, and me on board. And of course, Chris, who continued to sit, tied up with a furious face.

Once the other EMTs were in place on the ground, the ones on board set up a stretcher and lifted the pilot onto it, cinching straps tight around Marvin's body. They lifted him over the side, where Angelica rushed to his side. He was taken to the ambulance with his wife holding his hand and talking to him the whole way.

Then a policeman climbed aboard and looked at Chris and then at me. "So, this is the culprit?"

I said, "Yes, sir. He admitted to killing a person a week ago, and then we saw him kill his sister today."

"He killed his own sister?"

"No. The sister of the guy he killed last time."

The officer made a face and pulled Chris to his feet. He checked to make sure the ropes were secure and then nodded to me. "After you, Miss."

I climbed from the basket, and Joey helped me down the ground. Ahhh, that was what I needed. I hugged my big man and said, "It sure is good to be on solid ground."

Joey's brother, Jett, stood behind him and said, "Maria, you'll do just about anything to get publicity for our shopping center, won't you?" The twinkle in his eyes was cute, but he wasn't kidding. Beyond him, I saw the Channel 13 news team. We were about to get more publicity.

I shrugged. "I guess last year's events at my shop weren't enough – had to have an emergency landing too. But, this time, you can partly credit Joey and Julie for putting out the big, white landing X."

Jett said, "I'm glad you're ok, girl. I need to get back to the pub." He waved to the news crew as he headed to Rusty Railroad, leaving me with Joey.

The other passengers stood around, wondering what to do. I told Joey, "Let me talk to them for a sec."

I walked over to the group that had assembled to the side. "I want to thank you for being so helpful. If that was your first balloon ride," I looked at Chad and Cindy, "or even your second, please know that was not normal. Ballooning is generally safer than other forms of transportation."

Nurse Janet started a slow clap for me, and the others joined in. I shook my head. "Please, no. You all helped. The real hero is my good friend, Finn O'Brien." I hollered, "Granda, come here."

Everyone cheered and clapped for Granda, who waved us off as he came near. With a big smile, he told the group, "Ah, Darlin's, it was nothin'."

He hugged me and whispered, "Thank you, dear Maria, for giving me my wings again."

I told the group, "After we speak to the officials, I'm sure we can find people to take us back to the park."

Chad said, "We're planning to take an Uber, but thanks."

Before anyone else could comment, all eyes turned to something beyond me. I turned back toward the balloon where the officer was escorting Chris over the edge of the basket. Just as Chris was on the last step, his ropes got caught on a piece of the wicker, and somehow, loosened enough for him to wriggle out of his binding.

Chapter 19

We all stared as Chris jumped from the basket, hands completely free. The fit 30-year-old gave a maniacal smile and said, "Bye bye, suckers!" and ran off toward the open space behind my shop.

No! Without a thought, I raced off after him. Chad, Joey, and Josh joined me as we neared the back of my shipping container.

I yelled, "The bowling balls!" Joey caught on and grabbed one. He rolled it at Chris, but the escapee just tripped over the ball, faltered a bit, then kept running. I picked up a ball, but it was too heavy for me. The second was too light, and just like in the Three Bears story, the third ball was perfect. I rolled the ball and missed him entirely. I gave up the ball idea and took chase.

Josh, the baseball boy, grabbed a few bowling pins as he ran by and chucked one at the madman. The first pin hit Chris's leg. All it did was make him limp a little, so he kept running.

Meanwhile, Chad dug through his pile of bicycle parts to find a rusted bike with a pink basket. The kids' bike looked like it was fully intact. Chad hopped on it and chased after Chris. The old bicycle wobbled with the big man peddling as fast as he could. I worried the wheel might pop off, but Chad gained ground on Chris.

I heard sirens. Hopefully, the police would catch Chris if we couldn't.

Joey wasn't far behind Chad's bicycle.

Josh held another bowling pin as he ran. When he got close enough, he threw it, expertly missing both Joey on foot and Chad on the bike. The pin hit Chris square in the back, causing him to fall flat on the sandy gravel.

Chad jumped off the bike and reached Chris just as he started to stand up. Joey joined him, and the two pinned him on the ground. Wow, that was amazing!

I was out of breath and slowed to a walk. Somewhere along the line, Emma, arrived and walked next to me. She held her phone to her ear and said, "I'm in contact with the police, and they are on their way."

I huffed, "Thanks. It takes teamwork to capture a killer."

The policeman, who had lost his hold on Chris in the balloon and had let him escape, came up behind us. He was panting and sweating, but that made sense since he was wearing a wool uniform.

As we neared Chris and the guys, I asked, "Hey, did you find Scarlett's body?"

The cop wiped his forehead, then wrinkled his nose. "I have no idea what you are talking about. I just got a call twenty minutes ago directing me to arrest a guy in a balloon." He then leaned over and finally cuffed Chris. Within seconds, two police cars screeched to a stop in the gravel area next to us.

Of course, wouldn't you know it, Sergeant Barnes had to be one of the men heading toward us. He barked to the officer, "I see you caught our guy. Good work." He turned to the cop. "But next time you have to arrest someone in a balloon basket, Chavez, make sure you cuff him first."

I chuckled. How often would that happen again? Grumpy ol' Barnes did have a weird sense of humor.

The cop didn't seem to know it was a joke and said, "I know. I'm sorry. I should have taken care of that first thing."

Barnes turned to me and sighed. "So, I see you managed to get in the middle of another crime scene and needed to be rescued."

I started to point out that I wasn't rescued, but then I realized I had been - by Granda, so I closed my mouth.

Chad stepped forward and said, "Actually, she saved us. Nobody else took charge. She stepped up when needed."

Barnes, wearing his usual rumpled suit, nodded and growled, "Yeah, I heard that, and I guess Stoney's death wasn't an accident." The detective looked pained to admit he had been wrong.

I smirked. "Thanks for admitting that I was right."

The detective rolled his eyes.

I leaned over the killer. "And you don't remind me of Keanu Reeves anymore. He would never harm anyone."

Barnes scoffed, "Actually, Reeves played the villain in nine films, so you are really wrong about that. Keanu would have no problem tossing a person out of a balloon in a movie. You probably wouldn't know because you only watched *Speed*, or *Bill and Ted's Excellent Adventure*, right?"

I snapped back. "No. I watched *The Matrix* and…" I thought hard. "Well, I can't think of any other movies." Gee, there we were sounding like 10-year-olds again. But then I brightened and added, "*John Wick*! Yeah. I saw one of those." Remembering how violent that movie was, I scrunched my lips and admitted, "Okay, so maybe Keanu's character would have done something like that."

While Barnes and I bickered about Keanu's movies, two other officers shoved a grumbling Chris into their cruiser.

I bent to pick up the bowling pin that had hit Chris. While leaning down, I removed some of the Goathead thorns that were stuck to my shoes and socks. I hated those things. They could puncture a bike tire in nothing flat. Speaking of flat, how had Chad ridden through the desert without getting a flat tire?

I held the bowling pin out to Josh, "Hey kiddo, do you want this as a souvenir?"

He grabbed the pin and said, "Hell, yeah. Thanks! My friends are gonna think I was badass."

Emma and I said in unison, "You were."

Joey smiled and took hold of my arm. "Maria, let's go. We owe Jill and Granda a cold drink."

I said, "Good idea. We all need to take a minute to relax. Plus, I'm thirsty and could use something to eat. And they need to see your surprise behind the counter!"

We turned to walk back when Barnes asked, "Anyone want a ride back to the balloons?"

Chad and the teenagers took him up on it, but I said, "Thanks, but we'll walk."

Joey added, "We'll take the bike back."

Chad thanked us, and Joey picked up the bike. As he pushed it, we came upon another bowling pin, and I put it in the basket.

I looked at my watch and was surprised to find it was after 11:00. No wonder I was hungry. Then I turned to Joey and said, "Wait. I can't have a drink with you. I need to get back to my shops. How had I forgotten that? Gosh, Angelica sure wasn't watching my booth." I shook my head. "I should never have gone on that balloon ride."

Joey stopped me and said, "Good thing you did. You knew who to call, and from what I heard, you were quite the little hero up there."

I leaned up against him and said, "But I abandoned both of my stores. What kind of businessperson am I?"

He tilted his head wryly. "Well, they weren't exactly abandoned."

I stopped and regarded him. "What do you mean?"

"While you were in the air, Jill called and filled me in on everything she knew about your situation, including that you lost your phone. I figured you hadn't handled your shops in the middle of an emergency." Joey bent over, picked up a bowling ball, and put it in the basket.

I said, "Okay?"

"Yeah, so I called the manager of the Artisan tent and asked if they could put up a closed sign at your booth and Angelica's too, but they said they already had it under control."

I sighed. "Good. Thank you for calling. But what about the store here?"

By this time, we were approaching my shipping container. Joey didn't answer me, but nodded toward my door, then proceeded to put the balls and pin away. When a woman exited my shop, I hurried to the door and flung it open, only to see my junior salesman looking up at me. Bart told the man standing by the counter, "Sir, you can confirm everything I told you about the making of the chair with the artisan, Maria Olson."

I cracked a smile and said, "Well, hello Bartholemew. Thank you for filling in for me again."

The boy nodded. "I enjoyed it a great deal. I can stay longer if you like. Grandmother Louise was happy I would spend the day here."

I smiled, then answered the customer's questions about the chair covered in postage stamps.

The man paid Bart and carried the chair outside just as Joey entered. When I raised my eyebrows, Joey shrugged. "You said he was a great salesman, so…"

"Yes. He is definitely that." I turned to the boy. "No offense, Bart, but I'm not sure it's legal to leave the shop in the hands of a nine-year-old. You know…child labor laws."

Bart lifted his chin. "Don't worry, Miss Maria. Miss Julie was here the whole time."

Joey's sister, Julie, came out of the back room carrying a stack of bags I had recycled from old jeans. She said, "Yeah, we figured we shouldn't let a child work alone. But I tell ya, he's nothing like any kid I've ever met."

"Right? Thank you, Julie. I'll make it up to you. Oh, and your idea to install the big landing X may have saved lives?"

"Yeah. We watched the landing. Not exactly what I envisioned, but it worked."

I walked to the door. "I should get going. I'm sure the police need to talk to me. Have fun, you two, and thank you so much."

Joey and I crossed the lot where the passengers were still giving their statements to officers and Detective Barnes. The balloons had been deflated, and the envelopes had been rolled up and packed into giant bags. The crew members were in the process of lifting the baskets into their respective trailers.

Joey said, "I should go back to the brewpub. Come get me when you are finished.

Before he could leave, I grabbed him and gave him a kiss. "Thank you for being here for me."

"I'm just happy you are alright."

I moved over next to Jill and Granda. A tall man with freckles and brown hair stood with them. Granda patted him on the back and said, "Maria, meet Seamus Flannery, owner of Lucky, the shamrock balloon."

In a very thick Irish accent, Seamus said, "So, you were the lassie who needed help."

"That's me. I don't know what I would have done if Granda hadn't flown your balloon and saved us."

"I see why the ol' fella had to give it a lash and borrow Lucky. Finn had to help his wee friend. I was in bits this morning with a fierce dose of the tummy bug, and so I couldn't have helped earlier. I'm glad he got to fly even if it was just once." He slapped Granda on the back.

I was instantly relieved that Granda wouldn't be charged with theft.

Jill leaned over to me and whispered, "By the way, we didn't tell the FAA that Granda's license had lapsed, and God forbid they find out it expired fifty years ago."

All laughter stopped when Sergeant Barnes appeared in front of me and grumbled, "Now, for the troublemakers."

Jill stood tall and countered, "We didn't cause the trouble. We stopped it, Sir Barnes."

He flattened his mouth and voice. "Yeah, I heard. Let's start with you, Mrs. Standing Wolf. Tell me what happened in your own words."

She puffed out her cheeks and said, "It's Standing Bear, if you don't mind."

While Jill told Barnes everything she knew, Granda and Seamus walked over and started talking their balloon crew, who were just finishing up.

I watched as Chad and Cindy got in an Uber, which made me sad. I'd probably never see them again. Nurse Janet stood with an older man whom I assumed to be her husband. She gave Coco a hug, then walked off with him.

When Carmen and the other two girls joined me, I asked, "Where are the teenagers?"

Carmen pointed to the parking lot and said, "The boy's parents picked them up."

I nodded and turned to Bianca. In Spanish, I asked, "How are you doing?"

She told me she was still in a bit of shock but knew he was just a short-term romance. It wouldn't have worked out with the distance between them.

I was glad to hear she wasn't completely heartbroken over Chris.

I smiled. "I just want to thank you all for your help." Then, I spoke to each one of them in turn. "Bianca – I'm glad you were tall enough to reach the valve. Coco, you might want to go into nursing if you don't become an artist. I loved the little picture you drew for me. You are very talented. And Carmen, you handled the burner valve and walkie-talkie like a pro. I sure hope the rest of your trip will be much calmer."

Carmen said, "It has been very exciting. None of us will forget today. I'll tell Abuela how you flew a big balloon, too."

I gave them each a hug. "Where are you going now?"

Bianca said, "We go up to top." She pointed at the mountains.

"Oh, are you going to ride the Sandia Tram?"

They nodded, yes.

I said, "You will love it." Riding the tram was a must-do for tourists. After my high-flying adventure today, it may be a long while before I get in the aerial tram hanging from a cable over a mountain.

Sergeant Barnes glared at me as I finished giving the girls hugs. "Your turn, Olson."

"Okay, Barnes."

Jill joined Granda and Seamus while I described the entire episode from start to finish to the detective. He listened and wrote notes in his worn old notebook.

When he looked up, I asked, "Do you know how Marvin, the pilot, is doing?"

He nodded. "He's over at Presbyterian Hospital and is in stable condition."

I felt relieved. "Good. Where did they find Scarlett's body?"

He shook his head. "They are still searching."

For some reason, that really bothered me, but it had only been two hours. I said, "Well, if it helps, she should be somewhere near the Bosque, just South of Paseo del Norte. I stopped short. "Wait. Didn't the crew see her fall? They would know where her body is."

"Nope. As far as we know, nobody saw where she landed. I'll let the search party know about the location, but the body could have hit the water and floated downstream a bit."

I recoiled at the thought of Scarlett's body floating down the Rio Grande. When Jill joined me, Barnes turned and walked away without saying goodbye to either of us.

She looked at me and said, "How rude," ala Stephanie on *Full House*.

Jill said, "So I hear Julie and Bart are covering for me… covering for you. Do you think I should go relieve them?"

"No. they are fine. Take the day off. It's been a lot."

I looked around at the nearly empty parking lot. The ambulance, police cars, and balloons were all gone. "Isn't it strange not to have our own cars here? I'll ask Joey if he wants to take us back to the Fiesta. He was going to help me pack up."

"If he can't, Seamus will drive us."

As we walked over to the pub, I said, "I'm anxious to see what's happening in my Fiesta booth."

"I'll bet you are."

Joey was wiping down a table when we entered and looked up. "How did the interview with Barnes go?"

I shrugged. "He was as obnoxious as usual."

"Well, I'm sorry, but I can't leave until another busboy comes in at 12:30. It's tough finding reliable employees."

I felt bad for him and tried to ease his guilt. "Don't worry about coming if you can't get away. I'm sure I can handle it alone."

He winked, "I'll be there."

Jill, Granda, and I caught a ride with Seamus. It was fun sitting in the back seat with the two old Irishmen who sat up front. They told funny stories of the good old days in Dublin. It brought back memories of the two of us riding with Jill's grandparents when they took us to the park years ago.

Jill said, "Since you didn't have your phone to take pictures of our two balloons, I got some from that Emma girl in your basket, and I took some of my own. I'll send them to you. And when you get a new phone, you can have them."

She showed me her phone. The first picture was of Jill, posing like a silly model. And there I was at the helm of the balloon, and another of Granda Finn at his controls. Those were great, but the pic of the two balloons tied together was my favorite. "Oh, thanks, Jill. I'll treasure these."

I hugged her until she tickled me to let go. The rest of the ride, we goofed around, as if we were carefree six-year-olds again. Where had the time gone?

Chapter 20

When we arrived back at the Fiesta Park parking lot, I hugged Jill, Granda, and even Seamus, thanking them profusely before heading to my booth. "You are all lifesavers!"

There were only a few customers in the area since it was almost closing time. Some artisans had already packed up their booths. I walked faster. When I arrived at my spot, I was surprised to find Jenny, the candy girl, there showing a purse I made from the *Wicked* book cover to a couple.

"Jenny?"

She looked surprised. "Oh, good, you're back. Help them and I'll explain afterwards." She scooted back to her area.

Was this the plan? Did the artisan manager make my young neighbor take over my sales along with hers? That didn't seem fair.

I answered a lot of questions the couple had about the making of the book purse as they hemmed and hawed. Finally, I gave them a special 'End of Fiesta' sale price, just to help them decide. I wanted them to leave so I could find out what happened during my absence.

Lowering the price worked, and the lady beamed as she carried her new, unusual purse from my shop.

There were no other customers around, so I rushed to Jenny's booth. "I'm so sorry that management asked you to watch my booth. There was an emergency with our balloon. Now I regret going on the ride. It was irresponsible of me."

"Oh no! That's not what happened at all. When Anglica left, the manager put a closed sign on both of your booths. All was fine for an hour, and then a customer walked up and threw a fit. Apparently, she had paid the entry fee just so that she could come back and buy the framed print she had looked at yesterday. I didn't have any customers at the time, so I sold her the print. Then, a bit later, a couple came to your booth wanting to buy one of your bowling balls covered in pennies?" Jenny made a face, as if it were a ridiculous thing to buy, but continued. "I asked for cash or a check, but they didn't have that, so I put the money in my account until you tell me what cash-type app you have."

I waved my hand. "Forget it. You keep that money. I just appreciate you stepping up. How did that couple get in? They certainly hadn't come here just for the book." I pointed down the aisle, as if the *Wicked* couple were nearby.

"Oh, they were walking by and spotted the purse. They asked me if I could help them."

"Well, I appreciate you looking out for things. How were your sales, overall?"

"Pretty good. They improved once I came up with a good sales pitch." She started stacking bags of candy in a box. "Do you think you'll come back next year?"

I shook my head, "Probably not. It's been a lot of stress, especially since I can't afford to pay help."

When a man walked behind us, I turned and was startled to see that it was Smith. Why was he here?"

I walked around the corner just as he shoved the Moores' sign out of the way.

I marched into the booth. "Um, are you supposed to be here?"

His head turned slowly, and he glared at me. "Yes. My sister-in-law, Angelica, asked me to start packing up their booth by noon. It is noon. Are ya gonna call the police on me?"

I felt dumb and said, "No. Of course not. I'm sorry. Today has just been crazy." I now felt bad that he had been my main suspect. Just because he was rude didn't make him a killer.

"Crazy? What's crazy is that my brother-in-law is in the hospital fighting for his life because of you."

"Me? How did I cause Marvin's medical issues?"

He lifted his chin and spouted, "All I know is, if I had been on that flight, none of that would have happened."

What a jerk. I thought back to the events. Even if he knew what Chris had in mind or why Scarlett was there, he couldn't have stopped anything. He would have been just as shocked by what happened as everyone else. Realizing he was just being a jerk, I rolled my eyes and said, "Whatever, Barry. My main concern is Marvin. How is he doing? I'd like to stop by and see him at the hospital when I leave today."

He shook his head dramatically and looked so arrogant that I almost laughed. He sneered, "That's impossible since you aren't family."

I was disappointed, but asked, "Well, can you at least tell me how he is? I lost my phone on the flight, so I can't call."

He gave an annoyed sigh. "Well…they say he's going to recover, but you sure put him in a bad situation by not landing the balloon earlier."

I couldn't stand being around the bully any longer and turned around. As soon as I got back in my booth, I made sure my curtain was pulled far enough forward that I couldn't see any part of the annoying man.

I packed up the smallest items into a tub. While I was practically upside down, reaching under a table for another tub, I heard, "How's my beautiful pilot?"

Without looking up, I answered, "I'm not a pilot and am definitely not beautiful today. I'm a mess."

Joey chuckled when I stood upright. "Well, you look beautiful to me, but your hair does look kind of like you chased a murderer through a desert while carrying a bowling ball."

"I wonder why? I'm also upset with that Smith guy that I told you about. He's next door now and was blaming Marvin's medical episode on me."

He turned serious. "Are you okay?"

"Yeah. Just stressed out."

"Want me to go rattle his cage?"

"No. He will drive you insane, and I like you just the way you are." I threw my arms around Joey's waist and squeezed.

"Well, then, let's get to work so we can get outta here."

Joey and I talked as we packed up the remaining products from my booth into boxes. It was cathartic to discuss all that happened, especially with someone who wasn't judgmental. The packing didn't take us nearly as long as the setting up had.

I brought my truck around to Main Street so we could load up. When I returned to my booth, I overheard Joey next door talking to Smith.

"I don't care what you say. Maria never did that. She's the nicest person I know. If someone was in trouble, she would help out. So, stop making her out to be a troublemaker. If you ever see her again, I expect you to apologize or at least be cordial."

I blushed to hear Joey's kind description of me. When I noticed Joey's phone sitting on top of a box, I figured he wouldn't mind me making a quick call. He had told me his password six months ago, and I made fun of it. Who would use 123456?

Once I unlocked it, I called Angelica. I said, "Hi girl, it's me, Maria. I'm using Joey's phone because I dropped my phone out of the balloon this morning. I don't want to bother you, just checking on Marvin."

"Oh, he's so much better. They're going to do a simple procedure tomorrow and then keep him for observation for a few days. He should be able to go home by Tuesday."

"That's so great. I wanted to stop by, but Smith said only family could visit."

"Well, he's lying. Nobody said that. You just come on by, sweet thing. Marvin would love to see you."

I was so relieved to hear that. "Okay. I will. I might bring Joey along, too. Anything you need me to do for you here at your booth?"

"No, Hon, I wrote a list for Smith. He's very good at following written directions, even if he is the most unpleasant person around."

I giggled quietly, then remembered something. "Oh, Angelica, the girl in the candy shop across from me, sold one of your paintings. Can you talk to her for a sec?"

"Of course."

I carried the phone to Jenny. Meanwhile, Joey had returned and was stacking boxes. I said, "I heard you sticking up for me with Mr. Lovely, next door. Thanks!"

"Yeah, you're right. He's a complete ass. You ready to start loading?"

"Yep. Oh, I hope you don't mind, but I borrowed your phone to call Angelica. I'm going to stop by Presbyterian Hospital to see Marvin. Wanna come with?"

"Sure – but just for a bit. I'll need to drive my own car."

I looked across and saw that Jenny had just finished talking to Anglelica, so I went to her. "Did you get that straightened out?"

She handed me the phone. "That is one nice lady. She said to keep the money for dealing with her customer."

That made me smile. I said, "It's been so nice getting to know you, Jenny."

Joey suggested we drop off the display pieces and boxes at my shop before heading to the hospital. "You don't want to risk someone breaking in and stealing all your merchandise."

So that's what we did. We took two cars to the hospital and headed for room number 419. We rode up the elevator with a man and a little boy carrying flowers. When we got to the third floor, those two got off. Beyond the man, I caught a glimpse of a woman with a broken arm who was waiting for the down elevator. Even with a bandage covering her right eye, I could swear she was staring at me. As we continued to the fourth floor, I felt uneasy.

Joey said, "Maria, we're here. Are you coming?"

I hadn't realized the door had opened. I stepped out and said, "Did you think that lady with the broken arm looked familiar?"

"What lady?"

The one waiting to get on at the last stop."

'Oh, I didn't see anyone. It was probably just one of your customers. I can't tell you how many times I see familiar faces and have no idea where I know them from."

"Yeah. Probably." The feeling continued to nag at me as we walked down the hall."

"Hello there, you two!" Angelica sang as she rushed to greet us at the door.

I handed her a bouquet of paper flowers made from New Mexico maps. They were in a pretty, red glass vase.

Angelica hugged us both and said, "Aren't you just too sweet?" She turned to her husband. "Marvin, wakey wakey. Maria and Joey are here."

I held my hand up. "Oh, don't bother him. Let him sleep."

Marvin lay with his torso elevated in the hospital bed, still looking peaked, but not nearly as pale as he did on the balloon.

"It's just the meds making him groggy. He wanted me to wake him when you arrived."

He opened his eyes and grinned. "Hey, Maria. Thanks for coming by. You too, young man."

Joey said, "I can only stay for a minute. It looks like you are on the mends, probably because you have such a beautiful nurse here to be with you."

He wheezed out, "Don't I know it. She's my guardian angel. But I understand it was your girl who saved the day."

"She did. Better watch out. She may be taking over your piloting job."

I laughed and said, "Don't worry. I'm never going to get in that kind of predicament again."

Joey looked at his phone and said, "I'm sorry, but I need to get back to the brewery. Good to see you are improving, Marvin." He turned to me, squeezed his eyes tight, and explained, "Another employee problem. I've gotta head out." He kissed me and waved to my new friends before leaving.

I approached Marvin's bed and took his hand, avoiding the IV port on the back of it. "I'm so glad to see you are doing well. You sure gave us a scare."

"Well, if I remember correctly, there was a lot to be nervous about that day. When was that anyway?"

Angelica squinted at her husband. "Marv, honey. That was just this morning."

I jumped in. "I don't blame you for being confused. It seems like a long time ago to me too, and I'm not on any pain meds."

He nodded. "Well, I may have had an episode on the ride, but I was aware of what was going on. I know you took charge and saved everyone on board. You did good, Maria."

I scoffed, "Well, I wouldn't take it that far. Surely someone else would have stepped up before the balloon crashed. But thank you."

"I have a question," Marvin said. "When I got here, and the nurses changed me into a gown, I saw something stuck on my shirt. Angelica looked at it and discovered it was Stoney's lucky pin. Do you know how it got there?"

I was a little embarrassed to tell him, but I did anyway. "Well, just before the flight last Sunday, Stoney gave it to me for good luck. I felt terribly guilty that he didn't have it during his last flight, thinking it might have been my fault. I wore it in his honor every day afterwards. When I saw you were in such bad shape this morning, I gave it you for luck."

He smiled. "Well, thank you for that."

Angelica nodded, then asked me quietly, as if to keep from upsetting Marvin, "Did they find Scarlett's body?"

I said softly, "Not that I know of."

Of course, Marvin could hear us. He closed his eyes and said, "I still can't believe our Chris did that."

I agreed and said, "It was definitely the most bizarre thing I'd ever seen." Then I realized Scarlett had threatened Marvin, so Chris may have saved his life. Someone needed to stop her – he just chose a very traumatic way.

Angelica stretched her arms and said, "I need coffee and am starving. Do you mind staying here while I run and get a bite?"

"Of course not. Take your time. I'll hang with Marvin." I walked her to the door and watched her walk down the hallway. I called out, "Can you bring me a Coke?"

She gave a thumbs-up as she headed to the elevator.

I took the seat next to Marvin's bed and wondered what we could talk about. After a few beats of silence, I asked what I hoped was a safe question. Maybe it would take his mind off the tragic day. "Do you and Angelica have kids?" I could only imagine the beautiful skin tones, talents, and skills their children might have with those two as parents.

"No. I have a grown son, by a previous marriage, who lives in New Jersey with his family. We all get along great, but once Angelica and I got married, we chose not to have kids of our own. It has been good for us." He leaned his head back as if thinking. "But, maybe that's why we took Stoney in as if he were a son. And Chris, too."

Darn, I thought that was a safe conversation, but it came back around to Stoney and Chris. Marvin looked so sad.

I said, "So, if you were awake and listening to what went on in the basket, did you think it was weird for me to have my friend tow us in?"

He said, "Actually, it was pretty smart. With no trained pilot on board, you needed someone to help. If I had been more coherent, I could have given you directions. You all handled it remarkably well."

"Just so you know, my friend's grandpa was an award-winning pilot in Ireland." I leaned in and whispered as if the FAA were listening, "But he hasn't had a license in almost fifty years. He brought us down as smooth as butter."

Marvin gave me a painful laugh. "For that, I am thankful. I promise I won't turn him in."

I changed the subject again. "I brought you some flowers I made from New Mexico maps." I handed him the vase.

He studied the flowers curiously, as I explained. "I know some people are allergic to latex balloons, and others sneeze with real flowers, so I figured paper shouldn't bother anyone."

He nodded. "I really like these. There's Las Cruces, where I grew up." He pointed to one petal of a flower. "And I can see Taos, where I met my lovely Angelica."

I was glad he already enjoyed the unique flowers. Just as I took the vase back from him, I heard someone come through the door behind me. It was pretty early for Angelica to have returned from eating, but maybe she brought the food back here to eat.

What I didn't expect was to see Marvin's eyes widen. He started to shake as though he saw a ghost.

I turned around. There stood the girl I had seen outside the elevator. One eye was bandaged, the other was bulging red and black. She was not one of my customers. That was Scarlett!

Chapter 21

At the shock of seeing the dead woman standing in Marvin's doorway, I tried to steady myself by putting my hand on the metal hospital tray. That didn't steady anyone or anything, and I ended up dumping his water cup onto the floor. I got hold of myself and took stock of the situation. I stared at Scarlett and gasped, "You're alive!"

She scoffed. "You can't get rid of me that easily."

I stuttered, "How d d did you survive that fall?"

"I didn't fall. I was thrown out. Remember? Lucky for me, I fell on a tall Cottonwood tree. It broke my fall as I bounced from limb to limb. I broke my arm and leg on my way to the ground. Yeah. That was really fun. Not."

It was then that I noticed that she had a cast on her leg as well as one on her arm.

Marvin moaned, and I turned to see if he was choking. He coughed out, "What is it you want, Scarlett?"

"My money. I am the rightful heir to my brother's fortune. If I have to get rid of you to get it, that's what I'm gonna do."

At that, she lunged forward, knocking me off balance. I fell to the side, but I recovered before falling to the floor. She put her hands around Marvin's throat, and I watched in horror as she squeezed tight. The worst thing was the gurgling sound he made. The scene was as terrifying as the one I experienced earlier in the morning. What could I do? I wasn't strong enough to move her away and didn't have time to run for help.

I tried pulling on her good arm, then kicking her bad leg, but she wouldn't release her hold on him. So, I did the only thing I could think of. I lifted the glass vase holding the map roses and slammed it onto Scarlett's head. The vase fell to the floor and shattered, as Scarlett collapsed onto Marvin's chest.

Marvin took a deep breath and rubbed his throat, glad to be able to breathe again.

As stunned as I was, I knew Scarlett would come around soon, so we needed to do something. I said, "Marvin, do you have an emergency button attached to your bed?"

He felt around on the side of his mattress and picked up a cord. He repeatedly punched the button. It wasn't ten seconds before a nurse entered, asking sweetly, "Can I help you, Mr. Moore?"

When she saw Scarlett slumped across his body, she yelled, "What is going on?"

"This woman attacked him. Get help quick."

The nurse rushed into the hallway and yelled, "Code White, room 419."

I wasn't sure what that meant, since the only code I knew was Code Blue, but I trusted she knew what she was doing.

Moments later, the nurse returned with two male orderlies who lifted Scarlett off of Marvin's body. The movement brought Scarlett back to life, and she struggled to get free.

She yelled, "You haven't seen the last of me, Marvin Moore. I'll get my money one way or another."

I was pretty sure that wasn't going to happen. Anyone who strangles a patient in a hospital would undoubtedly do some time behind bars.

After processing her threat, Marvin shook his head. In a strangely strong voice for someone who lay in a hospital bed, he said, "I tried to tell you while we were on the balloon. Your brother didn't have a fortune. He was in debt up to his ears. Stoney was a terrible bookkeeper and donated everything he had to people in need and his charities and forgot to pay his bills. That's all I inherited – his debt and some photographs – most of which were donated after his death.”

She screamed, “You’re lying. I know he made lots of money with his photos. You’re just trying to keep me from getting what’s rightfully mine.”

Two police officers arrived and handcuffed Scarlett, which was a difficult process with her cast covering one of her wrists and with her struggling.

Marvin was now so stressed, he could barely talk, but managed to croak, “That means you had your brother killed for nothing. You are a true monster.”

Marvin faded closed his eyes, and the nurse checked his vitals. She turned to the policemen. “He’s had far too much excitement. Get that woman out of here.”

As the officers ushered Scarlett from the room, I could hear Angelica’s voice. “You? What the hell is going on here?”

While the nurse was attending Marvin, I rushed into the hallway, where Angelica stood with my Coke and a shocked face.

Scarlett strained to reach Angelica, but wasn’t able to with her restraints. She spat on her and then screamed, “You two are holding out on me. I’ll be back to get my money. You better believe it.”

I wondered how the woman thought she would be released to come after anyone, especially after her attempt on Marvin’s life. The officers finally dragged her away, and Angelica joined me, baffled as expected. When she saw the water, the red glass on the floor, and the nurse leaning over Marvin, she ran to him. “Are you okay, Honey?”

He didn’t answer, and she began to panic.

The nurse raised her hand. “He’ll be fine. He just had another traumatic experience and needs to rest. I gave him something to help him sleep.”

I held Angelica's hand and described how Scarlett had come in, pushed me aside, and started to strangle him. I continued to explain. "All I could think to do was hit her with my vase."

"Oh, Maria, thank you so much for being here." She wrapped her arms around me tight. Then she straightened and stepped back. "But…I thought she died in the fall. What the hell?"

I shrugged. "Apparently, a Cottonwood in the Bosque broke her fall, but I have no idea how she got from there to the hospital with a broken arm and leg."

"And why was she angry with Marvin? What did he ever do to her?"

"She said she deserves her brother's money."

"Did Marvin tell her Stoney had none? We used our own money to pay for his funeral costs and all his bills."

I said, "Marvin didn't have time to tell her before she struck. And when he did, she didn't believe him."

We moved to the bedside chairs and discussed the whole situation while Marvin slept. It wasn't an hour before Sergeant Barnes barged in and looked at me. "And of course, you're in the thick of things again."

I replied with a shrug. "Lucky me."

He shifted his feet and held up a finger. "I guess now we know why we couldn't find her body."

Barnes stood over us and took my statement. After he was finished grilling me for the second time in a day, I asked him, "How did Scarlett get to the hospital to get fixed up without the police knowing she had survived?"

"I interviewed her, and she is a piece of work, by the way. She said a couple of young guys walking along the river heard her calling out for help. They put her in their jeep and dropped her off at the emergency room door. They didn't even come inside."

I said, "So it was just a stroke of bad luck that she ended up at the same hospital as Marvin?"

"Yeah." He smirked. "She said she wouldn't have known Marvin was here if she hadn't seen you on the elevator. She followed you to see who you were visiting."

I cringed to realize I had inadvertently given away Marvin's location.

Angelica saw the worry on my face and took my hand. "It's okay, Sweetie. I know that girl. She's obsessed. She would have found him sooner or later."

I asked Barnes, "You know she had this whole murder thing planned for weeks, right? She convinced Chris to kill Stoney. Then, when she found out Marvin was the beneficiary instead of her, Chris was supposed to get rid of Marvin so she could get the inheritance. I've never met anyone so selfish and evil."

Angelica nodded. "But the worst part is that it was all for naught. Stoney had no money. Nothing except some photos."

Even Barnes looked surprised at that revelation. He patted Angelica's shoulder. "Well, we have enough evidence to lock her up for a long time. Don't worry about her or Chris anymore. Just get Mr. Moore healthy and enjoy life."

I was pleased that the grumpy detective was so kind to Angelica. The frumpy detective always managed to redeem himself, somehow.

But it wasn't seconds after I praised the man internally that he pointed to me and told Angelica, "I'd stay away from this one, though. She's trouble with a capital T."

I rolled my eyes and said, "Hey, my upcycled roses stopped Scarlett from hurting Marvin even more. So, there's that."

"Yeah, sure." He turned and walked out without another word.

Angelica said, "He's a strange one, isn't he?"

"You don't know the half of it."

I stopped by Jill's house on the way home from the hospital. I needed to retrieve my little Zia for good. I filled Jill and Kelly in on the 'rest of the story.' They were shocked, as expected.

Kelly said, "You must be exhausted. Have you eaten today?"

I realized I hadn't had anything since the little donuts this morning. "No. I'm actually starving."

Jill said, "Let's go to the brewery and get you something to eat. You'll sleep much better tonight on a full stomach. And just think, you have tomorrow off to do nothing."

Even though my bed was calling me, it was only five o'clock, and I needed to eat. "Let's do it. I'll see if the girls want to go along. Hey, maybe Granda can meet us too. I owe him big time."

I stopped by the house and found my three guests relaxing in the living room. They looked much more refreshed than I did. I said, "Carmen, can I borrow your phone for a sec?"

She nodded, and I took it, thankful I had Joey's number memorized. I told him what had happened at the hospital after he left. He was shocked, of course, but I said I'd see him soon.

I said, "Come on, girls. Hop in my truck. I'm taking you out to dinner!"

I put my tiny pup in my jacket as we squeezed into my front seat. As I drove, they talked a mile a minute about their trip up the mountain on the tram. We planned to spend the rest of the week together, after I recovered from today, of course.

We parked by my container, and I took them inside for the first time. While they looked around, Julie showed me what she and Bart had sold. I immediately paid her for the day, which she didn't want to take, but I insisted.

I grabbed cash and handed it to my junior salesman. "Bart, you are a very special boy. Thank you again for your help."

"I won't be able to assist you for a while. My mother is taking my sister, Lisa, and me back home to Texas in the morning. I must go back to school to work on my education."

I wondered what grade the little smartie was in. Was Bart one of those "Doogie" kids who was five grades ahead of his age? I shook off the idea when Louise popped in to pick up her grandson.

I introduced my loud friend to the girls. It was funny how they stared at the woman, with her bedazzled butterfly shirt and pants, not to mention her big hair.

Louise said, "So, these are the little señoritas you were talking about. From what I heard, you gals have been out on the town, just a 'whooping it up goin' here and there all around the Duke City. She pinched Coco's cheek and said, "Aren't you just as cute as a bug?"

Even Carmen had trouble understanding the woman's thick Texas accent. But anyone who met Louise was bound to be pulled into her arms for a big hug, and that's just what happened, one at a time. Finally, she released the last one and left to take Bart to his mother.

As Julie, the girls, and I walked to the pub, we ran into Mike and Pat, who had stopped by their bakery to pick up the starter for some sourdough. I introduced the girls and invited them to come along.

Jill and Kelly had already arrived and were sitting at a big table with Sophia, and Granda. Sophia bounced in her highchair when she saw Zia's head poking out of my jacket. I knew I had to sit by her so she could pet the pup. I put my purse down in the chair next to hers to save my place.

Jill popped up and greeted Julie and my three guests. When she saw Pat and Mike follow us in, she squealed, "It's the fabulous bakery boys! This is a full-blown party, now!"

I looked over at Carmen and her friends, who seemed to get on beautifully with Mike and Pat. It sounded like Pat was fluent in Spanish. Who knew?

While Julie played with Sophia, I grabbed Jill's hand and said, "Jill, Kelly, and Granda Finn, come with me."

The trio followed me to the bar, where I said, "Check this out." When I pointed behind the bar, their eyes grew wide as they stared at the piano, which now displayed beautiful wine bottles.

Joey and his brother, Jett, stepped up behind the group. Jett said, "You like?"

Jill, still shocked, said, "I thought you took it to the dump!"

Jett grinned. "We were on the way there, but neither of us had the heart to get rid of the gorgeous piece of furniture and we brought it here as our special feature."

When I looked at Granda, I saw he had tears in his eyes. He said, "I'm delirah about it. Now I can come see the ol' fella any time I want."

Joey patted him on the back and said, "You are always welcome. And by the way, your dinner is on me tonight. I can't thank you enough for saving Maria's life today."

Granda waved him off. "Grand, thanks, but I already decided that I'm paying for the whole table. You see, I had a mighty good day getting to fly again. Plus, I sold my house and now I'm rich!"

I kissed him on the cheek. "You are the best."

Joey leaned into my ear. "I can't believe you have the energy to hang out tonight after all you went through. Are you okay?"

I took his hand and pulled him outside with me. Once we moved off to a secluded side of the big porch, I hugged him. As he rubbed my tight shoulders, I said, "I'm just glad it's all over."

He whispered into my hair, "I'm so sorry I didn't stay with you at the hospital. What a nightmare."

I pushed away from him and shook my head. "No, Joey. You couldn't know something like that would happen. It turned out just as it was supposed to, and everything is fine. Besides, as much as I love having my strong, handsome boyfriend around, I need to be able to save myself sometimes."

I rested my head against his chest again and gave a big sigh. My worrying days were over. Carmen and her friends ended up being a joy to have around. My savings account got a big boost from the Fiesta booth sales. The perpetrators were all locked up. My friends were here with me, and Joey was a dream come true. What more could I ask for?

Epilogue

Two Months Later

I opened the front door to find Joey standing on my porch wearing a sleek, dark suit that accentuated his broad shoulders and thin waist. He was clean-shaven, and his blond hair was pulled back in a ponytail.

I gulped at the sight and said, "Wow, you look amazing, Mr. Roth."

He pulled his hand from behind his back and held out a bouquet of beautiful flowers in every color imaginable. He grinned. "I have to step up my game if I am going to be seen with the most beautiful girl in New Mexico." He stepped back and studied me with eyebrows raised. "And look at you. All eyes will be on the lady in red tonight."

Blushing, I stood on my tiptoes and kissed him. "Thank you."

I ran inside and put the flowers in a vase of water, but took one white rose from the bunch and pinned it in my hair. I grabbed my wrap and then rejoined him.

After I shut the door, we both looked at the window where Zia sat on the back of the couch, patting her tiny paw on the glass. She hated to be left behind, but events like tonight's didn't permit dogs. Simultaneously, we said, "Bye, Zia. We'll be back later."

As Joey drove to the venue, I said, "Wow, you even cleaned your Jeep."

"Only the best for you. Besides, I could hardly see out of the windows after off-roading last month."

When we parked, Joey turned all gentlemanly on me. He walked around to my door and helped me out as if I were a princess. As we walked to the uniquely designed International Balloon Museum, he said, "This place is so cool. I love how the exterior represents a half-inflated hot air balloon."

"I know. I think it's amazing. I can't believe they rented the whole museum as their venue. It's fitting, considering…"

He nodded, and we entered the 75-foot-tall glass and steel gallery, which mimicked a fully inflated balloon. Since the museum is located on the south end of Balloon Fiesta Park, people pay extra during Balloon Fiesta to sit at the museum's observation decks for prime viewing of the balloons. The unique space held artifacts and materials related to ballooning. We passed giant gondolas, collections of ballooning materials, and the largest grouping of balloon pins I had ever seen. The pins made me think of Stoney and his silly hat.

I remembered touring the museum on a middle school field trip with Jill. As I walked by the flight simulator, I flashed back to the two of us in it, pretending to be balloon copilots. She would say, 'Westward Ho!' I'd pull a lever, and we moved that way. Who knew we would indeed be flying balloons 15 years later?

Just as I thought of Jill, her voice rang out loud and echoed in the museum. "Maria and Joey, come on! You're missing the fun." She stood in the doorway of the big hall, wearing a dark green cocktail dress. The color always looked amazing on her, since it contrasted with her gorgeous red hair.

Joey passed a sign labeled Prescott and Garcia Wedding, with an arrow pointing to the spot where Jill and Kelly stood. I hugged Jill, while Joey and Kelly gave each other a manly hug. I was so happy the two guys had become good friends over the past year. We were a fun foursome, unless Sophia was included, then we were the fab five.

I smiled when we entered. The space looked like a Christmas wonderland. All the decorations were red, green, or a combination of the two. Guests had been asked to wear the Christmas colors, so everyone fit in perfectly with the theme. Lucky for Joey and Kelly, black was also allowed since red and green suits were harder to find than dresses. Neither of them relished the idea of wearing a green or red suit, but they did each come up with colorful Christmas ties.

I had provided the centerpieces made from pinecones collected at my friend's cabin in the Jemez Mountains. I painted some of the cones red and even more of them green. Each table decoration was different. Some were bouquets, some Christmas trees, and others were just pinecones in baskets. Every centerpiece was surrounded by greenery and included mason jar candles. At each place setting, I placed a pinecone dipped in wax as a fire starter. with a tag that read, 'Your presence warms our hearts.'

Jill and I helped Pat, Mike, their parents, and friends set up in the afternoon. Pat was so excited and nervous that he rushed around getting in people's way. He was no help, so we finally banished him from the place and sent him shopping with his mom. Mike, always the calm one, stayed and delegated jobs to different people.

At the gift table, I slid our wedding card into the big slot of the globe I had upcycled for the wedding. On the side, I painted the words, "Love doesn't make the world go round; Love is what makes the ride worthwhile" – Elizabeth Barrett Browning.

I had glued the tiny Swedish bluebird I'd gotten as a gift to the front of the envelope. I hoped it would bring good luck to their marriage. I was happy it fit through the card slot.

Next, I slipped in a card sent from Carmen and Bianca. Coco, on the other hand, had mailed me a small canvas she had painted for Mike and Pat. It was a beautiful, abstract scene of hot air balloons. Joey placed her painting alongside the other gifts.

The four of us found seats in a row beside Larry, who was dressed in a handsome black cowboy shirt and black jeans. He looked pretty good. His date, Sally Ann, seemed smitten by her new boyfriend.

Jett sat in the row in front of us with Amy, the sweet Rusty Railroad server, as his date. The two of them were so beautiful, they looked like models. Joey thumped his brother on the head when he sat behind him.

In the next row up, the three odd, antique store brothers looked uncomfortable and out of place. They probably didn't attend that many formal affairs. Next to them sat Louise. The woman stood out even more than usual in her glittery red and green ensemble. She looked more like a Christmas tree than a woman in a dress. I sat behind two empty seats next to her on the aisle. I was happy I wouldn't be sitting right behind her, or I might not have been able to see around her bouffant hairdo.

When the music started, Mike came out from a side door, flanked by his tall parents. He was dressed in a hunter green tuxedo. They were a handsome family.

When I saw movement on my left, I turned to see a small girl passing me on the aisle. It was little Lisa, throwing red flower petals. She wove down the aisle in a sort of funny dance. Walking stiffly behind her was Bart, holding a pillow with a ring tied to the top. He was counting his steps methodically, and when he reached the end, he stopped abruptly, apparently following his directions with exact precision.

How adorable. I didn't know the kids would be in town for the wedding, but it was December, and they probably came to New Mexico for Christmas with their grandmother.

Once the little flower girl and ring bearer were in place, the music from the sound system changed to the upbeat song, *Let's Hear It For The Boy*. We all laughed when Pat, wearing a dark red tuxedo, danced down the aisle with his parents. His mom and dad seemed to be just as fun as he was. The whole audience clapped to the beat of the music, while Mike shook his head happily at his silly future husband and in-laws.

Once the grooms were in place beside their parents, Bart grabbed Lisa's hand and led her back to sit beside their Lou Lou.

The service was brief but beautiful. Pat surprised everyone by singing an original song he wrote for Mike. It was sweet. How nice that they did special things for each other.

Then came the wonderful reception. The buffet was catered by Tio's Kitchen. We all smothered our New Mexican meal with red and green chile. Gotta have "Christmas" at Christmas time.

Our table was too much fun. Joey and I were seated with Jill, Kelly, Jett, and Amy. After the meal, we drank Joey's new Christmas brew and laughed about its funny name, Brewdolph the Red Nosed Grainbeer.

When the grooms stopped by our table and sat for a while, Pat took in a deep breath and shuddered with excitement. "Just think, tomorrow we will be on a beach in Hawaii!" He went on to describe the resort where they would be staying for their honeymoon.

Mike leaned over and asked me, "How have you been holding up after all the excitement at the Balloon Fiesta. I'll bet that was traumatic."

"It had its terrible moments, but I made new friends and even made some money. Since then, one of my new customers, Sandy, has taught me to play pickleball. I go a few evenings after work. It's so fun, helps to relieve stress, and now I get exercise. Other than that, I've just enjoyed a less complicated life."

"Good for you. I have a feeling my life is going to be even more complicated, both working with and living with Pat."

"No. You are the perfect couple. Your relationship will be even stronger now."

When Pat popped his head between us, I hugged his neck. "Have a blast in Hawaii, Pat."

After the meal, we all danced like goofballs on the dance floor. Pat had made sure we could dance the Electric Slide and the Macarena. Then, when things wound down, we helped to carry gifts and centerpieces out to the grooms' family cars. Other guests started to leave while caterers began their cleanup.

Our group wasn't ready to leave each other yet, so we went out on one of the balconies that overlooked the Balloon Fiesta Field. It was dark, but the museum's lighting provided enough glow to enjoy as we sat our group of six in a circle to visit. The evening was unseasonably warm, so we were comfortable with just our light coverups.

I finally said what I'd been wanting to say. "I have a story to tell you all."

The others looked at me as I started my tale. "Last Monday, on my day off, I drove down to the Rio Grande to take a walk with Zia. We walked along the Bosque until she got tired, then I carried her. Along the way, she perked up as if she saw something. On the way back to the car, at the same place, she squirmed, and I let her down. She rushed into the brush, and I chased after her, trying to grab her leash, but she seemed hell bent on finding something."

Jett laughed. "Tiny Zia tracking? That's a laugh."

"I know. It was crazy. When I found her, she was sniffing all around the area. Then she pawed at a bunch of leaves and sat, staring at it. She looked up at me, panting, as if she were proud."

Jill said, "Ok, so is this story going somewhere?"

I nudged her. "Be patient." I sighed and continued, "I asked her, 'What is it, Zia?' and leaned down to brush aside the

Cottonwood leaves. There, caked in dirt, was a 35-millimeter camera."

Amy said, "Oh, nice find. Did you keep it?"

I shook my head slowly with my lips tight, wondering if the others suspected what I had found. All of a sudden, Joey's eyes widened. "Was it Stoney's camera?"

"I didn't know, but I suspected it was. I picked up the camera and Zia, then drove directly to Marvin and Angelica's house."

Jill turned to Jett and Amy, saying, "It's the coolest house ever. So big and in the foothills. Maria took us along for a party there last month, and the view is…"

I interrupted. "Jill, do you mind?"

She zipped her lip. "Oh yeah. Continue. What did they say?"

"Marvin said it was definitely Stoney's. He said, 'I can't believe you found it.' But I told him, "I didn't, Zia did."

"At that, Marvin and Angelica stared at the dog on my lap. That's when I explained to the two that she was pretty smart and had even helped solve a murder last year."

I could tell Amy was confused, since she came here after all that excitement, but figured Jett could fill her in. "Angelica called her a wonder dog." I laughed, and the others nodded knowingly.

"That's when I asked Marvin if there was any chance the film in the camera might still be good after months outside. He said he wouldn't know until he checked, then he hurried off with the camera to his darkroom."

My group sat with mouths open as I continued to tell them bout last week's find. "Angelica, Zia, and I stood out on their beautiful balcony as we waited for Marvin to come back with news. I was so impatient that after twenty minutes, I started pacing and watching the sliding glass door for him to reappear. When he finally returned, his eyes were bright. He said, 'We have some beauties!'"

My group asked questions all at once. "Cool." "What were the pictures of?" "Did he take one as he fell?" "Were they any good?" "How many did he salvage?"

I said, "I don't have to answer your questions. I can show you." I took a small manila envelope from my purse and handed out the extra 4x6 copies Marvin had printed of Stoney's last photos. My friends all turned on their phone flashlights and looked through the photos as I waited for their reactions.

I picked up my new iPhone to turn on my flashlight too. When my face unlocked the screen, I smiled at the wallpaper. It was the photo of Marvin's purple balloon and Seamus's green shamrock balloon tethered together. That was a crazy memory.

"Wait. These are black and white. I thought Stoney shot in color." I looked up to see Jill shining her light on a photo.

I agreed. "He usually did use color, but on that flight, he chose black-and-white film, which turned out to be easier for Marvin to develop quickly in his darkroom."

Joey said, "Ooh, look how eerie these balloons are with the sun behind them."

He held it up for us to see, and I remembered what Stoney had named a similar photo. "Stoney called that a 'ballooner eclipse'."

Everyone thought that was perfect.

Jill said, "I'm kind of glad there wasn't a photo taken as he fell. That would be too much. Although a shot of Chris pushing him out would be pretty strong evidence against him."

Kelly said, "Not to worry. Chris will be behind bars for a long time. No evidence was needed. Too many witnesses heard him confess."

"This one is fantastic!" Jett, the artist in the group, held up a photo that had been taken as Stoney leaned out of the balloon and looked upward. It showed their balloon and the helicopter flying above them, just as they started flying through the mist of the cloud. Everyone looked at the photo and agreed it was spectacular.

I said with a frown, "Marvin said that was the last photograph Stoney ever took. He thought it was so good that he immediately entered it in a contest on behalf of Stoney. If the image wins, the prize money will be donated to Stoney's chosen charities.

But even if it doesn't win, a huge print of it will hang here in the museum to honor Stoney's adventurous spirit and his philanthropic legacy.

Jill said, "Wow. Who knows what would have happened to these if Zia hadn't found the camera? Nobody else would have connected it to Stoney."

One of the museum employees came out and told us they would be closing in ten minutes. The others handed me the pictures, and I put them back in the envelope and in my purse before staring out at the enormous dark space where hundreds of balloons had taken off just months ago.

It was too dark to see much, but I pictured the Artisan tent on the opposite end of the field and could almost feel the energy of tens of thousands of people milling about, excitedly. Main Street was now empty of food booths and balloon merchandise tents. It was surreal to see the space in total darkness and silence.

Joey said, "Maria, are you coming?"

"Yeah. I'll be there in a sec."

I stood there alone, realizing I would never forget the colors, the sounds, the fun, the excitement, and the devastation I had experienced during those ten days. I felt melancholy but knew the balloons would return next October, as usual, and with no major mishaps.

The balloon period of my life was now over. I gave a little sigh and turned to follow Joey into the building and back to my lovely, ordinary life.

What do Maria's products look like?
Works by real artists

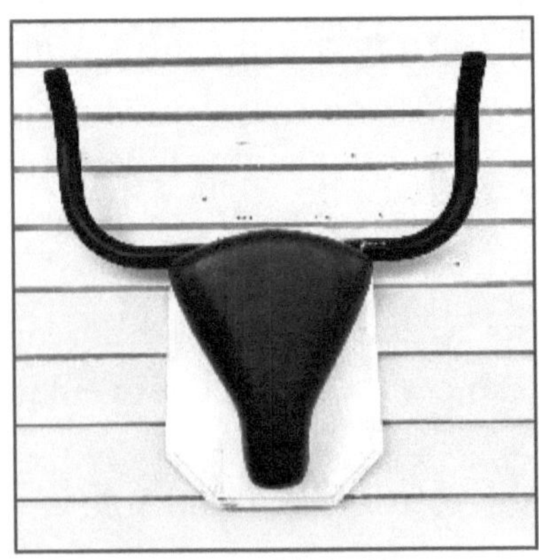

Bicycle Taxidermy
Blythe Davis
www.wildrecycled.com

Lightbulb Balloon
Veronique Marcoux
www.CapsuleCreations.etsy.com

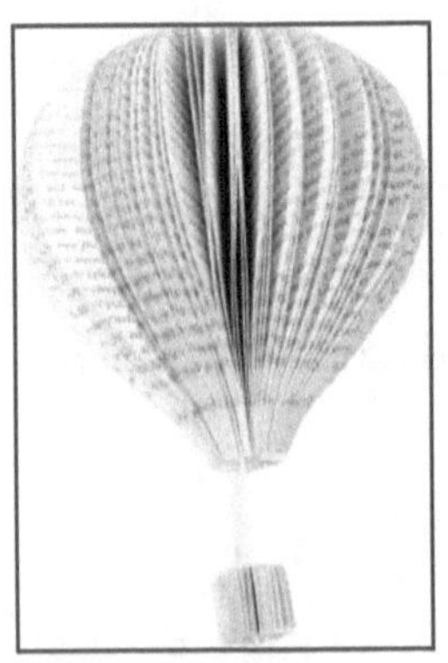

Book Balloon
Amy Geiser
www.RootToVine.etsy.com

Map Flowers
Victoria Wheeler
www.BloomingPotential.etsy.com

Player Piano Deconstruction Photos
by Author - Martha Landes

Piano with half the keyboard

Piano - usable parts removed

Rows of billows

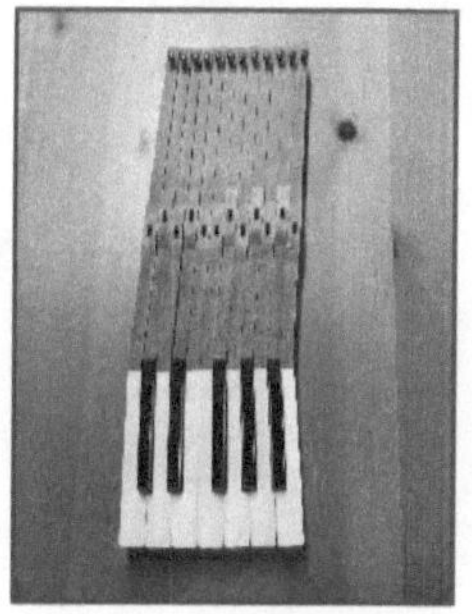

Full length keys

Key rack

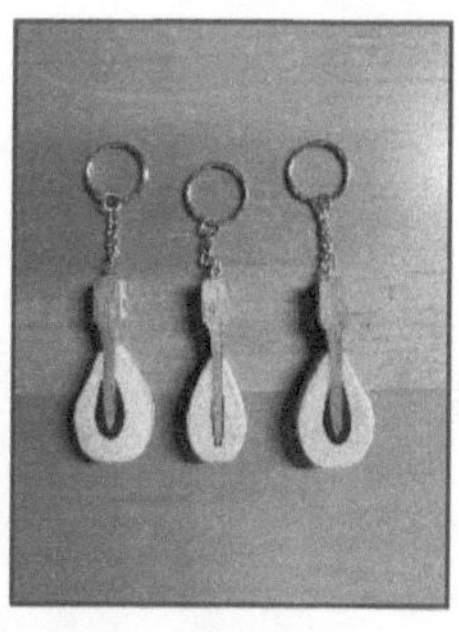

Hammer keychains

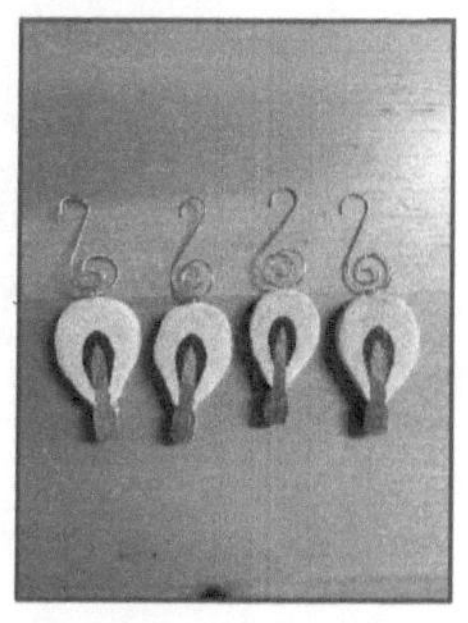

Hammer
balloon ornaments

About the Author

Martha Kemm Landes is a former Oklahoma public school music teacher. Besides writing musicals for her students, she is known for writing the Oklahoma State Children's Song, <u>Oklahoma, My Native Land</u>. After moving to New Mexico in 2011, she began her transition from composing music and musicals to writing light mysteries.

Martha lives in Rio Rancho, New Mexico, with her author husband, Dan, and their adopted Old English Sheepdog, Pepper. They enjoy spending time at their cabin in the nearby Jemez Mountains and traveling.

Besides writing mystery novels and renting out the cabin, Martha's other activities include quilting, playing pickleball, biking, gardening, and hosting movie nights in their backyard theater.

Scan the QR code for a quick link to Martha's website, where you can find fun news, giveaways, and even subscribe to her newsletter, Mini Morsels from Martha.

www.ingramcontent.com/pod-product-compliance
Lightning Source LLC
Chambersburg PA
CBHW061756190726
48289CB00007B/1972